MAIJA'S CHILDHOOD HORROR HAD COME TRUE

When I heard the trolls' sirens, I knew that death was near. No human can hear such sounds and live.

"Jump! Jump!" they demanded.

Flames had burst through the trapdoor and climbed to the roof of the attic. But beyond the attic, just outside the window, was a shaft of pure air that one could breathe—without pain or limit—while plunging to the earth below.

I forced myself into the window frame, dropped my head and hurtled into space.

White Midnight

CILLAY RISKU

PLAYBOY PRESS
PAPERBACKS

Then old Väinämöinen sings in a low voice. He sang the wind into a gale, worked the weather up into a fury; he speaks these words, made this magic utterance: "Take him, wind, into your vessel, cold spring wind, get him into your boat for you to speed him to gloomy North Farm."

The epigraphs in this book and Grandfather's songs at the wedding feast are from the *Kalevala*, the national epic poem of Finland.

CHAPTER ONE

We Finns are fond of telling a story about ourselves. Admittedly, the story may be more fable than fact, but our origin is obscure and we can get away with legends.

It is said that a Finn was often included in the crew of a Viking ship because Finns were thought to be warlocks, possessors of supernatural powers and "far sight." Though it is also said that the warlock was not a particular favorite of the crew, the staunch but superstitious Vikings felt it prudent to include a Finn rather than leave him in his mysterious northern country, plotting for the wrong side.

Knowing my countrymen, I'm sure they delighted in their mysterious reputation and took every opportunity to enhance it. There is also the possibility that they really did have these powers.

Despite the "gift" of my ancestors, I found myself devoid of any glimpse into future events as I sat in a gently rocking boat and looked across the vivid blue northern Finland lake. I was not even able to summon an emotion for this sight that I had longed to see for many years. All I could think of was that once Janne had told me my eyes were the same color as the lake's waters.

Dots of islands punctuated the lake's smooth surface, and birch and pine trees edged its shoreline with a brilliant green. Grandfather's island was hidden behind a bend in the lake, and soon I would be home.

Why couldn't I feel the wonder of that moment? I was on the final stage of a long voyage home, and I was caught in an emotional limbo. My adult self could not relate to the reality of the moment; the child who still dwelled within me feared a flood of bittersweet memories.

I leaned over the side of the boat and mindlessly drew circles with my fingers in the cool water. Behind me, Helge cursed and tugged at the motor's rope. I smiled at his easy flow of Finnish profanities. The succinct American curses had never seemed quite as expressive. Perhaps one always feels his native language is the only one suitable to express strong emotions.

I had experienced a good many strong emotions during the last ten years, dating from the day when Grandfather announced his sudden decision that I be sent to America to "broaden" my education. Sending me away had also severed my relationship with Janne, a young worker in Grandfather's mill, and I never doubted that that was the real motive behind the decision.

Janne and I had known one another since we were small children, and our friendship had grown during the golden days and white midnights of the island's summers. The dark winter months that I was forced to spend at school in Helsinki had seemed endless, and I would count the gray hours until the precious summer sun would again emerge and I could return to the island. Janne attended the village school, but Grandfather insisted that I receive my education in the capital, under the stern eye of my Great-aunt Ida.

Despite the agonizingly slow progress of the dark winters, summers did come and I always returned to Grandfather's. As soon as I exchanged dutiful greetings with my relatives, I sought out Janne and listened in red-faced delight to his exclamation of how I had grown during the winter months.

"Ha, it's you again. You've grown taller, Maija, but you're skinny as ever. Doesn't that great-aunt of yours feed you, or do all the girls in the capital look like boys? Your grandfather should leave you in the village during the winter so you could become plump and pleasant to a man's eye on good country food. Well, come over after I have finished my chores, and maybe I will take you fishing."

As we grew into our teens, his teasing reference to my lack of womanly development ceased and it was *his* turn to be red-faced and confused on the occasion of our summer reunions. His passion for fishing remained, but I found a certain satisfaction in noting that he paid almost as much attention to me as he did to a pull on his line.

We were no longer children, and there were strange new stirrings that we felt for one another; but we had not, as Grandfather feared, become lovers. Janne was three years older than I and was filled with precise plans for his future: "Someday I will own a lumber mill even more prosperous than *Herra* Leinonen's."

My future plans were limited to what I would wear to the next midsummer festival. Even though I sensed his awareness of me as a woman, Janne treated me as a silly younger sister. Nonetheless, Grandfather drew his own conclusions about our relationship and denied us the right to pursue it. Aarno Leinonen seldom allowed others to make their own choices.

The sound of men's laughter drifted across from the tavern on the wharf, and then their voices blended into a Finnish drinking song:

> *If you drink, drink to the end.*
> *If you love, love the night through.*

I was reminded how much my countrymen enjoy their drink, songs, and lovemaking. A disgruntled countrywoman had once remarked that they often seemed to enjoy their pleasures in that *order,* too.

Helge kicked the motor and solemnly rewound the rope, addressing each loop with a "helpful" word. He gave a mighty tug, and the motor was jerked into hiccupping life. As the outboard subsided to a dutiful roar, Helge turned toward me and grinned, the width of his smile making up for the absence of teeth. He made a sign of victory over the motor and pointed toward the bend in the lake.

"It is good you are home, *Neiti* Maija. Soon you will see The Island."

I nodded. There are sixty-two thousand islands in Finland, but Grandfather's would always be *the island* to the people of that area because he was the owner of the biggest lumber mill in the north of Finland, employer of thousands.

I had gone to the tavern on the dock to arrange for a boat to take me to the island and found that Helge still operated the shuttle. As usual, his face was flushed from a combination of wind, sun, and the contents of several empty bottles of beer that sat in front of him. The wrinkles in his rosy face were more deeply etched than I had remembered, the blond hair whitened, but he looked much as he had ten years before when he ferried me across from the island to begin a journey to an alien land.

It is said that the Finns are a hearty lot and slow to show their years. I pushed back the long blonde hair that whipped about my face and wondered if the past ten years had treated me as kindly as they had Helge. I was twenty-eight, practically a spinster in the youth culture of America. Perhaps I wouldn't be regarded as such an old maid in my own late-marrying society.

The men at the tavern had shown signs of interest in me—reassuring after having been out of circulation for so long. Some had recognized me and called out their welcome and a joking conjecture as to why I had returned.

It was obvious that no one knew about Grandfather. That didn't surprise me. He always sought to conceal his personal affairs—and death is a very personal affair.

I thought how much easier it would be if I had been able to return as a sophisticated woman of the world, one who knew how to control her emotions, knew the right things to say. I tried to smooth a wrinkle from my blue linen shift and looked regretfully at my sneakers. I should have dressed more smartly for my return, but I knew I would have to scramble up the wooden ladder of the old pier. Eight years of chasing after twins had trained me for practicality rather than chic.

I could feel the pulse pounding in my throat as we approached the bend. Soon I would be at the island. Almost thirty, I remonstrated to myself, and my heart still pounded as it had in childhood when I was to come under Grandfather's scrutiny.

My carefully nurtured feeling of independence had vanished upon the arrival of his telegram. How often I had fantasized about just such a summons: He would send a tearful plea, begging me to return; I would send a scathing rejection.

When the wire came, it was not tearful, but its message precluded rejection: "COME HOME AT ONCE. I AM DYING. WIRE ESTIMATED ARRIVAL TIME AT ISLAND TO MRS. SAARINEN AT MILL OFFICE. TICKET ARRANGED THROUGH VIKING AIRWAYS. HURRY. GRANDFATHER."

The years and resentments that separated us disappeared. Grandfather was dying, and he wanted me to be with him. It was only after the shock of the message wore off that I realized he had, as usual, assumed that I would obey his command. No thought was given to the complexities of leaving my life in America. No reference was made to the fact that he had not communicated with me in over eight years.

Two years after I had been sent to America, I wrote to seek his permission to drop out of the university and return to Finland. I could no longer withstand the alienation and purposelessness. His reply had been to lecture me on the value of education and *sisu*. *Sisu* is the little Finnish word that represents a special quality of character that is said to be found in Finns. In English it is invariably translated as "guts."

My reply was that I would be happy to complete my education—*in Finland*. I would earn my own passage money home by accepting a temporary job as a baby-sitter for motherless twins. The job had been offered me through the employment bureau of the university because the father had specified a Scandinavian girl. I didn't bother to mention that, technically, Finland isn't a part of Scandinavia.

Grandfather's response had been swift and stinging: "You are not a Scandinavian nursemaid, you are a Finnish scholar. You may not return to my home until you have completed your education."

But I wasn't a scholar, and *sisu* can also mean stubbornness. I dropped out of the university and accepted the job as a substitute mother for the two-year-old twins. I refused to believe that Grandfather would remain adamant, but my subsequent letters went unanswered.

My step-grandmother, Mummo, sent Christmas and birthday cards, but no words of her own were added to the printed greetings. I guessed she had been forbidden to write me. She also sent me the clipping from the village newspaper when Kaarina received her medical degree.

In the beginning of my exile I had written long letters to Janne, but never once in the ten years I was gone did I receive a letter or card from him.

Time passed, the twins grew dearer to me, and I found a certain satisfaction in my existence. Their father, Dr. Kincaid, often said that none of them could have survived without me. When I thought of it at all, I imagined he would someday ask me to marry him. Perhaps I had to believe that because my life was so isolated. My substitute mother role rarely put me in contact with other young people, especially available men. My days were filled with feedings and romps with the children and my evenings quietly shared with Dr. Kincaid when he was free from calls.

I wonder if I would have replied with such alacrity to Grandfather's summons if Dr. Kincaid hadn't announced his engagement to his office nurse. The sudden engagement had been a shock, but, I admitted frankly, I really hadn't been as upset at losing the doctor as at the thought of sharing the twins' affection with a stepmother.

Although the boys and I exchanged tearful goodbyes and promises of long letters and possible trips across the great ocean that would separate us, I knew that their memory of me would dim in the delight of having a real mother. And that was only right. They needed a real family, and so did I.

The boat rounded the bend, but I deliberately delayed my first sight of the island and looked instead at an elbow of land that jutted out. As a small child, I had often hidden in the tall reeds that crowded its banks. It had been a favorite "secret place," made especially attractive because I had been ordered to stay away from the marshy area. In later years I had climbed out of my bedroom window to meet Janne there. We would lie in the cool marsh grass, the midnight sun above us, and share our dreams. My dreams never involved becoming an outcast.

Grandfather and I had a special relationship because he raised me. My mother had no living relatives and died when I was born. Five years later Father contracted flu and wasn't strong enough to withstand the pneumonia that developed.

He and four other Finnish soldiers had tried to hold a small grain mill in the eastern province against advancing Russian forces. His comrades were killed, but he was captured. When he was finally released, he

seemed a very old man—much older than his vital
father. I could barely remember him.

When Russia allowed the Finns to travel through
their forfeited eastern section, Grandfather and I took
the tour bus to Leningrad and passed the ruins of the
mill. There was nothing to mark the site except a pile
of stones and remnants of a waterwheel.

"Why did Father fight so hard to defend that?" I
asked.

"Because it is part of Finland," Grandfather answered simply.

We drove through acres of uncultivated land and
deserted farm houses.

"The Russians asked the Finns of this area to remain and work their farms."

"And did many stay?" I asked.

"Only those who were six feet under the ground."

Large granite rocks studded the nearby fields, some
of them lined up in rows.

"Look over there," Grandfather directed. "You can
see how the farmers used those boulders to build a defensive barricade against the advancing Russians. Yes,
child, there are many who understand why my son and
his comrades fought so hard to keep a little mill."

Father had been an only child and Grandmother was
killed in the final days of the Winter War. Many years
later, Grandfather married his housekeeper, a plump,
placid little woman whom everyone addressed affectionately as Mummo, or "Granny," rather than by her
Christian name of Lilya.

A widow with three sons and a daughter, she was
pleased that her children had come under the protection of such a wealthy and important man. She
never tired of reminding her children of their good
fortune. And that, I suspect, is how the first seeds of
antagonism toward their stepfather were sown.

There are three racial types in Finland. The Swedo-
Finns are descendants of Swedish settlers and im-

migrants from the Baltic area and Germany. Many retained their Swedish language or adopted it in preference to the more difficult Finnish tongue. The Leinonens are of that descent.

The Tavasts, or so-called typical Finn, came from the southern shores of the Baltic Sea early in the Christian age and settled in Central Finland. Mummo, a Tavast Finn, had the typical stocky build, round face, blue eyes, and upturned nose. Broad, high cheekbones gave her face a slightly oriental cast, which is also a characteristic of the Tavast Finn.

Her first husband had been a Karelian, a descendant of the settlers of eastern Finland, who are thought to be of Russian origin. Her three sons and daughter had inherited their father's dark Karelian looks—and moods.

The boys—Paavo, Eero, and Heikki—were nine, four, and two years older than I. They were slim, graceful boys, with eyes as gray as a winter sky and as likely to shift from silver sunshine to threatening storm clouds, depending upon their ever-changing moods.

Though the boys were slim, their sister, Kaarina, was thin and had none of their easy grace. She was seven years older than I, and even from childhood it was predicted that she would be a spinster. Her narrow face seemed to be cast in a perpetual expression of disapproval. Her gray eyes were an impenetrable cover for whatever emotions she may have felt. She must have been no more than nine when Mummo and Grandfather married, but I could never remember her as anything but grown up and disapproving of my childish antics. She resisted my attempts to adopt her as a sister and even insisted that I call her *tati*, "aunt." I did, but I also gave her other titles, for which Grandfather reprimanded me while trying to suppress a smile.

It occurred to me at times that our family had been formed through a series of tragic deaths. No wonder there were strange undercurrents and black moods in a household that was haunted by so many ghosts.

Not that I had always been aware of this. I had been, on the whole, an oblivious child, intoxicated by my joyous youth. It was only after the alienation from Grandfather that I had felt the lack of family solidarity. Whatever their feelings might have been, no one had spoken out against Grandfather's decision to send me overseas. Their only comment had been that I should be grateful for the opportunity to travel. Was it because they were afraid of incurring his wrath, as I had, that no one spoke out in my behalf? Or were they pleased to see me go—and stay away?

But we are a family, I proclaimed to myself as I finally looked at the island, which loomed in front of us. *Grandfather will not be with us much longer—pray God I've arrived soon enough to see him alive—and we must join forces, as a family does in time of loss. We must learn to love—and forgive.*

Although it was almost nine o'clock at night, the island was bathed in golden light. But the sun couldn't penetrate the dense woods behind the house, and the tall trees cast sinister shadows over its mansard roof.

A little balcony protruded at each end of the second story. The east balcony served the boys' bedrooms, which were dubbed by them "The Lords' Chambers." I had often dashed under that balcony to keep from being pelted with objects, usually vile ones, that the boys enjoyed throwing at me.

On the west side of the second story was what I called "The Ladies' Chamber," the large bedroom I had shared with Kaarina. Its balcony was perfect for retaliatory raids on any "uncle" who was foolish enough to walk near it.

The boys and I had loosened some shingles on the roof so that we had convenient foot- and handholds for crawling across from one side of the house to the other. When we were very young, we had held midnight meetings in each other's chambers. After the boys outgrew the thrill of these clandestine meetings, they used this means of exit to sneak off to the wharf and row across to the mainland for late-night rendezvous with the village girls.

In the distance, the balcony of the Ladies' Chamber was shadowed by birch trees, but I thought I saw someone standing there, looking out at the approaching boat. I waved and hailed the observer, but there was no answer. The figure, if there had been one, disappeared into the shadows.

No one was waiting on the pier to greet me. Of course, I reminded myself, they would all be with Grandfather.

Helge brought the boat smoothly alongside the pier. The splintery old ladder had been replaced, and the fresh lumber contrasted sharply with the weathered planks of the dock. The old boatman helped me ascend the steps and then handed up my one large piece of luggage and my cosmetic case. I secured the boat to the pier, and Helge clambered up, carrying a large wicker basket that I presumed contained groceries.

"Just carry those as far as the front path, Helge," I shouted. "The boys can bring everything in later."

Since no one had come to greet the boat, I assumed that Grandfather's condition was critical. He wouldn't want Helge near the house or the news of his illness would be spread throughout the village as soon as the old man returned to the tavern. Grandfather always preferred to make his own announcements. Although he would be unable to issue this one, he would still want it handled in a dignified fashion, rather than spread through village gossips.

Helge looked disappointed that he couldn't go into the house. News of *Herra* Leinonen's household was always good for several free beers at the tavern. He shrugged philosophically and proceeded up the pathway on his short, bowed legs, carrying the heavy luggage, while I trailed behind, deliberately delaying my entrance.

It was June and the intense sun had baked the earth along the pathway to a fine dust. Bits of black granite glinted on the ground, but hearty weeds and butter-cups broke through the hard-baked surface with de-termined bursts of green and gold.

Finns seldom waste their energies on the carefully tended lawns one sees in America and England. They accept the natural beauty of the landscape. The trees had been removed from the front of the house in order to give an unobstructed view of the lake, but a thick forest of birch, spruce, and pine encircled the back and sides of the house.

Helge settled my luggage on the grass path. I shook his rough, callused hand and watched him totter back to the pier. The motor started on the first pull and shattered the mournful silence of the island.

I looked at the large front door, expecting to see someone emerge, but no one came, although the roar of the outboard must have been heard in the farthest interior of the house.

Arrivals had always been an exciting event, breaking the isolation of island life. It had been a contest to see who could be the first out on the pier to greet an ap-proaching boat and identify the passengers. Even Kaarina had responded to the excitement of arrivals.

Only one motorboat and an ancient rowboat were now at the pier. It had always been Grandfather's custom to keep two motorboats for the convenience of the family. Had he been taken ashore—back to "the mainland"—to the hospital?

But the revelry of the men at the tavern. . . . If Aarno Leinonen had been taken to the hospital, the whole village would have been aware of it, and the men would have talked in hushed, respectful tones, concerned for their employer—concerned over their own future wel-fare, with the mill passing out of the hands of the old patriarch. And surely Helge would have said something.

No telephone had ever been allowed on the island, and so I had sent a telegram to the mill office upon my arrival in Helsinki. It had been impossible to quote my exact arrival time at the island, but surely someone was expecting me.

My heart gave a painful thump as I realized the implication. *He's dead, and no one wants to be the one to break the news to me. They're all waiting for me inside so I can read the news on their faces without the awful words having to be spoken.*

My legs were weak as I walked to the door. My hand felt strangely heavy as I lifted the large brass knocker. The coat of arms of Finland was engraved in the brass: a rampant lion standing on a Viking sword and grasping a two-edged, sharply pointed sword in its mailed fist. Arranged around the lion were nine heraldic roses, representing the nine provinces of Finland. The knocker was now a curiosity because the lion faced to the east.

After Finland's defeat in 1940, the Russians had insisted that we turn our lion to face the west as a testimony to our disloyalty. Finland had been an autonomous grand duchy of Russia for 108 years, and the Soviet bear felt we had showed ingratitude for its protection.

Grandfather had refused to change our ancient door knocker, saying, "My lion will continue to keep a watchful eye on the Russians."

I brought the knocker down sharply and waited for the sound of footfalls in the wooden entry hall. Moments passed, but there was no sound. I lifted the knocker again, but before I could bang it down, I heard a curious whimper. I stood very quietly and heard the noise repeat itself. It seemed to come from the walkway. I looked about, but there was nothing to see except my luggage and the large wicker basket that Helge had placed alongside it.

The peculiar sound became more persistent as I turned from the door and stepped off the pathway to search in the tall grass, thinking I would find a kitten or other small creature among the weeds. Then the whimpering turned into a full-scale cry—the unmistakable wail of a human infant.

The lid of the wicker basket was moving, so I stooped and took it off. Inside lay an infant, wrapped in a blanket, redfaced, the little fists and legs flailing in frustration.

I lifted the baby from the basket and held it against me. The dampness of the blanket could explain the child's discomfort, but question after question raced across my mind. Had it been asleep all during the boat ride? Or had the motor muffled its whimpering? Why hadn't Helge heard it when he carried the basket to the walkway? But Helge, I remembered, was hard-of-hearing. Nevertheless, he surely wasn't unaware that there was an infant in the basket!

I hugged the crying baby closer to me while the questions whirled about. The shuttle boat was a small speck on the lake's surface. No chance of hailing Helge back to answer my questions about the baby.

I didn't hear the door open. *"Maija!"* a male voice called, and I whirled about, clutching the baby so tightly that it screamed in protest.

A tall, dark-haired man stood in the doorway. Oblivious of the howling infant, I watched the expression on the man's face change from delight to bewilderment and, finally, to unmistakable anger as a flush suffused his cheeks. He turned from me and spoke to someone who stood in the shadow of the entrance. I couldn't hear what he said, but his voice seemed to tremble with suppressed rage.

Then Grandfather stepped into the wide doorway. His hair was totally white and his broad shoulders were slightly stooped, but for an eighty-three-year-old dying man he looked extremely fit. He reached out and put a hand on Janne's shoulder, whether for his own support or to comfort Janne I couldn't tell. For an instant, the three of us stood frozen in place, staring at one another dumbly. Even the baby, seeming to sense a strange halt in time, became quiet.

Grandfather patted Janne's shoulder and appeared to be about to speak, but Janne shrugged his hand aside.

"So it was all an elaborate scheme to cover your *real* motive—preserving the precious honor of the Leinonens," Janne said bitterly.

"I know what you're thinking, but I knew nothing of *this*," Grandfather responded, gesturing in my direction. "Perhaps there is an explanation. . . ."

Janne's lips tightened into a cruel smile. He glanced at me and said, "I heard the explanation for babies quite some time ago."

Grandfather's voice became loud and commanding. "All that I said was true; so don't be a fool and let pride allow you to lose——"

Janne's voice matched Grandfather's in volume and strength. "*Herra* Leinonen," he said, "you have taught me to be a businessman, and a businessman does not pass up a profitable deal even though he finds there is an extra, shall we say, *clause*." He turned to face me, but there was no trace of delight in his sea-green eyes.

I had often told myself that I had forgotten him—even forgotten what he looked like—but I had lied to myself. Still, I remembered a boy, and a man stood before me—with no trace of boyishness left. He had always been lean and straight, but now the leanness had toughened into the hard muscles of a man, and there was more than a hint of arrogance in his posture. His face had none of the humorous mobility I had loved. Its hard-set planes and suggestion of lines attested to the trials of life. Janne, my childhood friend, was now a man, and one who obviously disliked me.

"Maija, forgive my rudeness," Janne said unrepentantly. "Welcome back—and congratulations." With a curt nod, he strode around me and down the pathway.

"Well," Grandfather said at last, looking at the child, "is that another of your nursemaid charges or have you brought me a great-grandchild?"

CHAPTER TWO

Grandfather stepped back into the hallway and said in the rich, commanding voice I remembered so well, *"Tulkaa sisään!* Or have you forgotten your Finnish? Come in, come in!"

The last phrase, a heavily accented attempt at English, sounded so incongruous that I smiled despite my bewildered state and stepped into the house.

"What do I have—a great-granddaughter or a great-grandson?" He reached out and took the baby from me, grimacing as he touched the damp bundle.

"Neither," I answered. "I mean, I don't *know*. I mean, you don't have *any* great-grandchild. Oh, let's sit down."

The old man nodded and handed the infant back to me. He led me into the sitting room and sat down in the large rocking chair that had always been regarded as his throne.

I stood in the middle of the room and looked about at the familiar surroundings. Hand-woven rug runners still protected the highly polished floor. The only suggestion of the passage of a decade was their more subdued colors.

Mummo's housekeeping abilities could be seen in the immaculate condition of the room and its furnishings. The only exception was the table at Grandfather's chair, which held a messy array of pipes and cans and packets of tobacco, arranged exactly as he wished.

Neither Mummo nor any of the occasional maids was permitted to tidy it.

Standing in front of Grandfather made me feel as vulnerable as when I had been caught using one of his pipes in a bubble-blowing contest with Heikki.

"Sit down, Maija. Don't stand about like a fool. Sit down and explain yourself."

I retreated to a long wooden bench along the wall and opposite his chair. It was very hard and cold, as I remembered it—a torture seat for a hapless victim who was about to be interrogated. The infant stopped crying and stared up at me with very wide dark-blue eyes.

"It seems that your house guest is a boy. I know it's hard to believe, but we met just a few minutes ago, when he'd had enough of a wicker basket. Helge had the basket aboard the boat and unloaded it with my luggage. I presumed it held groceries."

Grandfather's heavy eyebrows, now as white as his mane of hair, drew together as he frowned. The years had not dimmed the blue of his penetrating eyes.

"It's true," I said. "I just *found* this child. Look"—I opened the blanket—"would I bring a naked baby? Would I *make up* such a bizarre story?"

"Your imagination has never been faulty, Maija."

"Well, if I wanted to foist off an illegitimate child, I think I could have worked up a better explanation."

He picked up a meerschaum pipe and examined it before beginning to fill it. The process was meticulously performed, and it seemed an eternity before he finally placed it, unlit, between his teeth and settled back in his rocker. A low rumble formed in his throat, and then the bass tones of his laughter filled the room.

Finally, controlling his merriment, he said, *"So,* what a homecoming! You gave me quite a fright. And Janne. . . ." Another roar of laughter burst forth.

The mention of Janne brought me to my senses. "What is this all about? You said you were *dying.* I was terrified, thinking I wouldn't arrive soon enough to see you alive, though you appear to be in glowing health. And what was *Janne* doing here? When did *he* become welcome in your house? And what in the world was he talking about? I think *I'm* the one who deserves an explanation."

My attack destroyed his amused expression. His brows drew closer together, and he coughed elaborately before replying. "Yes, well, we will talk of that later. First, do something about that child. You'll find suitable garments in the chest in the back hall. Mummo's kept every garment that you children ever wore." He snorted derisively. "She thinks Kaarina might use them someday. Ha!"

He rose from the rocker, and for the first time I saw that his movements were not as sure as ten years ago. I detected a tremor in his hands as he pushed against the arms of the chair. "I will make some coffee while you tend to the child," he said.

"Where is everyone? Where's Mummo? Do the boys and Kaarina still live here?"

He snorted again and replied, "They're here more often than I would like. Yes, they all stay very close to the feathered nest. Kaarina's been in Germany for almost a year, or so she says. It's very mysterious. She told Dr. Tami he wouldn't have heard of the clinic. It's some sort of an experimental program in a rural area. She's been home for a week now, but she took off somewhere today and said she wouldn't be back here until tomorrow.

"I made 'the boys,' as you call that gang of parasites, take Mummo to the Gypsy festival in the village. I wanted to talk to you alone."

I wanted to ask more questions but was silenced by an imperious gesture "Go now. I will make the coffee. I still make better coffee than that old woman, though she wouldn't admit it." With what I suspected was conscious effort, Grandfather walked vigorously out of the room.

I carried the baby to the back hall. The large
wooden chest did seem to hold every garment that we
had ever worn. The styles were old-fashioned, but at
least the clothes were dry. I washed the infant with a
hand cloth and dressed him in a diaper, a knitted
"soaker," an undershirt, and a flannel gown. He
watched me solemnly as I tended to his needs.

He seemed to have cried himself into a state of
fatigue, and I hoped he would sleep long enough for
me to figure out a way to feed him. Mummo had never
used bottles to nurse her babies, so there were none for
me to borrow. Then I remembered my toy chest and
the tiny bottles I had used to nurse my dolls. It was
an improbable solution, but so was the situation.

I picked up the infant and climbed the back stairs to
my chamber. The long hallway of the second story
was as shadow-laden as I remembered, and the huge
linen closet, where my uncles had told me trolls lived,
seemed almost as ominous as it had in childhood. I
found myself wanting to tiptoe past it.

In my childhood, when I was with an adult, the
closet was nothing more than a flower-scented storage
room for the mountains of linens that were required to
last throughout the dark months of winter. There had
been no automatic washers and dryers in our village.
During the last days of summer, all the linens were
washed, meticulously ironed and stored on the wide
shelves of the closet with sachets of dried violets and
rose petals tucked within the folds. As a final touch,
colored ribbons were wrapped around each stack.

In the daytime, accompanied by Mummo or one of
the village girls who assisted with the laundry, I thought
the linen closet was a feast of sight and scent. But at
night, my uncles told me, it was the home of trolls—
wicked, grotesque forest creatures. I was told that a
colony of these evil dwarfs lived in our linen closet as
in a cavern, and used the ribbons for playing games.
They peeked through the crack under the wide door
and watched to see who passed. Anyone who did not

hasten by was captured, dropped through a trapdoor in the closet (known only to the trolls) and carried off to the darkest part of the forest. The unlucky captives were cut up—just as Mummo shredded our worn-out woolen garments—spun into pillowcases and returned to the closet.

At the far end of the hall was the door to the Lords' Chambers, I turned right and entered the large bedroom that Kaarina and I had shared. The room had always had, as it were, an invisible line down its middle. One side of the room housed Kaarina's possessions and reflected her personality, the other side mine.

Even now, the difference was evident. Kaarina's bed was covered with a plain beige bedspread, tasteful and expensive-looking—the selection of a woman who lived without frills. There was no clutter of cosmetics on her dressing table, but only a tortoise-shell brush-and-comb set and a crystal jar that held large hairpins. Apparently she still wore her hair in the neat bun she had worn since young womanhood.

My half of the room still looked exactly as I remembered leaving it; the typical taste of a teen-ager was carefully preserved. My frilly dotted-swiss bedspread was freshly washed and starched. My vanity, the antithesis of Kaarina's, was cluttered with perfume bottles and toiletries.

I removed the top from a bottle I remembered as holding my favorite perfume and was assaulted by an odor like vinegar—the scent of yesterday's sweet memories, I thought, as I replaced the stopper. The toy chest, which I had also used as a bench for my dressing table, had not been moved from its position. What's more, it still held my childhood possessions. Had Mummo's sentimentality preserved them, or had Grandfather ordered them kept for my return? Whatever the reason, it was comforting to see that my existence within the household had not been erased.

I placed the baby on the bed and tried to soothe

him, as he had resumed whimpering, but I suspected that pangs of hunger were fast eroding the contentment he felt from the warm, dry garments. Suppressing the temptation to reminisce over the contents of the toy chest, I searched for the doll bottles. But my memory had distorted their size—they were much too small to use for feeding a real infant, who was growing more fretful.

Since there was no telephone on the island, I would have to take a boat to the mainland. That would take at least twenty minutes, plus the time it would take to borrow a baby bottle from a friend or drive to the hospital in the neighboring city. A small dispensary served our village, but I doubted that I would find a bottle there. I had to find a quicker way to feed the child. Perhaps, I thought, I could find a rubber glove and construct a nipple from it. I had seen that done on TV shows to feed abandoned newborn creatures. But would it work in real life, for a human baby?

While I tried to think of a solution, I rummaged through the chest. Near the bottom I found Poika, my well-loved, and well-worn, doll—a harmless facsimile of a boy troll. We had often huddled together under the bed linens, Poika vowing to protect me from the bad trolls of the closet if they dared to venture forth. Poor Poika was practically bald because of my habit of dragging him about by his once gloriously scruffy mop of woolly hair.

I smoothed the remaining tufts of hair and picked him up for a hug, uncovering, as I did so, a paper bag at the very bottom of the chest. I couldn't remember the bag or what treasure I had stored in it. I was puzzled to find an inner package, its paper crinkly and fresh after a decade of storage, and inside the package was a woolen baby blanket. Wrapped in the blanket were diapers, undershirts, gowns, nursing bottles, and even a pacifier.

In the joy of finding the nursing bottles, I didn't bother to ask how they got there. I brushed the pacifier against my skirt and popped it into the baby's mouth, hoping it wasn't too unsterile. The child's eyes widened as he began a furious sucking on the nipple.

I gathered up the baby and the contents of the bag and went downstairs to find Grandfather. The smell of rich, strong coffee directed me to the kitchen, where I found him pouring two steaming cups from a large copper pot. He had also set out a platter of cold meats, bread, and cheeses. There was a small pan on the stove.

"I'm warming some goat's milk," he explained, nodding toward the pan. "Lilya believes it has mysterious benefits. I don't think it can be more harmful than the milk we get from Helge's cow."

I handed the infant to Grandfather, who didn't object now that he was dry, and washed one of the bottles and nipples in boiling water. The milk was tepid, but I remembered that Dr. Kincaid recommended a moderate temperature. It sounded sensible to me, since even my virginal mind doubted that the human body dispensed hot milk. The baby had spit out the pacifier and was howling for real food, so I filled the bottle quickly.

A Russian blue cat crept across the kitchen floor and peered up at the bundle in Grandfather's arms. "This is Pai-Pai," Grandfather said, nodding at the cat. "I believe he thinks we've gone mad."

"We have," I said as I thrust the bottle into his hand. Momentarily disconcerted, he managed to fit the nipple into the infant's searching mouth. Then nature took command and the child began to nurse.

I sat down, sighed in relief and sipped the hot coffee. The only sounds were the baby's sucking and the thump of the cat's tail, twitching nervously against the floorboards.

"Explain," I said finally, breaking the tranquil mood.

Grandfather lifted his head and gave me a puzzled look. "*I* don't know where he came from," he said.

"I didn't mean the child, though we'll soon have to see about that. I mean the telegram. You said you were dying."

He settled the baby in the crook of his arm and fussed with the blanket, not looking at me. "I thought that would be a less shocking way of putting it."

"Less shocking!" I startled the baby with the shrillness of my voice.

Grandfather frowned at me, silencing me with his look. "Just as I said—*less* shocking. I think you would have been considerably *more* upset if I had wired that I am going to be murdered."

CHAPTER THREE

Surely I had misunderstood him.

"I said someone is trying to *kill* me, and may soon succeed," Grandfather repeated calmly. He indicated the platter of food. "Now, eat."

I reached for a piece of black rye bread and a thick slice of Finnish ham. I had often hungered for these remembered delicacies, but now I had no appetite.

"Eat, because you will need your strength. But eat quickly, because I don't plan to remain a nursemaid forever," he said. But I saw that he smiled at the nursing child and was pleased that he seemed content in his arms.

I gulped down my food and said, "Grandfather, why would anyone want to kill you?"

"It is my guess that someone has decided I have lived too long and is impatient about the inheritance."

"You mean someone in the family? Surely you don't think——"

"Surely I *do* think that, Maija. Oh, I have made enemies in my time, but I can't think of anyone who'd bear such a grudge that he would want to kill me. I am considered a fair man."

That was true. In his business dealings, Aarno Leinonen had the reputation of being a hard but fair man. But that could not be said for the opinion of his family. I hadn't been the only member to suffer from his stubbornness. His was always the correct opinion, ours the result of "immature thinking and desires." I doubt that Grandfather had ever deliberately set out to make us unhappy, but it often turned out that way.

His opinion usually proved to be correct, but he was unable to allow for human weakness. He'd never been a weak person, and he found it impossible to understand weakness in others.

"Was it *fair* that you didn't allow me to come home?" I asked softly.

Anger flashed across his face, but the baby prevented him from banging his fist on the table or answering as loudly as he would have liked. The vehemence in his words made up for the soft tone in which he answered.

"You were sent to America to receive a good education, but you gave up as soon as you felt homesick. No granddaughter of mine should give up to such weakness."

"Grandfather, you know that wasn't *my* purpose. It was *your* purpose for me, and I doubt that my education was your only reason for sending me away."

"I don't know what you mean," he answered blandly.

"I mean Janne."

"Nonsense! Janne is a fine man. He's the manager of the mill."

Whatever his previous opinion of Janne's character and worth, it had changed; and no one had ever made Grandfather admit that he had once held an opposite opinion.

I was wise enough, or maybe tired enough, not to argue the point with him. But Janne—manager of the mill? That explained why he had been in the house, but certainly not the angry, mysterious words he had hurled at his employer.

"I'm glad that you've changed your opinion of Janne," I said, "and that he's in such a responsible position." I could feel my face begin to flush. *Ridiculous,* I chided myself, *twenty-eight and still blushing over a childish romance.* I was so provoked at my emotion that I spoke more fiercely than I intended. "Anyway, you wanted me to get a broad education and I did."

"Ha, from being a *nursemaid?*"

"Yes," I retorted angrily, trying not to startle the baby. "I learned about love and patience and understanding, which I would never have learned in *this* house."

I was sorry as soon as the words were said, but I felt it was the truth. Grandfather's house had always had an underlying current of hatred and misunderstanding. I knew that the boys and Kaarina felt it. Grandfather had always treated them in a condescending fashion. He had given them material goods but had reserved his respect and love.

A combination of tragic reasons contributed to his attitude. Mummo's children were her only treasure, and she spoiled them. After the marriage, Mummo subtly thwarted Grandfather's attempts to discipline her brood while nevertheless lecturing them on their duty to be appreciative of *Herra* Leinonen's generosity.

The wars had deprived Grandfather of his own family, and it seemed to me that he had barred his heart against further suffering. Somehow I had crept through that barrier, but all the others were kept at an emotional distance.

I suspected that was the reason why he married Mummo. She was a faithful and faultless housekeeper, a woman so humble that she barely rippled the surface of his existence. I believe he married her because he needed the convenience of a wife, and by filling that position with such a bland woman, he avoided the possibility that he might someday meet someone for whom he could feel genuine love—and the attendant emotional suffering that inevitably is a part of love. I doubted that he could withstand further emotional suffering.

He always treated Mummo well, if not affectionately,

and she seemed to ask for nothing more. He accepted her children, but he never loved them. Perhaps he might have learned to if they hadn't been as they were.

Grandfather's shoulders sagged and his head bent low over the infant. His voice sounded old as he asked, "Have I been such a poor grandfather?"

I went over to him, knelt and put my arms around him. "Oh, Grandfather, *no*. It's just that you are so stubborn. Can you imagine how I felt when you wrote that I would never be welcome in your home unless I followed your command to stay in a land that was so far away from you—from everything familiar? America is a beautiful, wonderful country, but not *my* country. I thought surely you could understand how I felt. I tried so hard in my letters to express my feelings."

He put a hand to his forehead. "It's been so long ago. Was I really so hard that I couldn't understand your emotions?" He shook his head and sighed. "I must be getting old. All I seem to remember is your refusal."

We sat in silence, caught up in our suffering. Finally I said, "I guess we are both stubborn."

He lifted his head and looked at me. For a moment the color of his eyes seemed faded, but then the blue caught fire and he replied softly, "*Sisu*, Maija. I prefer to think that we both have a bit too much *sisu*."

I laughed and hugged him. It was the closest he had ever come to admitting he was stubborn. I was more than willing to let it rest there after a decade of separation.

"Well, now, take the child. I believe he is asleep. What are we to do about him?"

I took the infant and for a brief moment wished he were mine. The baby's eyes were shut tightly in sleep, and a fringe of blond lashes lay upon his fat cheeks. His mouth, still puckered, occasionally moved in a sucking action.

Despite his apparent abandonment, it was clear that he had been well cared for. His body was plump and he seemed to be healthy. He appeared to be a little over a month old.

"What indeed?" I muttered. "Who would discard such a lovely baby?" I remembered the paper bag. "Do you have any maids now?"

Grandfather grunted, disgusted. "Everyone is too good nowadays to go into service, especially on an island. They prefer the villages and cities—all but the rejects. Mummo discharged the last girl—I think her name was Pirkko—nearly a year ago. I'm not sure what her problem was, but I know she was always fluttering, fumbling and quaking—especially around me. A pale chicken of a creature."

"I can't imagine anyone being intimidated by *you,* Grandfather," I replied, but he ignored the quip.

"Why do you ask? Is there something you need? Mummo will return soon."

"No, I asked because I found a bag in the bottom of my toy chest with a simple layette, necessities for a baby."

Grandfather looked at me sharply. "So you think that chicken of a maid may have left those things and then sent back the baby? Seems preposterous—but then she was a preposterous girl."

"Aren't there excellent assistance programs in Finland?"

"Of course, more than ever. *Taxes* . . . ah! They grow worse every year, but that's the price for our being a humane, progressive country." His pride in the social system was evident despite his complaint.

"Then, why would a girl give up her child if there's so little social stigma attached to having an illegitimate baby?"

"Who can say what goes on in the head of a chicken?" Grandfather replied with a shrug. "Perhaps she found another man, who wouldn't accept a child.

Of course, there is the possibility that one of your uncles is the father. . . . Ah, this is pure speculation. In the morning I will contact the authorities and make inquiries about the maid. Mummo hired her from the tavern, and it's possible that Reino will know about her."

"Reino still works there? I thought he would have——"

"——made something of himself?" Grandfather interrupted. "Ha! He always talks of becoming an architect, but his mother wants him to stay at home and be near her. Of course he complies. He's married to a village girl—a trembling little thing whom his mother can dominate. He doesn't even have children to show for the match. God may have given him good looks and a fine physique, but He forgot to give him a backbone."

"I always liked Reino."

"You, too? I thought you had better taste. It's bad enough that Kaarina goes about mooning over him. She thinks no one suspects, but I've seen her face. He's just the sort of weakling she'd be attracted to. No *sisu!*"

"Grandfather! If you talk like that, it's no wonder. . . ." My voice trailed off as I remembered his horrible allegation.

"Maija, I have always said what I think and done what I feel is best, and I plan to continue. They might kill me, but they aren't going to turn me into a mindless coward. And they *aren't* going to kill me now that you are here."

"Please tell me what this is all about. Have you gone to the authorities?" I knew as soon as I asked that he hadn't. It would be too shameful.

"You think I can't outthink this group of weaklings by myself? No, Maija, I have come up with another way to outsmart them—and to ensure my safety."

"Stop talking in riddles and tell me what happened to make you think——"

He interrupted again. "I don't *think*, I know. There have been three attempts on my life. But I don't want to waste this time telling you about them. Mummo and the boys will be back soon, Kaarina may walk in anytime, and we have other things to discuss. But I have it all written down for you to read." He drew a thick envelope from a pocket and handed it to me.

"I intended to mail this to you, but then I decided it would be better if you returned so that I could discuss the solution with you. It occurred to me that you might be a little startled and, ah, make some objection if I didn't explain it to you in person." His words sounded carefully rehearsed.

So, I thought to myself, he hadn't been as confident of my loyalty as he pretended.

"Whom do you——"

He held up his hand. "I don't know, as you can tell from the letter. It could be any of them, but I have to be realistic. They all have the same motive—money.

"After you left, I adopted them. Don't look so surprised. I didn't know if you were ever going to come to your senses, and I had promised Lilya that I would do so someday. In fact, it was in our marriage contract. I had to honor both the promise and the document.

"They are now my legal heirs. Several years ago I could see they were disappointed that I had inconvenienced them by living so long, so I decided to settle a good amount of money on each of them. I didn't give them a fortune, you understand, but enough that they could realize their ambitions—such as they were!

"Predictably, they've all gone through that money by now. Eero pretends to be a successful writer, but all I've ever seen has been published in those so-called intellectual reviews that pay no money. And it's his money that supports the goings-on in his apartment in Helsinki—which he prefers to call his salon. In other words, he pays for a fawning audience who will agree with all his advanced thoughts.

"This summer he's spending his vacation on my island. You can imagine what *I* say to his foolish prattlings. No, there is no fawning audience on this island. Even the doddering old fool, as Eero considers me, can figure out that he came here out of desperation. He ran out of money. He claims he's writing, but he must have a silent typewriter.

"Paavo—he used his money to buy a souvenir shop in the village. You can imagine how profitable that has been, considering the number of tourists who come to our area," he said sarcastically. "But it gives him plenty of opportunity to visit the tavern and the girls. And girls are expensive, even village girls.

"Heikki invested his money in a trade-school course to learn fabric design. I will say, though, that he's an accomplished designer and has begun to earn a name for himself with adaptations of ancient Finnish patterns."

"Then, it doesn't sound as if Heikki has squandered his money."

"No, he hasn't squandered his money; he's allowed his lover to do that for him. A thoroughly despicable individual with very expensive tastes. *His* name is Arvo and *he's* gaining quite a reputation for distinctive fashions, thanks to Heikki's talent and money. Arvo repays Heikki by living with him and treating him like a lap dog."

Eero, I thought, the razor wit, but always in need of an audience to applaud him and agree with him. Paavo: handsome, indolent, overly fond of alcohol and women. And Heikki: artistic, shy, submerged by his stronger-willed brothers and sister, pampered by his mother. All had allowed their weaknesses to ruin their lives. But was any one of them so flawed that he would commit murder?

"What about Kaarina? She's a doctor, and surely you don't suspect that she would do such a thing. Besides, didn't you say she's been away for nearly a year?"

"So she says, but there's no proof that she was in Germany all that time. Someone thought they'd seen her in Helsinki a few months back.

"Who knows what Kaarina would do? She has always been so controlled. It is impossible to read her. I suspect that type of woman—or man, for that matter. She's neurotic, for all her medical degrees. I know she hasn't made any money on her own. I paid for her education; so none of her inheritance was used.

"Doctors in this country don't become as wealthy as in America, but they make a decent living. Why doesn't she have any money? Has she used it to hire an assassin? Who knows what goes on in the life and mind of a neurotic spinster?"

The baby stirred in my arms, so I went and sat in Mummo's little rocking chair. I settled the infant comfortably and rocked back and forth, savoring the familiar squeak of the chair.

As a child, I had often come to talk with Mummo as she rested in that chair. Usually it was because I had been teased by the boys or rejected by Kaarina. Mummo would rock and listen to my tales of woe with a sympathetic cluck of her tongue while she knitted one of her many scarves. (As a small child, since they all looked the same to me, I had assumed that she worked on one never-ending piece of knitting.) Her sympathy was limited to tongue clucks and head shakings, but her presence was always serene and soothing. She was the mother and the grandmother I had never known, and if she seemed somewhat distant, I supposed that was the way of mothers and grandmothers.

Soon they would all be home. The sun was bright, but it was nearly eleven o'clock at night, and I doubted that Mummo would stay for the all-night revelry of the festival. I also doubted that the boys would risk their stepfather's wrath by refusing to escort their mother home.

Grandfather filled his pipe, lit it and tossed the match into an opening in the porcelain stove, to be engulfed by the flames of its wood fire. The stove's blue-and-white tiles were as spotless as usual, and for a moment I forgot the horrible suspicions—facts, as Grandfather believed—and absorbed the peacefulness of the kitchen.

Grandfather drew thoughtfully on his pipe and exhaled a series of smoke rings that floated upward to the wood-beamed ceiling. One of the rings hung over the top of the bearskin on the wall, giving an incongruous halo to the headless creature.

"This is what I plan to do," Grandfather said suddenly, shattering the peace. "Since I have failed to raise these children to avoid temptation, I will remove the temptation.

"They want me dead so they can inherit the estate. I have made a point of telling them that all my money is tied up in the mill and that it took all my available capital to give each of them an advance on their inheritance. I've also told them that the economic situation has not been good and that it has been necessary for me to put all the profits back into the mill.

"If I were to die, they would promptly sell the mill—at a loss, no doubt—and proceed to squander that money, too. I don't intend that the mill I have devoted my life to, and all the people who depend on it for their livelihood, be put out of business. *I* am going to sell it."

"What? That doesn't make any sense. It comes to the same thing."

"You are interrupting again. I said I'm going to sell it, and I am, but I am going to sell it to Janne." He sat back and blew a large wreath of smoke, then looked at me.

If he had been expecting a dramatic reaction, he

was disappointed. I was so surprised that I could only stare at him. I thought, *He's lost his mind or become senile. After all, he is eighty-three. A small stroke, not noticeable physically, but the collapse of a small blood vessel in the brain—that could affect his thinking.*

"Ah, no reaction? Well, maybe the rest of my plan will draw a response. And no, I haven't become foolish-headed, if that's what you are thinking behind that blank mask of a face." His blue eyes twinkled, and it was difficult to hold to my belief that he was senile.

"I will sell the mill to Janne for the sum of—since you are more accustomed to thinking in terms of American currency, I will state the amount that way—one dollar! Do you think that's a fair price?" He raised his eyebrows in an innocent expression.

A fair price? He proposed to sell one of the largest mills in the north of Finland for only a dollar, to a man from whom he had sent me five thousand miles away?

I didn't know what to say. He certainly didn't look senile—but the strain of the years? Again I thought of a minor vascular collapse. That would also explain why he believed that someone in the family was trying to kill him and why he would, in effect, abandon the mill he had devoted his life to.

Should I humor him? Should I prevail on his better judgment, or did he still have the power of judgment? And what about Janne? Why would a man who was about to receive a productive mill for the ridiculous sum of one dollar speak so angrily to his benefactor?

Did he think he had been the butt of one of *Herra* Leinonen's crude jokes, or had he, realizing the man was slightly senile, hoped to shock him back to his senses? I decided I must talk to Kaarina as soon as she returned. Surely, as a doctor, she would have recognized the signs of a stroke.

Grandfather tapped his pipe against the stove and poked a match into the bowl, gathering the last bits of tobacco embers—the best part of a smoke, he once told me. The silence seemed to last many minutes. I rocked back and forth in the squeaky chair, thinking frantically. If only the baby would wake up and demand attention, I thought. But the child slept soundly within my arms.

"In case you are convinced that I have lost my senses, I will tell you the rest of my plan. I have no intention of allowing the mill to pass out of the Leinonen family, and you are the only remaining blood descendant."

He looked away for a moment, and I could see sadness in his face. "Strange that this should be. Once there were so many of us. My brothers, your father, the children that Lea and I would surely have had if she'd lived. They all paid the price for the freedom we enjoy, freedom that allows these whelps to scheme my murder." The soft expression on his face was replaced by fierce determination.

"The mill will stay within my family. You aren't capable of running it, but Janne is. He has proved to be a fine and knowledgeable man. I have told Janne I will sell him the mill if he promises to marry you. Tonight I plan to tell the others that it will not do any good to hurry my departure, as they will not benefit from my death.

"The contract for the sale will be written in such a manner that you will be the major shareholder. Should Janne divorce you or prove an unfit husband, you will have the controlling interest. I'm sure this will never happen, but it pays to be cautious in such matters.

"It is only five days until Midsummer Eve. As usual, the celebration will be held on a Saturday so that everyone can attend. It will be a romantic night for a wedding, don't you agree? We will toast the new bride and groom and remember our old gods. Ha! Now, *there* was a fierce lot. How they will laugh when they see how we outwit the schemers. What a midsummer celebration this one will be!"

"You must be senile! You *must* be. Do you really think you can send for me after ten years and use me this way? What do *I* have to say about all this? One day it is 'Maija, you must go to America and broaden your education, cultivate friends who aren't just simple mill workers.' A *decade* later you send for me, through the ruse of a horrible lie, and say 'Maija, you are to marry Janne on Midsummer Night.' And what of Janne? What kind of man would accept such terms? He used to be so proud. Oh, how could you *think* of such a thing, Grandfather?" I began to cry.

He got up and looked down at me. "Maija, Maija. Do you think I would ever deliberately hurt you? I know it seems that I am ordering you, but it is for your own good—*and* mine, I admit. Yes, and Janne's. It is an ideal situation. There is no other way I can disinherit that band of hangers-on. You are only my grandchild but they are my legal sons and daughter. Don't you see, I want to care for you? It is not for myself that I care. I am old and it doesn't matter about me, but it matters about you—and all the others who have worked for me and look to the Leinonens for their livelihood.

"Maija, don't cry. I thought you would be pleased. You and Janne always seemed so fond of each other— too fond, I rather suspected." He began to stroke my hair as he had done when I was a child.

The gesture blocked my anger and increased my tears. It took all my determination to force them back and say, "Can't you understand? That was *ten years ago*. I was eighteen and Janne was twenty-one. We were practically children. We haven't seen one another in all that time. He's never written me. I've changed . . . God knows how much Janne must have changed."

He cleared his throat. "There are reasons why Janne

didn't correspond with you. The point is, he is a fine man, and you have several days in which to become reacquainted. Maija, I approve of him. I would never entrust the mill to anyone I don't feel is worthy."

"What about me, your granddaughter?" I said, wiping the tears from my eyes with a corner of the baby's blanket.

"Both are my children, Maija. Both the mill and you were brought into being through my body and brain. Don't look so insulted. I love you and want what is good for you, but I also love the business I created and all the people who, because of it, are able to live decently. The mill is not an unworthy sibling."

"What about love, Grandfather? Has it occurred to you that I might want to marry a man who loves me . . . whom I love?"

He turned away from me. "The kind of love you are talking about—the romantic love of fiction—is a fragile thing. It is shattered by the first blow of reality. Respect is the foundation of a good marriage." He paused and added softly, thoughtfully, "Sometimes we are fortunate enough to be granted the type of love you are referring to *and* respect. Perhaps you will find that combination with Janne. Your Grandmother and I——" His voice broke, but he cleared it almost immediately and stood up to his full six feet. "Respect, *sisu,* that is the real foundation of marriage. Janne will not fail you in that."

He was so sincere that it was difficult to keep the resolve with which I meant to counter his plan. I could not agree to it, but I needed time to think—to formulate an alternative, to grasp the full implication of all I'd heard.

"Listen," Grandfather said, "I hear our motorboat. It is almost at the pier. Dry your eyes. Say nothing of what we've discussed. We will talk again tomorrow. Tonight, when you are alone, you will read what I have written in that letter.

"Ha!" he exclaimed, his mood shifting to good humor. "I can hardly wait to see their reaction to the baby."

The sound of the motor died, and voices drifted through the open windows of the kitchen. I put the letter in a fold of the baby's blanket. Though it was midnight, the sun was high in the sky. A white midnight —and I would have to pretend that it was good to be home again.

CHAPTER FOUR

We heard the front doors open and Mummo's unsuccessful attempt to quiet Paavo. He sang out in a rich, slurred baritone voice:

> *Dance, little fairy, dance,*
> *But dance quickly:*
> *The liquor store*
> *Closes at four o'clock.*

His song drew laughter from his brothers but a snort from Grandfather. "It would take more than a 'little fairy' to keep that one away from the *Alkoholiliike*."

Paavo, the first to reach the kitchen, stumbled through the doorway and brandished a bottle of Finnish vodka.

"Good morning, Father," he said drunkenly and began a formal bow that ended in a comic crouch when he caught sight of me.

Mummo, hard on his heels, nearly fell over him. "Paavo, you foolish boy," she started to scold. She was rounder than I had remembered, and her oval body was matched by the shape her mouth formed when, surprised, she saw me.

I read malicious delight in Grandfather's expression as he watched everyone's reaction. Eero and Heikki, who stood behind their mother just gaped. Heikki spoke first. "Maija, you—you have a child?"

"Well, it isn't Paavo's 'little fairy,' " Grandfather

said, glaring at Paavo. "Get up, you drunken fool."

Paavo managed to rise unsteadily, but instead of moving into the room he waved the bottle in my direction. "Cheers!" he said, raising the bottle and gulping vodka.

Mummo pushed him into the room. "Foolish boy, sit down. What will *Herra* and Maija think of you?"

She was nearly twenty years younger than her husband, but nevertheless in her sixties. The neat bun that nestled on the nape of her neck revealed silver hairs mixed with blonde. Her plump figure was clothed in a plain blue dress. I had never seen her wear any other color. In the winter she wore navy blue and in the summer lighter shades of blue. Her eyes darted across me and the child and settled on her husband, as if asking for a clue to her proper reaction. He refused to return her look and studied his stepsons' faces, as if expecting one of them to break into a confession. Recovering from their shock at finding me, they drew down their habitual masks.

Every eye focused on Grandfather. His expression was bland as he puffed on his pipe and continued to look from one face to another.

Heikki gave me a tentative smile and sat on the far end of the table bench, trying to make himself inconspicuous. Eero raised an ironic eyebrow and gracefully seated himself at the table. Paavo stood swaying in the middle of the kitchen.

I was unable to assume any facial disguise. I felt like an idiot, and no doubt looked like one. The baby woke and stared about in wide-eyed wonder. I hoped that he would begin to wail so that the awful silence of the room would be broken.

But it was Mummo who broke the silence. "Well, we must all have some coffee." In Finland, coffee is suitable for any occasion, and it was a "safe" suggestion. She bustled about the kitchen, gathering mugs and filling them from the copper coffee pot.

Paavo pushed his cup aside and took another swig

from the bottle, which caused a fit of hiccups. I began to titter nervously. Grandfather glared at me and, turning a fierce expression on Paavo, said, "I think it would help if the rest of us have a drink, too. We might be better able to tolerate Paavo. Get my bottle, Lilya."

Mummo, delighted to have something to do, immediately rose and fetched a large bottle of vodka that was reserved for the master of the house.

"Perhaps the ladies would rather have *mesimarja?*" he said, referring to the special Finnish liquor made from cloudberries. I nodded in agreement and watched as Mummo found the bottle and poured two glasses of the lighter liquor, one for me and one for herself.

When everyone was provided with a drink, Grandfather raised his glass and said in a loud voice, "*Kippis!* We drink to Maija's return and to a new addition to our family."

I almost gagged on the sweet amber liquid. Surely I hadn't heard him correctly!

Grandfather tipped his glass, downed the vodka and handed the glass to Mummo with a gesture that indicated he wanted another. "If all of you have followed my suggestion that you read the Bible daily," he said, "you will remember the injunction: 'He that is without sin among you, let him first cast a stone at her.'"

His fearsome look swept over the room. "Maija has chosen to return to my house. I have welcomed her and assured her that the rest of you will, too. It seems I have a great-grandson, and I have decided that we will not press her for the details—unless one of you has something to ask or say?" His eyebrows lowered as he looked around the room.

No one had anything to say, with the exception of me, but I couldn't make my mouth move. On top of the strange circumstances of my arrival and the subsequent revelations, he was heaping an inexplicable lie.

When I was finally able to speak, Grandfather forestalled my attempt. "You need not explain yourself, Maija. I have said all that is necessary. You must be very weary from your journey. Lilya, please help her to bed and see that she and the child are made comfortable."

Mummo jumped at his command and came toward me. She peered into the baby's face and asked in a shy voice, "What is his name?"

"I believe she said his name is . . . ah, what is it? A typically American name, eh, Maija? Ah, yes, Ya-ne. My great-grandson's name is Ya-ne." His eyes were as innocent as the infant's as he looked at me for confirmation.

"I suppose you mean Johnny," I said, returning his look and giving the name the correct pronunciation.

"That is what I said, Ya-ne. A common American name. Now, off with you two. I must hear all about the festival and share some news of my own. Go on, Lilya, see that Maija goes directly to bed, and do not make her more tired with your chatter. Off, both of you!"

I was too exhausted to do anything but obey, and without a further word Mummo and I left the room. She offered to take the child, but his warm body radiated reality, and I held him to me tightly. He seemed my only link to sanity. Mummo took my overnight case from the hallway and led the way up the back stairs.

Neither of us spoke on our way to the Ladies' Chamber, but when the bedroom door was shut, Mummo began to chatter in just the manner her husband had cautioned her against. I marveled at her ability to say almost nothing while talking incessantly. It was impossible for her to remain either

silent or idle for long, and she busied herself talking,
turning down my bed and unpacking the suitcase.

The baby was sound asleep again. I nestled him
in the blankets of the bed. Mummo's flow of half-
expressed thoughts continued as she helped me into
my nightgown. But my nerves finally gave way under
her barrage and I broke in urgently. "Please, Mummo,
something is very wrong, and I must talk to you about
it."

She looked around the room and said, "Oh, I am
sorry. What is it you lack? Ah, I shall have to bring
the cradle down from the attic. Perhaps one of the
boys will assist me——"

"No!" I spoke more sharply than I intended. "I
mean, that would be very nice, but tomorrow is soon
enough. We'll be fine tonight. I don't think you understood what I was trying to say. Oh, there is so
much to explain. I don't know where to start."

The old woman looked nervously at the door and
said, "We will talk tomorrow, Maija. Your grandfather will be angry with me if I stay here too long.
It is all right, child; I know you have much to confide,
and I will be happy to listen to you tomorrow. I
confess," she said with a sigh, "the years are catching
up with me. I feel very weary from the festival. So
we talk in the morning. You and the baby have all
you need tonight?"

She was standing in the doorway, anxious to leave.
"Yes, thank you. We will be fine."

"So I shall see you in the morning. *Hyvää yötä*
—good night." She closed the door gently.

As she had stood in the doorway, I noticed that
several strands of her blonde-and-white hair had
broken loose from her bun, making her look, in
silhouette, like a plump troll. Trolls could be cuddled,
like Poika, or feared, like the ones in the linen closet;
but they were not to be confided in. I decided to make
no further attempt to break through the barricade of

Mummo's unworldliness. I would seek advice from someone less insulated against harsh reality.

I sat on the edge of the bed, being careful not to disturb the sleeping child—Ya-ne, as Grandfather had christened him. I smiled despite myself and wondered if it were possible for so agile a mind to be damaged. Perhaps it was possible to be alert and aware in one area of the brain while confused in another. Fatigued and bewildered, I lay down and turned my face into the welcome softness of the pillow. My arrival and the subsequent events revolved in my mind like a kaleidoscope of meaningless words and expressions.

The trolls were coming! I could hear their stealthy footfalls. They were pushing at the door. Where was Poika, my protector? The hinges squeaked and the leader of the trolls called out a command.

I jerked awake. A small animal was pushing the door ajar and issuing a diffident command: *"Meow!"*

The cat, Pai-Pai, walked purposefully toward the bed and leaped onto my stomach. His large yellow eyes inspected me for a moment, and then he walked across my body and lay down beside the slumbering infant. My heart was pounding as I walked to the door and fastened it securely.

If I had been less tired, I might have found it amusing, but in my fatigued condition it seemed as ominous as everything else that had happened since I arrived. So many questions and no answers.

Suddenly I remembered the letter that Grandfather had intended to mail to me. I reached across the slumbering baby and the cat and searched through the folds of Ya-ne's blanket. The envelope was long and fat and not easily concealed, but I could not find it. In desperation and mounting panic, I unwrapped the child and searched the blanket, and then the bedroom floor. I looked down the hallway, then on the stairway, and then in the downstairs hall. As I approached the kitchen door, I heard angry voices, with Grandfather's bass voice dominant. It was not the time to interrupt in search of a letter that outlined the suspicions of an old man who believed that a member of his family was attempting to murder him.

I crept back to my bed. The cat purred in accompaniment to the small sounds of the sleeping child. My mind and body refused to search further for answers. I lay down beside them and fell into a heavy sleep.

CHAPTER FIVE

I woke at the sound of a motorboat drawing up to the pier. Automatically I reached for my bedside clock, only to upset several perfume bottles on the vanity. Even when my eyes opened, it took a moment to realize that I was back in Grandfather's house. The room was flooded with sunlight, but this gave no clue to the time. I felt so groggy that I was sure I hadn't slept for long.

A soft, warm form cuddled against my back, and all the previous events rushed back to me, routing my sleepiness and filling me with nervous dread. I rolled over carefully, grateful that I hadn't crushed the infant in my sleep. His blanket seemed curiously empty despite a rhythmic movement within it. As I started to gather the child into my arms, a furry head appeared, and Pai-Pai struggled out of the blanket and leaped from the bed meowing a protest at having his warm nest disturbed.

The baby was gone! One macabre possibility after another went through my mind as I searched for him.

I pulled on a robe and located my wristwatch. It was nearly nine in the morning. The door of the bedroom was ajar. My hand trembled on the banister as I made my way down the stairs. Approaching the entrance hall, I heard the sound of men's voices, but I didn't pause until I reached the kitchen. Mummo was bent over the sink, humming a tuneless little melody.

53

The sleeves of another blue dress were rolled up and her sturdy arms supported the infant, who was in a basin of water, content and gurgling. I sank down on the bench in relief.

Mummo smiled and continued bathing the child. "I decided you should sleep late this morning, so I went in at six o'clock and took the baby. He is such a wonder! My babies never would have slept so late in the morning," she said. Her tone seemed to imply that this had made them superior.

"You found his bottle?" I inquired.

"Oh, yes. I saw you had one last night. I haven't had much experience feeding an infant with an artificial nipple, but we managed, didn't we, Ya-ne? I also fed him a bit of porridge. I am puzzled about one thing, Maija," she continued as she lifted the child from the basin and wrapped a large towel around him. "I haven't been able to find any clothes for him, other than those in that bag."

"Ah, Maija, good morning!" Grandfather boomed from the doorway. "You look rested, and the little fellow seems quite content. Have you told Lilya about your lost suitcase? I will make inquiries for you when I get to my office. Don't frown so, Maija. It is a small matter. I am sure I can find it if you will just have patience. You always did lack patience. It is a virtue, you know."

He sat in the large rocker, took his pipe from his pocket and gestured with it at the soiled clothes that Mummo had removed from the baby. "I told Maija to take the children's old togs. I was sure you wouldn't mind."

"Of course, not, *Herra* Leinonen," Mummo said. She had never adopted a more intimate name for the man she married. To her, he was always "Mister."

"Well, Maija, did you go right to sleep last night, or did you get engrossed in the book I lent you? Interesting story, don't you think?"

In my panic over the child I had forgotten the letter. I glanced at Mummo, but she was absorbed in drying between the baby's toes. She hadn't seen my look of distress that Grandfather's innocent-sounding question evoked.

"No, Grandfather, I seem to have misplaced it, and I didn't want to disrupt all of you by coming back to the kitchen to search for it."

Lightning flashed from Grandfather's eyes. "How careless of you. I seem to remember you were always misplacing things as a child. I hoped you would have grown more responsible." His tone was so harsh that Mummo turned her head and looked at him.

"Do not become so provoked, *Herra*. The doctor warned you it is not good for your health. The book is unimportant, and the girl was very tired last night. Maija, I am going to look for a pair of booties for the child." She placed the infant in my arms and walked from the room.

We waited until we heard her footsteps recede down the hallway.

"How could you be so careless?"

"Why did you say this is *my* child? Isn't it enough that——"

The baby began to scream at our tirade. I tried to soothe him by sitting in Mummo's chair and rocking frantically. When he subsided, Grandfather and I glared at one another.

He sucked angrily at his pipe. "We must think," he said finally. "Where did you put the letter last night? Did you look for it upstairs?"

"I searched the entire room, and the back stairway and hall."

The baby was still fretful, and I shifted my position to make him comfortable. As I adjusted the cushion on the back of the chair, the missing envelope fell to the floor.

Grandfather immediately retrieved it, tapped it

against his broad hand and frowned. "Try to think what you did with it last night after I handed it to you."

"I'm sure I put it into a fold in the baby's blanket."

"Ah, I think I see what happened," he said as he turned the envelope over in his hand. It was crumpled but still sealed. "It must have slipped out of the blanket and become wedged in the chair. The cushion was pushed against it, so it couldn't be seen. Thank God."

He handed me the envelope and watched as I placed it securely in the large pocket of my robe.

"Now, Maija, you must listen to me and not interrupt. I know you are upset because of my story about the baby. It came into my mind after Paavo's performance, when it was too late to signal my intention. As I promised you, I will investigate the child's identity when I reach the mill office, which will be soon. Mr. Roine, the company lawyer, just arrived and I must go with him to attend to urgent business.

"I have a feeling that the arrival of this child on my doorstep is somehow tied in with the other, ah, matter. I have no idea how, but it occurred to me that if he is being used, it would considerably disrupt someone's plans if we simply claimed that he is yours. I doubted that anyone would expect that development, and I hoped they would show their guilt."

He shrugged. "Well, either they play a good game or the three of them are innocent. But I don't think it will hurt to wait them out a bit longer."

"But, Grandfather, you are talking about a human life and my reputation. You can't use us as if we were pawns in a game."

"I said don't interrupt. As you will see when you read that letter, this is no game, and I don't view it as such."

As the clock began to chime ten o'clock, Grandfather said, "I must go now, Maija. Mr. Roine is waiting for me in the parlor. All I ask is that you be patient for a short time. Read that letter, stay to yourself as much as possible, and, whatever you do, say as little as possible."

"When will you return?" I asked. I was afraid to be left alone in the web of lies he had spun.

"In a few hours, unless there are complications. Ah, one more thing," he said. "It might interest you to know that Janne bought the cottage on the east end of the island. I don't know if I mentioned that."

"No, you didn't," I answered coldly, "along with all the other things you haven't mentioned."

"Patience, Maija. Develop that virtue. It's very attractive in a woman. Janne should be home this afternoon. There were problems on the late shift, and he worked through the night at the mill. Till later."

He was gone before a suitable retort came to my muddled mind, and Mummo reentered the kitchen with several pairs of hand-knit booties. I heard the men leave the house and then the sound of the motorboat as they pulled away from the pier.

Mummo was discoursing about something or other, but I paid little attention to her. She appeared content to chatter to herself and the baby, apparently unconcerned that I ignored her. She put a thick pair of booties on the baby's feet.

"You must see that their feet are always warm and dry, Maija, and that only wool is next to the skin. Those man-made materials are unhealthy."

I vowed to rescue him from the hot, scratchy socks as soon as I dared, but for the moment I was only too glad to let Mummo take care of him. I had to find time to read the letter and think.

"Would you mind if I leave the baby with you while I dress?"

"Of course not," she answered, cuddling the infant against her ample bosom. "Ah, it is so pleasant to have a small one to look after again. How quickly they grow!"

"Thank you. I think I'll take a cup of coffee with me. It's too late to have breakfast, and from the aroma coming from your stove, I know that I must prepare for a wonderful dinner."

Mummo's plump cheeks reddened in pleasure. She was justly proud of her cooking.

"*Herra* told me that in America you eat only cold cuts and bread in the middle of the day. Is that right? It seems absurd!"

I smiled, remembering my initial reaction to the scanty American lunch. Now it would be difficult to force myself to eat a heavy meal in the middle of the day.

"Yes, that is so. Their customs are very different from ours. It is, well, a faster way of life. Everyone seems to be in such a hurry. I suppose that is why they have become such a powerful nation."

"Well, the Americans won't have enough energy to run their country if they don't eat a proper dinner. I am sure that is why they have had so much trouble lately. Finland could never have withstood so many wars if we hadn't eaten sensibly, and it was not always easy to do so in the bad days when food was scarce."

I smiled at Mummo's simple analysis of America's problems as I poured a large mug of coffee and laced it with cream and sugar. I had learned to drink the weak American brew black, but it is impossible to drink the strong Finnish coffee in that fashion. I groaned mentally at the thought of the calories I was imbibing.

"I'll be down in a while," I said, but the old woman seemed to have dismissed me already and was cooing to Johnny. I wouldn't be missed.

Back in my room, I dressed in a seersucker pantsuit and brushed my hair. I had arranged for my larger pieces of luggage to be sent to the mill office and hoped that Mrs. Saarinen, Grandfather's secretary, would see that they were sent to the island. The wardrobe I had with me would soon be depleted.

I took the baby's blanket from the bed, shook the blue-gray cat hairs out of it and made the bed. I fussed about the neat room until I admitted I was only procrastinating. It was time to read the letter. I took the envelope from my robe and turned it over in my hand, wondering if the contents would be hard evidence of the accusations or simply macabre fantasies of an old man.

I stepped out on the sunlit balcony and took a deep breath of the summer air. The lake shimmered like silver-blue satin under the bright rays of the sun. Again, unbidden, the memory came to mind: *Once Janne had said my eyes were the same color as the lake's waters.* Without realizing, I looked across the top of the thick forest, seeking the roof of a cottage on the far end of the island.

"Damn!" I said out loud, then thought how pleased Grandfather would be to see me staring dreamily in that direction.

My mind returned to the business at hand and I ran a thumbnail under the sealed flap of the envelope. There were minute tears across the flap, and as I pulled it back carefully, I saw that a loose layer of gum or paste formed the seal. I rubbed a particle of the sticky material between my thumb and index finger, making a tiny ball.

A neat job, I thought, and one that would not have been noticed if I had simply ripped the envelope open. Someone had opened the letter and carefully resealed it. It was possible that Grandfather had wanted to add something, but it didn't seem likely that he would have bothered to repaste the flap. He would have used a new envelope.

My hands trembled as I withdrew the four pages of the letter. My eyes had to adjust to the almost illegible, old-fashioned handwriting. Grandfather wasn't used to writing in longhand. For years he'd had efficient secretaries who handled his correspondence. His age, as well as his mental state, made his handwriting even more difficult to decipher.

I read the letter as quickly as I could, then went inside, locked the bedroom door and sat on the bed to reread it thoroughly. He began by explaining the advance inheritances he had bestowed on each stepchild and the manner in which each of them, to his way of thinking, had squandered the money.

The first "attempt" on his life involved the ladder that had served the pier for over fifty years. Grandfather rejected the idea that it might have simply succumbed to rot. It broke loose when he was climbing it, and he fell backward, suffering nothing more than a slight blow to his head when he landed on the deck. The ladder floated under the pier, and his attempt to reach it with an oar pushed it farther away.

His bellows finally brought Mummo, Eero, and Paavo. Ignoring his command that someone retrieve the ladder, they brought him into the house and forced him to lie down. He pushed aside the icepack Mummo attempted to put on his head, but Kaarina, who was home at that time, checked his eyes for a concussion and demanded that he remain in bed. No amount of railing succeeded in getting anyone to retrieve the ladder so that he could have it examined, and no one could convince him that it had simply come loose after many long years.

Grandfather, deciding they were preventing him from investigating the mishap, pretended to dismiss the incident and agreed to remain in bed. He told Mummo to bring Janne, saying he had to brief him on the day's business. As soon as Janne arrived, Grandfather ordered the others out of his room and told Janne to find the ladder and make a thorough examination of its fastenings. Janne later reported that the wood was rotten, but found it strange that the bolts had pulled away so cleanly. It was impossible to determine whether they had simply worked themselves free or had been deliberately loosened. Grandfather chose to believe that the ladder had been sabotaged, but I was not prepared to accept the collapse of a rotten piece of wood as proof of attempted murder.

The second attempt occurred in the mill yard, as he checked a load of lumber that had been carelessly stacked. Grandfather claimed there was no warning bell from the overhead crane that dropped a log so close to him that it dented the side of his hardhat. The hat saved his life by deflecting the blow that would have crushed his skull. He was knocked to the ground and saw only a blur of overalls as the operator jumped from the cab and disappeared among the piles of lumber.

As soon as Grandfather was able to summon help, a search was conducted, but no one could find the operator. Whoever it was had apparently fled from the area. The personnel records revealed that the regular operator, Uno Dahl, had failed to show up for his shift. Uno was a willing, capable worker when he didn't succumb to the temptations of drink. It wasn't unusual for him to take an extra day or two off each month, so that a temporary operator had been hired to fill in for him. The man was at the personnel office when Uno's absence was reported, and they put him to work without checking his references. His address and references later proved to be fraudulent.

It must have been a terrifying experience, but it hardly added up to a clear attempt at murder. More likely, it was a case of a man lying about his experience and supplying phony references in hope of getting a day's pay.

The operator's appearance was impossible to describe, beyond baggy blue overalls and a hardhat that was too large for him. He had answered the preliminary questions with his head hung down in a subservient fashion. The substitute operator, Grandfather speculated, could even have been a woman . . . Uno later stated that he had received a note telling him not to report for his regular shift, but he was unable to produce it.

As for the third attempt, Grandfather had slept late one morning, and when he awoke, everyone except the maid, who was later discharged by Mummo, was gone. The girl answered the summons of his bedside bell and brought coffee. It smelled bitter, however, and Grandfather asked the girl if she had prepared it. "Oh, no, *Herra* Leinonen," she responded. "I don't drink coffee. I took it from the pot on the table, under the cozy. Is it cold?"

It was piping hot and burned his tongue. This, plus his dislike of the fearful maid, caused him to berate her and send her away. After she left, he poured the coffee into the saucer and blew on it. He wasn't certain if it was his scalded tongue or the coffee itself, but it had a disagreeable taste, and after only one swallow he poured it back in the cup and pushed the cup and saucer away. They teetered on the edge of the bedside table, then fell to the floor.

I could almost hear him curse as he rang the bell for the maid, who was unwilling to return. As he got out of bed and bent to pick up the broken china, he felt dizzy, but managed to straighten himself and then fell backward onto the bed. A buzzing filled his head. The dizziness grew worse, and his limbs became numb. He lay helpless, pressing a finger against the bell and hoping he was pushing hard enough to make it ring.

He said he didn't become unconscious, but he didn't know how much time had passed before Mummo and Kaarina were beside him. Kaarina asked a number of questions about the numbness, and when he refused to answer, she sent Heikki to get Dr. Tami for a second opinion.

The doctor examined Grandfather and gave a frustrating series of "um's" and "ah's" in answer to his demand for an immediate diagnosis. The only definite statement the doctor made was that Grandfather should be taken to the hospital for a full examination. Grandfather refused. By that time he had regained some strength and the numbness seemed to have lessened. Still slightly dizzy, he crept to the bedroom door and listened to the conference between Kaarina and Dr. Tami on the probable cause of the incident.

"I've suspected that he may have been having minor strokes for some time now, Dr. Tami," Kaarina said. "He refuses to listen to my advice or allow me to examine him."

Dr. Tami agreed that it had been some time since he had examined *Herra* Leinonen. ("As if I weren't aware of my physical condition!" Grandfather appended hotly.) "Yes, *Herra* Leinonen always had a mind of his own, Kaarina, but we must humor him now." (Grandfather had underlined *humor*.) "His blood pressure is high, but that is not unusual for a man of his years. Keep him in bed for a few days. Do you have a sedative, or shall I leave something?"

"I have several mild sedatives. I shall take care of everything," Kaarina said. "I just wanted to get a second opinion."

"As I said, it is difficult to diagnose such an episode in a man of your stepfather's years without getting him to a hospital, but I know you will keep him under close observation."

Grandfather was infuriated to hear them say that he had suffered a stroke. He wrote that his physical condition and mental abilities were never better than during the days preceding his "seizure." He was going to inform Kaarina of the fact when she came in to administer her sedative, but Mummo and the maid accompanied her. They gathered the pieces of the cup and saucer and washed away the coffee. He told them to leave the mess, but Kaarina insisted that it be cleaned up before someone stepped in it.

Kaarina asserted the same authority with the sedative she wished him to take, but Grandfather was not to be bullied, and she finally gave up. He did submit to three days of bed rest, however. During that time the numbness in his limbs disappeared and the moments of dizziness became less frequent.

He wrote the letter while he was confined to his bed. "You will notice how quickly the coffee was disposed of. No time to get a sample for analysis. It was not a stroke that felled me, it was poison. Fortunately, I have always been fussy about my coffee—there was something other than coffee in that cup."

I lay back on the bed and stared at the distinctive handwriting. In the swirls of its old-fashioned script was the account, Grandfather said, that would convince me that three attempts had been made on his life. But it was not convincing.

Each incident had a logical explanation. The ladder was old and rotten. It could well have been a coincidence that it finally pulled loose as Grandfather was climbing it. It could have happened to anyone—any member of the family or any visitor to the island. Only someone who was mad would have attempted such a scheme, knowing how uncertain it was that Grandfather would be the one to ascend the ladder. On the other hand, of course, it could have been someone who was familiar with Grandfather's schedule.

It was understandable that a newly hired laborer would flee, having almost killed the mill's owner. And the coffee incident might have been no more than what Kaarina and Dr. Tami diagnosed. It wasn't like Grandfather to oversleep. Had that, in itself, been a warning of a stroke?

If one viewed the incidents in a detached way, they added up to evidence that Grandfather had suffered several small strokes. Perhaps he'd had one while attempting to climb the ladder and the backward thrust of his heavy body had pulled the bolts loose. Was his mind so muddled in the mill yard that he hadn't heard the warning bell?

I folded the letter and put it into a pocket of my jacket. I was even more confused after reading what was supposed to give me a clear picture of the events that, in Grandfather's mind, added up to murder.

I closed my eyes and pressed my fingertips against them. Fragments of color, like fireworks in a black sky, exploded behind my lids. Grandfather's spidery handwriting wove through the flashes of light and color. I felt dizzy, but it wasn't caused by the coffee I had drunk. It was caused by the confusion of thoughts that whirled about my brain.

It had become warm, and I was oppressed by the closeness of the room—by the house itself. The brilliant light that flooded my window drew me outside to let the sunshine wash my body and mind, to smell the clean fragrance of nature.

The envelope was addressed to me. What had prompted someone else to open it? If all the events that Grandfather chronicled were innocent, why had someone tampered with his mail? Could it be true that someone had tried to kill him?

CHAPTER SIX

I went downstairs to the kitchen, where Mummo was seated in her rocker, the baby cradled in her arms. Both were asleep and wore identical expressions of innocence. The baby's mouth puckered occasionally in a sucking movement, and Mummo snored in lady-like fashion.

The lid of a large pot on a rear burner of the stove heaved up and down, releasing an enticing aroma that mingled with the fragrance of newly baked loaves of bread. Pai-Pai was curled in a furry knot on the middle of a braided rug. He lifted his head, gave me an annoyed look, then resettled into his midmorning nap. The tranquillity of the kitchen contrasted sharply with the mood and accusations in the letter I had just read.

There was no sign of the men. Either they had left to pursue their various concerns or they were still sleeping off the effects of last night. The voices I heard issuing from the kitchen the evening before had been angry. Obviously, Grandfather had wasted no time in announcing his intention to sell Janne the mill in order to disinherit them.

It was clear that my services were not required, so I didn't feel guilty as I walked out of the house into the warm sunshine. I found the bicycles still stored in racks on the side of the porch. The one that I recognized as mine had been well cared for throughout the decade of my absence. I took it from the rack and, without conscious intent, turned onto the pathway that led to the far side of the island.

The path wound through the thick forest of trees, and I pedaled slowly, inhaling the fragrance of pine and birch. Sunbeams reflected off the smooth bark of the birches, making them glisten as if they were encased in silver armor. The sky was the radiant blue that I have seen only in my homeland—no trace of smog reminded me of polluted southern California skies.

A brown form raced across my path, almost upsetting me as I applied the brakes. The creature stopped and turned, as if to scold me, and thorny spikes rose up on its back. It didn't seem possible that this hedgehog was the same one I had tamed as a child, but when I called to it in a quiet voice, the animal eyed me curiously and began to lower its barbs. I continued to speak softly as I dismounted from the bike and slowly advanced on the wary creature. It seemed mesmerized as I bent down to it and extended my hand, remembering how soft those quills had been when my old friend allowed me to pet him. I had just succeeded in stroking the animal when my bicycle stand collapsed, startling it so that it embedded needle-sharp barbs in my outstretched hand. The pain, when I tried to pull them out, was more than I could bear.

Forcing my tears back, I climbed on my bike and began a wavering, one-handed course down the pathway to Janne's cottage. I hadn't intended (I told myself) to actually go to Janne's, but now it was the only logical thing to do (I told myself). The barbs hurt dreadfully, and I needed help in removing them. Even Janne would know that I hadn't petted a hedgehog just to find an excuse for seeing him.

My hand was throbbing and swollen by the time I came to the small cottage, which sat in a clearing. I caught a glimpse of the shimmering lake and heard the sound of someone chopping wood. Around the side

of the cottage, Janne was wielding an ax over a pile
of logs, splintering them into firewood. It was warm
work, and the northern sun beat down relentlessly.
Sweat coursed down his bare, sun-bronzed back. His
black hair glistened with perspiration, and two curls
fell over his forehead, giving him a boyish look that
contrasted with the hard planes of his face.

As I dismounted the bicycle, I drove a barb deeper
into my hand and gasped. Janne turned, saw me and
frowned. It was obvious that he was not delighted to
see me. Wordlessly, I extended my wounded hand, and
his frown deepened.

Then he threw his head back and laughed—the
deep, full-throated laugh that I remembered so well.
His eyes twinkled as he said, "I hope that is not the
hand *Herra* Leinonen expects me to ask for."

That "barb" entered my heart, and I started to
remount my cycle, but he put his hand on my shoulder
and said, "Come on, foolish one, go into the house
and let me see what first aid I can offer. I thought from
the look of things yesterday that you had grown up,
but I see that you still have the childish conviction that
you can pet anything that moves. Don't stand there
with those silly tears running down your cheeks."

He opened the door of the cottage and motioned me
to sit on one of the kitchen chairs as he looked through
his cupboards, finally locating a large pair of tweezers
and a small bottle. The tweezers were so large that I
suspected he used them to remove fishhooks, and the
fluid in the bottle was brilliant red.

My horror must have been mirrored on my face.
"Come on, Maija, be brave. This won't be the first
time I have mended your wounds. I seem to remember
that you always had a freshly skinned knee. Come to
think of it, you never were very brave when I dabbed
you with iodine."

"And I don't remember your being very gentle or

sympathetic then, either," I said, suppressing a wail as he pulled out the first quill.

"Be still and don't wriggle your hand or it will hurt worse." The expression on his face seemed to imply that he wouldn't mind that happening. I sat obediently while he twisted out the other barbs and poured the iodine over the palm of my hand.

"There," he said in satisfaction as he examined his operation. "Only one more bit of first aid is required." He brought my hand to his mouth and kissed it. Even through the sting of the iodine I could feel the warmth of his lips. His green eyes looked full into mine, and then he looked down at my hand again. He picked up my right hand and examined it in the same fashion.

"I think you got them all out," I said breathlessly, amazed by his kiss.

"I was looking for a ring. I see you wear none— neither on your right hand nor on your left hand."

"That is easily explained, Janne. I have never been married or engaged."

"I see," he said and released my hand.

"Janne, I don't think you see at all——"

"You don't have to explain. I thought I might have jumped to the wrong conclusion yesterday—and that you could be widowed or divorced." He shrugged. "But I could hardly expect you to remain a virgin all these years. I certainly didn't; why should you?" His tone was humorous, but his eyes evaded mine. "Did your grandfather tell you that I married?"

I felt the blood rush to my face. Another of Grandfather's neglected details.

"I see he did not. *Herra* Leinonen likes to skip over undesirable details if they don't serve his purpose. Oh, I am free now, Maija. His plan can still work."

"Did your . . . wife die?" I asked in a voice almost too soft to be heard.

"Oh, no, she was the picture of health the last time I saw her—but that was almost a year ago. She simply tired of being my wife. I went to the University of Helsinki, thanks to *Herra* Leinonen's scholarship, and she seemed to think me quite wonderful when we first met. Did wonders for my sagging ego, and it did sag after you left and I never heard a word from you. Your grandfather was always evasive about your address, so there was no way for me to contact you. I *did* think you would write me."

"But I did, Janne. I wrote you many times, but you never answered."

Janne turned around from putting the tweezers and iodine back in the cupboard and looked at me. "Maija, it is a little too late for lies. What does it matter now?"

"But that's *not* a lie. I *did* write—many times. When you didn't respond, I realized I was making a fool of myself."

He sat next to me at the kitchen table, searching my face intently, as if he could discover the truth with the power of his look.

He spoke thoughtfully. "My father must have made an agreement with *Herra* Leinonen to keep your letters from me in return for the scholarship." He gave a short, ironic laugh. "I remember his lectures about 'practicality' and 'knowing one's place.' Well, the twists of fate, eh, Maija? There we were, two lovesick children, each thinking the other had forsaken us, while a couple of shrewd old men engineered our lives."

"Grandfather said there was an explanation for your silence, but he told me so many things that it didn't really register. Did you love your wife?" The question came out even as I tried to stifle it.

His face darkened. "Did you love your lover or did it just happen? I'm sorry. I shouldn't have said that. I'll tell you the truth. I was flattered that such a cosmopolitan girl would show interest in me, a simple country man. She was fun and bright, and she thought my unsophisticated ways were 'quaint.' I told her that after graduation I would become the manager of the Leinonen mill. I doubt she'd ever heard of the mill, but she seemed impressed.

"We were married as soon as I received my degree. I brought her back to the village. At first she found everything 'charming,' but it was only a few months before the novelty wore off and she begged me to move to Helsinki. I explained that I couldn't. All my life, and all my future life, was tied to the mill. I wasn't suited for any other type of work and couldn't live in a city.

"I tried to pacify her by suggesting she go on shopping trips to Helsinki. Soon those trips stretched into weeks, and finally months. She spent more time there than she did here. It's strange how gossip can seep into a remote village such as ours. No one had the nerve to tell me to my face, but I heard she had been seen with other men.

"The last time I saw her, she told me she had found someone else—someone more 'aware of her needs.' She demanded a divorce, and I refused. I believed in marriage for life—for better or worse. But I wasn't prepared for her final argument.

"She told me that she had an abortion while she was in Helsinki on one of her 'shopping trips.' She said she knew that if she had my child I would never let her go. And if I insisted on forcing her to remain married to me, she would find a way of aborting any future child that might be conceived. It's not a pretty story, is it? The story of a fool."

He forced a small smile and said, "Despite my sneering remarks, I am glad you kept your child. Perhaps, given enough time, I can make myself believe it is my own."

"Janne," I said, "you must listen to me. The child you saw is not mine."

"What?"

"I know it sounds unbelievable, but I found it in a wicker basket that Helge had aboard his boat. He unloaded it with my luggage. I have no idea where the infant came from. To make matters worse, Grandfather told everyone in the family that the child is mine. He has some strange notion that the infant is connected with what he considers to be a plot against his life, a plot by someone within our own family."

"He told me about his suspicions, but this is ridiculous. He can't just keep the child without telling the police."

"He's gone to the mill now, but he promised that he'd start an immediate investigation. In the meantime, he asked me to go along with this."

I took Grandfather's letter from my jacket and handed it to Janne. "Read this. He had intended to mail it but changed his mind and decided to make me come in person. He actually sent a wire telling me he was *dying!* Now can you understand why I was so bewildered when you saw me on the porch?

"Oh, read it and tell me what you think. Is his mind affected? He seems so sure that someone is trying to kill him, but none of what he's written supports such a wild charge. He sounds like someone who has suffered a stroke. And then this bizarre plan of his, to sell you the mill in return for your marrying me. I think he must be mad."

"What do you think of me, Maija? Do you think I am also mad? Do you think I would agree if I didn't still have love for you?"

My heart almost ceased beating as his words seemed to echo over and over again: ". . . *if I didn't still have love for you.*"

"Janne, do you love me? Did you ever love me? You never told me so. What kind of man have you become? What kind of man would marry a woman he hasn't seen in ten years just to get control of a business?"

"I will ask you a similar question, Maija. What kind of woman have you become? Or are you a woman even now? I married a girl-child once, and I don't know if even the Leinonen mill would be enough inducement to make me go through that kind of hell again.

"Yes, I love you, or I guess I do. I remember that foolish pounding of my heart and how muddled you made me feel. And you still have that effect on me. When I was a boy, I always assumed you would someday be my wife. Maybe I'm just in love with the memory of the girl you used to be and with the woman I hoped you would become."

This was hardly the romantic declaration I would have wished for. "Well, according to Grandfather, we have several whole days in which to become reacquainted before we are united for a lifetime," I retorted with sarcasm.

"Maija, we *have* known each other a lifetime."

"You seem to dismiss the last ten years as readily as Grandfather."

Janne tipped his head in acknowledgment of my statement, then said, "Perhaps it would be well for both of us if we adopted *Herra* Leinonen's attitude. Now, why don't you let me read that letter while you wash your face and brush your hair?" He lifted a strand of hair away from my face and touched my cheek.

I left him with the letter and went to the bathroom to do as he suggested. The face I encountered in the mirror startled me: despite my disheveled hair and tear-stained face, I thought I looked lovely—lovelier than I could ever remember. My cheeks were a bright pink and my eyes *were* as blue as the lake's water.

A brush on the bathroom shelf had a pink handle. Had it belonged to his ex-wife, or did he keep it for . . . guests? I pushed the thought away as I pulled the brush through my tangled hair. I made a center part, tucking the side strands behind my ears, and then washed my face with cold water, which came from the lake itself. My mascara and eyeliner disappeared during the scrubbing, but I wasn't displeased with my appearance.

Janne was still sitting at the kitchen table, which dominated the room. The pages of the letter lay in front of him, and he was staring into space. My reappearance broke into whatever thoughts occupied him and he smiled at me.

"Now you look more like Maija. All that makeup does not suit you." He returned to the letter and said, "Why don't you pour us both a drink? You'll find a bottle in the cupboard."

The only liquor I could find was a half-filled bottle of Koskenkorva, a vodka considerably less potent than the best Russian brews, but strong enough.

"Such strong drink!" I remarked as I looked for glasses.

"Don't act like a teetotaler, Maija. I remember when you used to nip at your grandfather's vodka. Or have you joined a temperance league in America?"

I laughed and my face flushed as I remembered filling my dolls' nursing bottles with vodka and smuggling them out of the house. Janne and I had felt terribly sinful and grown-up as we sipped the tiny potions. But now I poured the vodka liberally, thinking a large drink would be welcome after the nerve-wrenching morning.

Janne pushed the letter aside, picked up his glass and clinked it against mine. "So now we are grown up and don't have to hide in the marsh reeds to do our tippling." He spoke with the wide-open grin I had so often remembered.

"What do you think about the letter?" I asked, anxious to hear his opinion.

"It's hard to say, though I remember the ladder incident and the accident in the mill yard. I wasn't actually there, at either event, but I became involved shortly after they occurred. I didn't see anything sinister in them. I also remember when your grandfather was confined to bed, but he said he had the flu. But I must admit that I thought he was deranged when he made me that proposition yesterday—offering to sell me the mill, to give it to me, in return for my agreement to marry you.

"I'm sorry, Maija, I thought you already knew about the arrangement, and when I saw the child, I assumed I was being used to uphold the honor of the family. I just didn't *think*—it was such a shock seeing you with an infant in your arms."

"Then, you refused the offer? But he led me to believe——"

"No, Maija, I didn't refuse. After all, how could I reject such an offer? No matter what you had become, I would have the mill, and you know that owning a mill has always been my dream. Your grandfather has been a wonderful employer, but he has always resisted modernization. I have so many ideas, and I would be able to——"

"You thought only of the mill," I said, unable to conceal my disappointment.

Janne looked at me over the rim of his glass. "Yes, I admit it. It seemed too much to believe that I could also have the girl I loved. I also understood that it was a business arrangement that would allow the mill to remain in the Leinonen family and that you would have control of the major share. Your grandfather made that very clear to me."

"And you agreed?"

"I didn't say that. I told him I would consider it. *Herra* Leinonen chose to interpret that as agreement. It's hopeless trying to argue with that old—forgive me, Maija—with *Herra* Leinonen. You know that yourself. It was only after I saw you with the baby in your arms that I thought, 'Why not? What is there left for me besides the mill?' A man should be able to attain at least one dream in his life."

"So now you are agreeable?"

"I am. The question is," and his green eyes twinkled, "are you?"

"So we will fall hopelessly in love within the prescribed days and wed and bed on Midsummer Eve while the old gods cackle approval. Is that the idea? How romantic," I said.

"It could happen, Maija."

He stood up and pulled me to my feet. Taking my hands gently into his, he placed them behind my back and drew me toward him until my head pressed against his warm shoulder.

"We could make all our dreams come true." His kiss was gentle and controlled, but my mouth responded with an urgency I never suspected I could experience. In an instant, his kiss became a hard demand and our bodies were pressed so close together that I could feel the beat of his heart.

It was more than vodka that made my blood race, and he sensed my desire. His lips released mine, and he kissed my face and neck, as his hands caressed my breasts.

"Janne," I said weakly, pushing away his hands, "I know you won't believe it, but I am still a virgin."

"I don't care," he answered. His words were muffled as he kissed my neck.

I pulled away from him, afraid of my responsive body. "Well, *I* do."

He drew a long breath. "I'm sorry, Maija. I didn't mean to—*why* are you still a virgin?"

I laughed and couldn't resist the obvious answer. "Because I've never been with a man."

"But why not? God knows you are lovelier than you were when you were eighteen. There must have been opportunities. Are you afraid of men? Surely you're not——"

An angry flush suffused my face. "No, Janne, there is nothing wrong with me. It's just that I never had the opportunity. I mean, I never met anyone. . . . Oh, there were attempts, but it wasn't what I wanted. And my life with the children tired me out so that I could avoid such thoughts."

I was angry with my stumbling explanation, for the necessity I felt to explain my virginity. Janne placed a hand on my shoulder, and I pushed it away.

"I think it would be wise if we finished our drink." He emptied his glass in a swift gulp. "Now," he said, "about the letter. These 'attempts,' as *Herra* Leinonen views them, could be simple accidents or tricks of fate or the result of minor strokes. How can we be sure?

"You've been away a long time, Maija, and you haven't seen the family grow up. You might think it is jealousy on my part, but they are ungrateful. I know that he can be a hard man to live around, but he is not cruel. If he were, he'd have banned that brood from his house and life long ago.

"But let us say that his accusations are well founded. Have you thought that he has now placed your life in danger? Surely if one of them attempted to kill him, they—he or she—won't stand back now and wait to be disinherited. If, as you say, he has told everyone about the plan, it's not safe for you to remain in that house."

"That's been my home longer than it's been theirs. I won't be forced to go into hiding!"

"When you thrust your chin out like that and make such declarations, I see your grandfather. *Sisu*, he would call it, but in this case it might just be foolhardy stubbornness."

"What should I do? I can't ignore his suspicions. I

can't walk away from him. And I certainly don't want to leave Finland again. I could never leave again."

"You can marry me immediately. Tomorrow, if your grandfather has had the chance to draw the contract."

"Janne, I am not sure that I want to marry you. This has happened too fast. We really don't know one another. You've had one bad experience and I . . . oh, God, I've waited so long. I couldn't stand the thought of being your wife in name only."

"Maija, I think you love me. I could feel it when I held you in my arms."

"Was it love or passion? Are you really so sure that you love *me*, or is it the eighteen-year-old Maija? Can we build a lifetime on the hallucinations of an old man?"

"Control of the Leinonen mill is something very real. Just think what would happen if your stepuncles and stepaunt inherit it. They wouldn't waste a moment selling it. The mill is my life, too. You must remember that."

"The mill, the mill! I am sick of hearing about the mill. I know it's important, but I feel that I am important, too. I must have a chance to think, find out the truth—and be certain how I feel about you, and how you feel about me."

"So we have several days to make our decision—until Midsummer Eve, next Saturday."

"You seem to find that as reasonable a courting period as does Grandfather."

Janne shrugged. "People have married in shorter periods and with less knowledge of one another."

"We have only the knowledge of children. What are you like now? What do you believe in? What is important to you?"

"The mill, and you, of course."

"I don't like the order in which you list your priorities," I said. "In other words, you see me as a way to get ownership of the mill—as a stepping-stone to power."

"Maija, be reasonable and stop looking for rejection where none is intended. I admit we do not know one another now, but we have a little time. I wish that you would marry me now so that I could get you out of this dangerous situation. I fear for you, and I don't want to lose you. I *can't* lose you."

"Is it me you are afraid of losing or the mill?"

He looked at me soberly, while only the tick of a clock broke the silence, then said, "I thought I'd made that clear. I don't want to lose either you or the mill."

"I must go now," I said. "Mummo will have dinner prepared, and I want to talk to the others." I rose to leave, but Janne put his hands on my shoulders.

"Don't be hasty. Give it a chance. Will you meet me at the tavern tonight? I think it might be wiser if I didn't call for you at the house. You could take a boat."

I nodded and smiled. "I might have to climb out the balcony window and sneak away to you."

"It wouldn't be the first time, Maija. Do that and maybe the feeling you once had for me will return." Then, solicitously, he asked, "Does your hand still hurt?"

"It stings, but I can manage."

"If you get another urge to pet a wild creature, turn back. I'm available for petting."

"You have barbs, as well, Janne, and they reach deeper than a hedgehog's."

CHAPTER SEVEN

I put the bicycle back in the rack and walked down to the pier, where another of our motorboats was moored. I hoped that Grandfather had returned with news of the child. Then I washed quickly and went to the kitchen. With the exception of Grandfather, the entire family was gathered. Mummo was heaping everyone's plate from serving platters of delicious-smelling food. Kaarina sat at the end of the long wooden table, in the place usually reserved for her stepfather.

She was ramrod straight, and only a tightening of her lips acknowledged my greeting. Her icy gray eyes flicked across me, and I saw that the passage of years had not altered her opinion of me. But I was amazed that she had the baby in her arms, sucking lustily at the bottle Kaarina held for him.

"Well, little sister, I see you have been enjoying the island's excitement," Eero said sarcastically as Heikki rose to seat me.

I felt a flush rise, then realized that they had no way of knowing where I had been. "There was excitement of sorts," I answered, holding out my injured hand. "I thought I had found my pet hedgehog, but either I was mistaken or he had forgotten me."

Mummo, her back turned to the stove, said automatically, "Oh, you must put some medication on it. You might get an infection."

"No need for that, Mother," Kaarina answered,

glancing at my hand. "She seems to have taken that precaution already. Where, I wonder, did she receive first aid?" Her voice was heavy with irony.

"Ah-ha," Paavo said, putting down his glass. He had already started on his daily libation, and his face was slightly flushed from drink. "So you have been to see your betrothed and he ministered tenderly to your needs? *All* your needs, Maija? Come, tell us!"

"Paavo!" Mummo remonstrated.

"I suppose we must all congratulate you, or do we offer the bride best wishes? I never seem to remember the proper etiquette," Eero said.

"With Janne for a husband, she will probably need best wishes," Kaarina said.

Paavo snickered and took another swallow from his glass.

"Has he mentioned the child? Surely he isn't willing to accept this baby as another condition of the sale." Kaarina looked down at the tiny being in her arms, and for the first time that I could remember a tender expression softened the glacial gray of her eyes.

"The child——" I stopped abruptly, remembering my promise to remain silent.

"Yes—the child?" Kaarina asked. Her face was as gray as her eyes. "What of the baby?"

Heikki looked up from his plate and said, "Father has asked us not to question Maija. He cited the injunction against casting the first stone."

Kaarina's pallid face blanched even whiter. "How pious of him."

"He is a lovely child," Heikki commented. "But, of course, I know little of babies."

"No," Eero said, "your life-style does not include knowledge of children, does it?"

Heikki shot a black look at his brother, and I was surprised that such a seemingly gentle soul could be capable of such an expression. But Eero always knew where and how to strike the most painful blow.

It was Kaarina, however, who commanded my attention. Her head was bent over the infant, but I saw the prophecy of spinsterhood in every line of her face. She was thirty-five, and her child-bearing days were fast disappearing. Did she look at the infant and think of the children she probably would never bear?

"I'll take the baby, Kaarina," I offered. "It must be difficult for you to hold him and eat."

She tightened her grip on the child, but her voice was expressionless as she answered. "I ate before my return. I'll hold him while you have your dinner. Later, I would like to give him a thorough examination—with your permission, of course."

"Of course," I said. "The . . . journey was somewhat taxing. Do you think there is any cause for alarm?"

"I didn't say that. However, a layman cannot always assess an infant's physical condition. Rosy cheeks and a chubby body do not always indicate perfect health."

Paavo continued to concentrate on his glass. "Maybe you would give me a physical too, eh, sister? I've been feeling a little tired lately."

"Little wonder," Kaarina replied. "The way you drink, I wouldn't be surprised if your liver is pickled."

"Such sisterly compassion," Paavo said, a wry look on his face.

"Come, everyone, eat," Mummo said cheerfully, trying to smooth the riled atmosphere. "Maija, have some *Karjalan paisti*. I've been cooking it since last night. I remembered that it was one of your favorites."

She heaped a massive portion of meat on my plate, and I savored the spicy mixture of pork, beef, and lamb. Two large boiled potatoes were added and a ladle of meat sauce. A famished man could have shared my plate and I would still have had more than enough. She watched as I tasted it and reddened in pleasure when I expressed appreciation.

The men ate silently. Eero had a hearty appetite but

no praise for the cook, even when she prompted him. "A bit too much allspice, Mother," he commented, wiping his plate clean with a slice of freshly baked rye bread. He had always considered himself an expert on food, along with everything else.

Mummo clucked in annoyance and tested a bit of food in her mouth. "Perhaps you are right," she allowed, even though it was obvious that she wasn't convinced.

Heikki pushed more food around his plate than he ate, and Mummo's fussing made him become even more sullen than usual. "Please, Mother, you know I have a delicate stomach."

"Ah, my delicate brother," Eero said in mock sympathy, "you have a woman's stomach."

"Please," I said angrily, "let's enjoy this wonderful food that Mummo has prepared. This is my first day home, and it would be nice if we could all be civil to one another."

"Yes, little peacemaker," Eero replied with a short bow.

"Here!" Paavo poured vodka into my water glass. "This is an instant peacemaker." I pushed the glass aside and concentrated on my meal. After the main course was finished and the plates were cleared away, large bowls of fresh strawberries and rich cream were placed in front of us. I was barely able to finish them.

Kaarina rose from the table, still holding the baby. "I'll take him to the den for the examination. You look as if you could use a nap, Maija. Perhaps it is the excitement of your engagement, but new mothers do need their rest, you know." The words were compassionate but carried an overtone of scorn.

I tried to help Mummo with the dishes, but she gently shooed me away. No one else offered to help.

"Well, I must return to my writing," Eero said with exaggerated importance.

"When do we get to read some of your precious

prose, dear brother?" Paavo asked, his voice slightly slurred.

"Never. You wouldn't be able to grasp my meaning. In fact, I am so wearied from your company that I will have to lie down before I commence. It is impossible to compose my thoughts in this atmosphere."

Heikki and I exchanged a look of amusement. After his brothers and sister left, he said, "I have some sketches of the designs I have been working on, Maija. Do you think you might like to see them later? After you've rested, that is." His voice was shy and prepared for rejection.

"I'd love to see them. Grandfather told me that he is very proud of your accomplishments in fabric design."

"Did he?" Heikki asked eagerly. "He's never told me so—but, then, he disapproves. . . ."

"I know," I said, lowering my voice so that Mummo could not overhear. "The only thing I wonder is if you are happy with your . . . way of life."

He sat for a moment without responding. "I suppose I am. I don't expect you to understand, but I always felt so pushed before, trying to be something I couldn't be. My friend has taught me to understand that my feelings are not shameful."

"Then, you are happy?"

"I am until he threatens to leave me. He has such ambition. He's such a sensitive human being. I'm afraid I often fall short of his expectations. Maija, I don't know what I would do if he left me!" Panic rose with his voice. "He wants to start a chain of shops, and it's going to take a lot of money."

"Have you talked to Grandfather about it?"

"I've tried to, but you can imagine his reaction. He said he wouldn't give me a penny to finance my—well, I won't repeat what he said." He was quiet for a moment; then a surge of anger distorted his soft features and he said, "He'll be sorry for his attitude!"

Mummo turned from the sink. "Heikki, you must speak respectfully about *Herra* Leinonen. You know how grateful we all must be for his kindness and protection."

"I'm sorry, Mother," he said, but there was no sincerity in his apology. He looked at me searchingly and said, "Maija, I really am sorry, not for how I feel about him, but——" He broke off and turned to leave the kitchen. Before he reached the doorway, he looked back. "You know I've always liked you. I am truly sorry."

"Sorry for what?" I asked, but he had left.

CHAPTER EIGHT

As I entered the bedroom, I saw that Kaarina had unpacked her belongings and had set a few toilet articles on her vanity. Aside from a small bottle of lilac water, there was little show of feminine luxuries.

The rest of my luggage had been put aboard Kaarina's boat, and as I unpacked and hung up my dresses and pantsuits, I thought my wardrobe looked positively lavish compared to the severely tailored outfits that hung on her side of the closet.

I sank into the feather bed and was drifting off to sleep when Mummo knocked. "I'm sorry to disturb you, dear, but I thought I would tell you that I've had Paavo light the fire in the sauna. It should be the proper temperature by the time you've had your rest."

"How thoughtful of you," I said gratefully.

A true sauna would be wonderful. I missed saunas more than any other Finnish custom in America, where most of my saunas turned out to be what a Finn would term a Turkish bath, filled with clouds of steam, whereas a true sauna is so hot that the air is crystal clear. The water that forms on the skin is caused by perspiration, not water vapor. I'm afraid I often made a bore of myself by pointing out that fact—and by attempting to correct everyone's pronunciation of the word. It should sound like "sow-na," not "saw-na."

The combination of fatigue, a full stomach and the midday warmth carried me into a sound sleep. I was aware of nothing until I was wakened by loud knocks on the door. Paavo opened the door and poked his head in the room.

"Come, Maija, the temperature is just right in the sauna. Look, I have cooked an egg in there." He threw an egg at me and I watched it bounce on the bed. When I picked it up, it was still warm.

"You do prefer your sauna at one hundred and ten centigrade [230° F.], don't you?" he asked with mock innocence.

"I'm afraid my stay in America has made me a bit soft. I'll have to work up to that. I'll be down in a moment. Don't throw any more water on the rocks."

"Just as you say, little niece." He grinned and tossed another egg at me, which I caught in midair and which turned into a handful of raw yolk.

I jumped from the bed, still holding the oozing mess, and chased Paavo from the doorway. As I wiped the egg from my hand, I thought that he hadn't changed much in ten years. Then I stripped my clothes off and changed into a robe.

The sauna was a few yards behind the main house, almost hidden among trees that snuggled up to the small wooden building. Smoke rose from its stovepipe. I entered the dressing room and saw that everything had been made ready for my bath: a stack of large towels, washcloths, and a bundle of fresh birch leaves that had been fashioned into a whisk.

(Despite the notion that Finns "whip" themselves masochistically while enjoying the "torture" of a hot sauna, the truth is that we merely slap birch leaves against our bodies to stimulate circulation. The leaves are also dipped into a bucket of water and flicked on the white-hot rocks that produce the heat. After a sauna has been thoroughly heated, just a few drops are sufficient to create a sudden rise in temperature. Only the novice throws a bucket of water on the rocks, and it is not uncommon to see such a person race into the cool air—sometimes neglecting to grab a towel—in his haste to escape being scalded.)

The exterior and the interior of a sauna are made of wood, which absorbs the moisture, and most saunas, such as ours, consist of a dressing room and a bath, or sauna room. A stout door seperates them and confines the heat to the sauna room. Our dressing room had a long wooden bench with a mattress, wooden pegs on the wall for clothing and towels, and a shelf well stocked with *kalja,* a home-brewed beer made of malt, sugar, and yeast. It is necessary to drink to combat dehydration, and few Finns prefer to drink water.

A small brazier—in addition to the main fire beneath the sauna, which heated the rocks—had been lighted and its coals were turning white-hot. A plate of *makkara* (plump sausages made of pork and mutton) had been set out, ready to be roasted on the grill. There was also a Karelian *piirakka,* a rye-crust pastry filled with a rice mixture. A good sauna stimulates the appetite.

It was warm in the dressing room as I stripped off my robe and sat down to brush my hair. I hadn't thought to latch the outer door, and I didn't know it was open until Paavo said, "Everything all right? Yes, I can see everything is *very* all right!" He wasn't commenting on the room or its arrangements.

"Everything is just fine, Paavo—except for your presence!" I clutched a towel about me.

"My dear niece, you seem to have forgotten your Finnish etiquette. It would be most impolite of me if I didn't offer to wash your back."

As he sat down beside me, I saw that he had donned a robe, evidently in anticipation of joining me in the sauna.

"Thank you, but no thank you. Although I'm sure there are many girls who are just yearning to have you wash their back."

"That's true," he said with a smirk, "but village

life affords a limited variety of backs, and I grow bored. I'm a very good back scrubber, you know."

"I'm sure experience has made you one of the best, but I'll have to take your word for it. Now, get out and leave me alone. I remember another bit of Finnish etiquette: 'Two places are sacred: church and sauna.'"

"Well, I assure you I wouldn't do anything in a sauna that I wouldn't do in church—unless given the opportunity, that is."

I tucked the towel more tightly about myself. "Paavo," I said, "I don't find you amusing. Will you please leave?"

"Oh, don't be so prudish, Maija. We used to take many saunas together."

"Yes, when we were kids."

"So, now we are grown-up kids. We have had more experience playing." His look left no room for misunderstanding.

"Get out."

"You're very proper for a young woman who just brought home a little bundle. Surely you don't still believe the story that the trolls bring babies."

"Out!"

"All right, calm down. I really just wanted to talk to you. Since you seem to have lost your sense of humor, I'll get to the point."

"Can't it wait until another time?"

"No, I want to talk to you privately." He latched the door. "Now no one else will walk in and offer to scrub your back."

I drew myself up with as much dignity as I could manage. "If you don't get on with what you have to say, I'll start screaming."

"Tsk, tsk. You *have* forgotten your sauna etiquette. Remember, 'One must not talk loudly or move boisterously in a sauna.' This is a place where both the body and the mind are cleansed, and I have a little mind cleansing to do."

"Please get on with it."

He reached above my head, deliberately rubbing against me, and took two bottles of beer from the shelf. He opened them, handed one to me and took a large gulp from the other.

"Last night my venerable stepfather announced that you are going to marry Janne. He also said that he plans to sell Janne the mill for a ridiculous sum. Is this really true?" His voice had lost all trace of humor.

I sipped at my beer, thinking frantically. "I think we've all heard him make wild statements," I finally answered evasively.

"Then, it isn't true? You aren't going to marry Janne? And he isn't going to sell Janne the mill?"

"Paavo," I said, as if exasperated, "I just got home last night. Grandfather said many things that, well, that I found hard to believe. He does seem to have some notion that I should marry Janne."

"Frankly, Maija, you are welcome to marry whomever you wish. In fact, considering your little bundle, I think it would be a good idea, but I am surprised that you would settle for a common peasant."

"I seem to remember that your father was a peasant, too, since you choose to use that word."

Anger flashed in Paavo's gray eyes. "We can't all be descended from the aristocracy like the illustrious *Herra* Leinonen and you, but it isn't past history and bloodlines that I'm talking about. Janne is a peasant, no matter that he is now manager of the mill. I don't know what he's done to worm himself into your grandfather's good graces, but I imagine he has performed some useful deeds that a man of finer principles would have refused to do. There is some special explanation behind my stepfather's decision to send Janne to a university and then give him managership of the mill.

"Maija, you must listen to me. There have been many rumors about Janne. You remember him as a young boy, but you must also remember that he came from a poor family. His father was an uneducated man, and Janne always had pretensions far above his station in life. Ambition can twist people."

"Don't you think it's possible that Grandfather saw Janne's potential?"

"How very loyal of you—and naïve. Hasn't it occurred to you that your grandfather bribed him with that scholarship in return for his promise not to contact you? Janne had been using you to better his life. We all saw that. As soon as he was offered an alternative, he dropped all thought of you. Did he ever write or attempt to contact you?"

"There were reasons for that."

"Oh, yes, *reasons*. One of the reasons was named Ritva—a very tantalizing one. He certainly didn't stay heartbroken over your absence for very long. But he wasn't man enough to keep Ritva."

"Paavo, that's cruel."

"Perhaps, but it's true. I have good reason to know. She began to throw herself at me shortly after he brought her back to this godforsaken place."

"And you——"

"Yes," he interrupted. "If he couldn't keep his wife in his own bed, it wasn't my fault. It seems to be a common complaint, and I'm always happy to do what I can to console a woman."

"You make me sick."

"Why? Because I am honest? I'm not married, Maija, but if I were—if I had a wife worthy of me. . . ."

He set his beer down and reached over to stroke my hair. I sat frozen, unable to move away from the unwanted caress.

"Don't," I said in a firm voice.

"Why not? We aren't blood relations. You are not really my little sister or my niece. We've known one another since childhood. Why do you think I never married? I've never found another woman I wanted." His voice had become husky.

"Don't, Paavo," I repeated, unable to find other words.

He sighed and pulled my hair across my shoulders. "I wouldn't harm you, Maija, but I do want you, and always have. I know I have a poor reputation, that I drink too much, chase about too much, but if you were my wife, it would be different. And I assure you that you would not go seeking a more exciting bed if you were mine."

I felt paralyzed, unable to move, when he reached over and kissed me on the lips.

"Marry me?" he whispered.

"Paavo"—I searched for words—"I am fond of you, but I never realized that you viewed me as anyone other than a relative. If you love me, as you say you always have, why didn't you contact me while I was in America?"

He shrugged. "I couldn't get your address. I begged Mother, but she would only say that *Herra* Leinonen would be displeased. You don't know how I felt last night when I saw you. It was as if I had fallen into a dream."

"And the baby? Was he part of your dream?"

He gave a short laugh and replied, "No. At least, not a child who isn't our own. But who am I to be virtuous?" He turned the pockets of his robe inside out. "See? I don't have a stone. I certainly won't be the first to hurl one at you. Maija, answer me. Will you marry me?"

I sought words, kind words that wouldn't leave a breach between us. When I finally spoke, I was shocked to hear myself say, "I'm sorry, but I love Janne, and I want to marry him."

Paavo slumped against the wall. The twinkling silver of his eyes had turned to stormy rain clouds. "I see," he said at last. "Well, I tried, didn't I, little niece?" He stroked my hair again and said, "I'm truly sorry you've decided to throw your life away." Before I could say anything further, he walked out.

The towel slipped to the floor, and despite the heat of the dressing room my skin was covered with goose bumps. Indeed, the sauna room was so hot that it took a while for my mind to register the fact. I had climbed to the top bench but quickly descended to a cooler level when the dry heat took my breath away. I dipped the birch whisk into a pail of water and flicked it against my body. Small droplets of perspiration gathered, and soon my body was slick with perspiration.

I was so unused to the intense heat of a true sauna that I couldn't endure it for more than a few minutes. I reentered the dressing room, toweled myself and stretched out on the mattress. Listening to a sound on the roof that I thought must be the afternoon breeze brushing the branches of the nearby trees against the little building, I slipped into a state of tranquillity that did not allow any review of the incident with Paavo —or any other disturbing thought.

I remained in that mindless state until my body cooled, then decided to return to the sauna. It seemed even hotter than the first time—but, then, it always does. One's blood becomes, as it were, preheated. I made no attempt to climb to the top bench; the lowest level was almost too hot.

There was a sound of steady dripping, and I checked the tap, but it was tightly shut. The water was trickling from an opening in the ceiling. Ours was an old-fashioned sauna, and the water was supplied from a large barrel on the roof. A chain was attached to the barrel through a small hole in the ceiling, and, when pulled, it released water onto the glowing bed of rocks below. I tugged on the chain, but it was taut. The water, as it continued to flow, was turning the room into an inferno.

My lungs were near bursting when I found a wash-cloth and used it as a mitt to turn the door handle. The handle turned, but the door wouldn't open, and the cracks around the door were sealed with weather stripping to keep the heat from escaping.

Taking short breaths of scalding air, I made my way to the tap, held my head under the stream of water and splashed handfuls over my tormented body. Even so, dizziness threatened to overcome me. My lungs were being roasted.

I pushed at the wooden door, but it wouldn't yield. Apparently it was swollen shut. The only implement I could find was the bucket, and I shrieked with pain when I touched its hot metal handle. With the wash-cloth wrapped around the handle, I banged the pail against the doorknob, hoping to spring the catch. But the door wouldn't budge, and still the water splashed down, creating wave upon wave of scalding heat.

I wanted to scream, but that would only force scalding air into my already aching lungs. I poured another bucket of water over myself and lowered my head to lessen the dizziness. Then I banged the bucket against a weak section of the door and made a fracture in the wood. Pressing my nose to the opening, I in-haled some cool air from the dressing room. After taking several breaths of air, I bashed the pail against the crack until it was wide enough to let my hand slip through. I pulled at the wood, stopping frequently to refresh my lungs with gasps of the cooler air. I was finally able to loosen a panel of the door and climb through the opening.

The floor on the other side of the door was littered with wood, which I carefully stepped over to avoid getting splinters in my bare feet. It didn't occur to me to look in the litter for a piece of wood that might have become wedged under the door.

I hung my robe over the hole in the door as a

barrier against the waves of heat that poured through the opening. My body was red, and blisters were beginning to form on my hands and feet. I turned on the shower and stepped under the cold water. Then, my heart still pounding with hammerlike blows, I collapsed on the mattress, wincing as my skin came in contact with the rough ticking. When my heart returned to normal rhythm and the dizziness subsided, I tucked a towel around my body and made my way back to the house. Each step on my swollen feet was so painful that I doubted I would be able to walk the short distance.

Kaarina was in the hallway when I reached the back door. She looked startled. "Well, Maija," she said, "I'm surprised you didn't come in through the front door. You would have a larger audience."

I dropped the towel, and at first she seemed to shrink from my nakedness. Then her eyes widened.

"What happened?"

"I was almost scalded in the sauna. The chain was stuck, and water kept dripping on the rocks. And the dressing-room door wouldn't open. Please, can you help me?"

"Go upstairs. I'll see what I can do."

It was a slow, painful progress up the stairs. When I finally got to the room, I dropped the towel and lay down on the bed. The patterns of the bedspread dug into my flesh.

Kaarina entered, and again I saw that look of disgust. *A strange reaction for a doctor,* I thought. She overcame her repugnance and arranged ice packs around my body and applied ointment to my hands and feet. After lathering a pink lotion on my face and neck in a less than gentle manner, she gave me the bottle and suggested that I would probably prefer to apply it to the "intimate" portions of my anatomy. my.

"You'll be tender for a day or so, but I don't think you have a first-degree burn. The ointment contains an antiseptic, in case the blisters break." She took my pulse and seemed satisfied with the rate. "Steady enough, though fast. Panic could cause that. You always were the hysterical type."

"Hysterical!" I said almost hysterically. "How would *you* like to be trapped in a scalding sauna?"

"My dear child, I think you are unused to saunas and just overdid it. You probably put more water on the rocks than you realized, and then became overheated and panicked. No wonder the door swelled shut, after a great surge of heat and moisture. I've had it do that myself, but a hard shove usually opens it. If you'd had your wits about you, you would have been able to open the door."

"The chain on the water barrel was stuck."

"I'll have someone check it," she said, humoring me. "You had better rest. Mother and I will see to the baby and fix a supper tray for you. Keep those ice packs around you and apply the lotion as you feel the need for it."

I lathered the lotion over my "intimate" portions and lay back, completely enervated. A good sauna causes temporary lethargy, but it is soon replaced by boundless energy—and a wolflike appetite. My sauna had none of those effects; I felt drained.

I dropped off to sleep, and when I woke the ice bags were sloshy. My skin was still tender, but at least I could move about without excruciating pain. The nightgown that Kaarina insisted I wear was now tolerable.

"Are you decent?" Eero called through the door.

"Come in," I replied. He fumbled with the knob and finally entered with a large tray.

"I have been put into service as a maid. The women claim to be too occupied with that baby of yours. They insisted I take this to you."

"Did you hear what happened?"

"Yes, Kaarina told us. Very strange. We've all been taking saunas there since we were children. It's never happened before." I could see by the lift of his eyebrow that he believed Kaarina's version that I had panicked.

"The chain was taut. It wouldn't snap back and just continued to pour out water."

"Well, Heikki said it's rusted and might have gotten stuck, but it seems to be all right now. No matter," he said in a dismissive tone, "you look pink and rosy and not too ill used, if you don't mind my saying so. We'll turn you into a real Finn again, given time."

He placed the tray on my lap and, to my surprise, pulled a chair to the side of my bed. He settled himself against the back and rested a leg on the bed. Eero was as negligently elegant as ever. His black hair was a little longer, more suited to the intellectual image he affected. The sprinkling of gray hair only added distinction. His hooded gray eyes suggested boredom, and his dark eyebrows were raised in one of their many acrobatic feats of amused irony.

"Summer soup, just right for an invalid, or whatever you are," he said, gesturing with a languid hand to the bowl of *kesäkeitti:* carrots, sugar peas, cauliflower, tiny potatoes and spinach mixed in a creamy base. "Mother insists that this is a light snack, and she's added a stack of pancakes with strawberry jam for dessert. Rather peasanty, but tasty."

I was puzzled that Eero stayed with me. Never before had he thought me worthy of his company, and I doubted that sympathy for my accident had prompted this solicitude.

"I suppose you want to talk about your discussion with Grandfather," I said, sipping my soup.

"I would hardly term it a discussion, since your grandfather never *discusses* anything. He gives ultimatums and decrees. An intelligent debate of issues is not his style. But yes, I *did* come to talk to you about his latest aberration."

I concentrated on my soup. When it became obvious that I wasn't going to say anything, Eero laughed.

"I see: 'No comment.' Should I take your silence

to mean that you plan to go along with this? Well, you always were a bit of a featherbrain, if you don't mind my saying so."

"I do mind, but you can think what you like."

"Oh, come; let's talk as adults. You know I tend to be sarcastic. All I meant was that you sometimes fail to think things through. You're not a child anymore, and it's time you learn to stand up for yourself."

"Have you?" I asked, giving him a level look.

He stiffened and checked his impulse to deliver a crushing verbal blow. His jaw muscles tightened, and he said in a constrained voice, "I have managed to create my own life-style quite independently of, and no doubt mystifying to, the good *Herra* Leinonen. Perhaps you are not aware that I have achieved a certain prestige in Finland's literary world."

"I'm afraid I've been out of touch with the Finnish literary community."

"Dear child, I mean no offense, but I doubt that you were ever aware of its existence."

"Perhaps you will educate me. I'd love to read your works."

"I'm afraid I haven't brought anything with me," he answered. "I knew they would be unappreciated. But that isn't what I want to discuss with you."

"Yes?" I said.

"As I was saying, it is time for you to take a direction in life—to separate yourself from your grandfather's tyrannical whims. You've allowed yourself to drift along for a number of years. A *nursemaid*. Really! And now you find yourself deserted and with a child." He held out his hand in a theatrical gesture. "I don't intend to ask personal questions. I'm just trying to point out that you have allowed yourself to be used, and if you go along with this scheme, you will forever remain a feather that is wafted in every breeze.

"You will only trade the tyrannical rule of one man for another if you marry Janne. Surely you can't believe that he loves you. It must be obvious, even to you, that he is willing to marry you only to satisfy the requirement that will give him control of the mill. As soon as *Herra* Leinonen is gone—and surely even he can't live forever—Janne will see that you are dominated, and then the good name of Leinonen, which I also bear, will be shamed. We can't allow that, Maija."

"I really doubt that Grandfather would have made Janne manager of the mill if he didn't have the utmost faith in him."

"That just shows how naïve you are. Have you ever heard of paranoia? Well, my stepfather is a classic example. He trusts no one close to him, and we've all speculated on just how Janne managed to ingratiate himself. It must have been through carrying out orders that a more honorable man would have refused. Your grandfather is even convinced that someone in this family is trying to kill him. Did he tell you?

"I see by your silence that he did. Well, do you know that he's had a minor stroke? Kaarina will confirm that. This notion that one of us is trying to kill him came about after Kaarina noticed the first indication of one."

"He appears to be in good shape for a man of his years."

"That doesn't always tell the full tale, Maija. I admit there are few outward signs, but it is the brain that is marred. You'll also notice that when he doesn't watch himself, his hands shake and he walks with a slight limp. He's always had a vindictive streak, but, really, can you imagine him selling his precious mill to an outsider? If his thinking were clear, he would see that there is no guarantee that Janne won't kill *you* after he's gained control.

"Maija, I'm warning you. You are placing yourself

in a dangerous position. Right now you seem to be in the throes of a childhood dream—marrying your childhood sweetheart and being happy ever after. Well, I'll predict the outcome of your adolescent dream—disaster."

"You're very solicitous, Eero. I never realized you cared so much for my welfare."

"Someone has to care for fools, and though you are a sweet girl, whom I've always viewed as a sister, you do tend to act like one. And you will be a fool if you go along with your grandfather's latest whim."

"And your only concern is that I not be a fool, as you put it?"

"Yes. Basically, yes."

He droned on, repeating his warnings, drowning me in a sea of words. I tried to listen as I ate the soup, but my attention wandered as he made the same arguments over and over again. I became so sleepy that it was difficult to lift the spoon to my mouth.

"Eero, I'm sleepy. Why don't you go now and take the tray with you? I just want to rest. What time is it?"

"About five, I suppose," he answered indifferently.

I tried to look at my wristwatch on the bedside table, but my vision was blurred and I couldn't read the tiny numerals. I knew I had to sleep or I would be unable to meet Janne at seven.

Eero took the tray, but even after I closed my eyes I could hear only the sound of his voice. I couldn't make any sense of his words.

CHAPTER NINE

It was as if pins were being inserted in my chest. My eyes felt glued shut, and when, with tremendous effort, I opened them, I looked directly into Pai-Pai's inquiring eyes. He had again intruded into my bedroom and was perched on my chest, kneading my tender flesh. I dislodged his claws and reached across to the vanity for my wristwatch. My hands felt numb as I fumbled among the array of bottles, silently cursing the eternal summer sun for offering no clue to the time of day—or night. I squinted. It was nine o'clock. Pushing the cat from the bed, I tried to get up, but my body refused to cooperate. I lay back, fighting to stay awake, but was again enveloped in a black, sleep-laden cloud.

"Too late," I heard myself say out loud. "Janne will know I'm not coming. Grandfather will be up soon and he will send him a message."

"It's a simple case of shock. I've seen that she's been kept warm and given sedatives."

"Why is her face so swollen? Does shock cause that, too? Maija, wake up!"

"Don't startle her. That can be dangerous. The swelling came from the incident in the sauna. I told you about that."

"That was two days ago! Why didn't someone send

101

word to me? Maija, listen to me. You must wake up. I've brought Dr. Tami."

"Doctor, as you can see, there's no sign of serious skin damage—only a slight reddening and swelling. The shock set in shortly after I put her to bed, and I felt it was best if we didn't attempt to move her."

"Yes, yes, Kaarina, I'm sure you did what you thought was best. If she was in shock, it would have been unwise to transport her to the hospital. One can't be too careful in cases of shock. But I don't know that I agree with your decision to sedate her. Careful, there, young man, her skin is still very tender."

I lifted my eyelids far enough to see through narrow slits. Janne was holding me.

"Wake up! You've slept long enough. Too long." He rocked me gently, drawing me out of my semiconscious state.

"Has she had anything to eat?" Dr. Tami asked.

"Liquids, when I could get her to take anything. She hasn't been a cooperative patient, I'm afraid. I was about to wake her and start her on solid foods when Janne barged in."

"Where's Grandfather?" I asked. "Why hasn't he come?" My voice seemed to come from far away. "Has something happened to him?" Sudden alarm drove away the mental clouds.

"He's in Sweden, Maija," Janne answered. "He had to fly there to finish an important negotiation, and I had to go with him. I left a message for you with Helge. When I got back, I found that you hadn't gone to meet me at the tavern, but the old sot claims he delivered my message to you here. Did he, Kaarina?"

"As a matter of fact, he did," Kaarina answered, "but I decided she was hardly in any condition to receive messages. Now, if you'll all leave, I'd like to examine my patient."

"No!" I said, frightened at the thought of being alone with Kaarina. "I want Dr. Tami."

"As you can see, she's still in a hysterical state, Dr. Tami," Kaarina said.

"Well, let's humor her. It's best not to rile the patient."

"Then, you do not want me to stay? But she has been my patient. I must say I hardly consider this a professional——"

"Oh, child, I know you are a fine doctor, but in my day we humored the patient rather than worry about professional ethics. I think it would be of more benefit to all of us if you asked Mummo to make some coffee."

When we were alone, Dr. Tami examined me thoroughly, giving special attention to my hands and the soles of my feet.

"Well, Kaarina did a fine job, I would say. Your skin looks healthy enough—no worse than what you could have sustained from a severe sunburn. You'll be tender for a day or two, but I don't think there will be any lasting damage. Ah, the human skin is marvelously resilient. Would you like to get up, young lady?"

"Yes. I'm terribly hungry, and I feel so stiff."

"And no wonder, after having been in bed so long. You'll feel a bit dizzy at first, so move slowly. I think you'll be more comfortable if you dress in loose-fitting garments." He cleared his throat. "I understand it's fashionable now for young ladies to go about without brassieres, and I would recommend that omission in your case. And wear a pair of soft shoes or slippers," he added. "Shall I send Kaarina to assist you in dressing?"

"I can manage, but I would like to know how the baby is."

"I've just seen the young chap, and he's the picture of health. You're lucky to have your own household physician. Kaarina is the soul of solicitude, and, of course, Mummo is having a wonderful time with a baby to fuss over. I understand there have been differences of opinion over the care of the child. Mummo does, ummm, have rather old-fashioned ideas." He chuckled. "You might say that the child is getting the best of the old and the new."

He helped me swing my legs off the bed. "Now, just sit there for a moment before you attempt to stand."

I was more than willing to follow his command. As soon as I sat up, the dizziness returned.

"Drop your head and take some deep breaths. Relax. You'll soon feel better."

I followed his advice, and the room came into sharper focus.

"Now, if you feel up to it, Maija, I would like to ask you a question."

"Yes, of course."

"When was your child born?"

My mind was still groggy. I said, "About a month ago, I guess."

"You guess?" Dr. Tami said in amazement. "Don't you know?"

I began to stammer. "Well, of course, I know—yes, he is a month old."

"When was he born?" the doctor asked sharply.

"June—I mean May, May 24."

"It is very unusual for a mother to forget the birth date of her child. She'll remember that occasion long after she's forgotten other birthdays."

"I seem to be confused. I suppose it's because of the accident."

"Yes, I can understand that your mind is still a bit foggy, but there is something I cannot understand. Why don't I see any indication of postpartum? Maija, a doctor can tell by looking at a woman's body if she has ever given birth."

"Dr. Tami—I. . . ."

"I have known you much of your life—and your grandfather, your father, and your mother. Certainly you can confide in me."

"Doctor, I'm not trying to evade your question, but

I must ask you something first. Do you think that Grandfather's mind is. . . . Do you think he's had a stroke?"

"It's hard to say for certain. When one gets older, there is a tendency for some of the small blood vessels to break. I gather you've heard about that spell he had a while back. Frankly, I was puzzled, and I won't try to tell you that I have an answer. If he sustained a minor stroke, he's recovered, or *adjusted* would be a better word. I am basing that assumption upon his observable mental condition. He won't allow me to give him a proper physical. In fact, we had quite a row about that. But, then, it's not the first argument we've had and, God willing, it won't be our last. He seems as sharp as ever, and I see no connection between his mental condition and the birth of your child."

"I found him."

"You what?"

"I know it sounds incredible, but someone had placed the baby in a large wicker basket—the kind we use to carry our groceries from the village. Helge had it on his shuttle boat, and it was unloaded with my luggage. When the child began to whimper, I discovered him in the basket. He was dressed in a soggy diaper and wrapped in a blanket."

"No note? What did Helge know of the child?"

"There was no note or any identification, and Helge had already left the dock. After I convinced Grandfather that I hadn't brought home an illegitimate child, he promised he would make an immediate investigation. Then he told everyone that the baby is mine. Doctor, has he said anything to you about the events . . . about his suspicions?"

"I'm not sure that I know exactly what you're talking about, but I know that he won't let Kaarina act as his personal physician. I suppose that's understandable. My own father would never believe I was a qualified physician. Is that what you're referring to?"

"That's part of it, Doctor. I wish I could tell you more, but I don't know whether I'd be disloyal to Grandfather. He asked me to be patient and leave everything to him. I think he suspected that one of the men of the family got a girl in trouble and the baby was sent to him for that reason. He wanted to surprise a confession from one of them."

"Did it work?"

"No, although they were certainly surprised. But not as much as I was to find that I had become a mother."

He shook his head. "I don't wonder that you're questioning his mental condition. Well, Aarno always likes to be in charge of everything. Usually does a good job of it, too. I imagine he has begun an investigation. If there is to be a family scandal, I can understand that he would like to be prepared. Janne tells me that he will return from Stockholm tonight."

"You won't say anything until then, will you? Heaven knows I would be grateful to have this cleared up, but I promised that I wouldn't say anything until after Grandfather returns. Do you think that Kaarina suspects?"

"Hard to say. I don't know whether she's given you a full examination in the past two days. If she discovered the, er, evidence, she didn't confide in me. I just wish she'd called me earlier. Not that she doesn't seem to have taken proper care of you, but I think you might have been better off if you hadn't been sedated. Ah, well, procedures change so rapidly that, I must confess, I am not always current.

"Well, my dear, all I know is that things have a way of sorting themselves out, particularly when people keep their noses out of them."

He glanced at his watch. "I've got to get back to the dispensary; we're giving booster shots this week. Now, don't tire yourself. If you feel fatigued or dizzy, take a nap, and don't stay in the sunlight too long.

Your skin is still very sensitive. I'll call back this evening, if I can, and talk to Aarno."

"You won't say anything to the others?"

"Not for the time being. The child is being well cared for, and I'm sure that Aarno is as good as his word as far as the investigation is concerned. We may be bending the law by keeping the little fellow here, but I suspect that he's better off with Kaarina to watch over his physical needs, and with Mummo lavishing all her maternal affections on him, than he would be in some institution. Besides, my memory isn't what it used to be. If I don't write everything down, I seem to forget. Can't even find a pen to make a note of all this."

I smiled and patted his breast pocket, which bulged with an assortment of pens. "I think I've located one —just in case you *do* need to make a note of anything."

"You see how easily I forget? I'll look in on you tomorrow."

I felt a certain amount of relief from hearing Dr. Tami's opinion, but it was tempered by an awareness of the doctor's age and his devotion to his old friend. I couldn't be certain how far that loyalty would affect his professional judgment.

There was a dull ache in my head, and my body was still stiff, but it felt good to move about. I put my mind on selecting suitable clothes, deciding on a shift and a pair of reindeer sandals I had splurged on in Helsinki while awaiting the northbound train. The shift was a gorgeous splash of abstract blues and greens —not unlike the color of our lake after a summer shower.

After slipping on the sandals, I went downstairs to the bathroom and peered into the mirror. I looked as if I had just received my first sunburn of the year. I creamed my face, removing the lotion that Kaarina had applied. Vanity overruled sensibility, which must have been a sign of returning health. Then I soaked some cotton pads in cold water and pressed them to my swollen eyelids. I finally decided that although I would win no beauty prize, I wouldn't frighten anyone; so I made my way to the kitchen.

Dr. Tami was refusing Mummo's offer of food. "No, no, Lilya. The coffee is enough; and I really must be off."

"Doctor," Kaarina said, "I would appreciate it if you would convince Janne that it would be most unwise to take Maija out today."

"Can't say that I agree with you, Kaarina. Just be sure that you don't get her overtired, Janne, and keep her out of direct sunlight as much as possible. I think a little fresh air would do her good. Make her wear a wide-brimmed hat or take an umbrella."

"I'll see to it, Doctor. Would it be all right if Maija and I take the baby, too?"

"The child stays here. Mummo has just fed him, and he needs a nap." Kaarina's voice brooked no disagreement.

"She's right, Janne," Dr. Tami said. "Maija doesn't need the fatigue of caring for the baby. Enjoy a little time together by yourselves."

I drank a large glass of goat's milk fortified with a raw egg, which Mummo insisted I take, and Janne promised to buy me a nourishing lunch in the village. Mummo outfitted me with a decrepit umbrella and the sunhat she wore when gardening.

Kaarina was rocking the baby, whose blond lashes fluttered against the powerful urge to sleep. Janne walked over and looked down at him, but Kaarina pulled the blanket over the child's face. I joined Janne, lifted the blanket, and we both looked down at the infant. Kaarina could hardly deny me that right, though I knew I had none. I wondered what thoughts went through Janne's mind as he gazed at the child.

The baby's eyelids popped open in defiance of sleep.

He yawned, twisting his rosebud mouth into a grin. That instant of animation brought a flash of recognition. I had seen that same smile on an adult's face. But this inkling of knowledge vanished as the child's sleep-heavy eyes snapped shut and his mouth relaxed.

Janne was frowning. Then he tossed his head as if to clear it of a troubling thought. Had he been thinking of his aborted child? "I suppose all babies look alike," he said.

Kaarina looked at him and said, "That's not quite accurate. Some are better formed than others. This child is a very healthy specimen."

I heard myself say, "Thank you." For an instant I had reacted spontaneously as the child's real mother.

Kaarina looked at me sharply, her gray eyes pinpoints of steel. "People should hardly congratulate themselves on God's work."

"Come, Maija," Janne said, taking my arm, "I've brought my motorboat. And don't worry, Mummo; I'll see that Maija gets a good meal."

"I'm sure you'll take good care of her," Mummo said softly.

"Oh, yes," Kaarina said, "we can be sure that Janne won't let anything happen to his future . . . wife."

The hesitation between *future* and *wife* sent a flush of anger over Janne's face, and I felt his hand tighten on my own, but he didn't respond to the taunt.

CHAPTER TEN

The breeze from the lake felt delicious against my skin—what little was exposed to it. "Do I really need this thing?" I asked, pointing to the black umbrella that Mummo insisted I take.

"I doubt that it will be practical after we get under way. Here, take this scarf," Janne said, "and tie down that charming hat. I think that'll give you enough protection from the sun."

I made a face at him and tried to give the battered hat a jaunty tilt as I wound the yellow scarf around the brim and tied it under my chin.

He started the motor with expertise and pushed the boat away from the pier. When we cleared the pier, he increased the speed, until it seemed that we were flying across a deep mirror. How good it felt to be on the water—especially with Janne.

"You forgot the fishing poles!" I yelled at him above the roar of the outboard.

"I *what?*"

"I said you forgot the fishing poles."

He reached beside him and picked up a pole.

"Oh, no," I groaned. "I was just kidding. I don't think I should sit in the sun and fish."

"You *what?*"

"I said," yelling as loudly as I was able, "I don't think——"

110

"Yes, I *thought* you said that," Janne yelled back, "Too bad. I'll have to take you back and get another fishing companion."

"I'll use the umbrella," I shouted.

"What? To fish with?"

"No, silly, to hold over myself so I won't get sunburned."

Janne adjusted the outboard, and suddenly I could hear without straining. "That was just a test. I wanted to be sure that you're still willing to go fishing with me. But I have other plans for our outing, so relax."

I assumed we were going to the village but, without explanation, Janne changed direction and we headed toward the jutting arm of the island, the marshy area near his cottage. He maneuvered into a narrow channel that was edged with reeds so tall that the boat was hidden among them. He brought the boat smoothly alongside a dock and jumped out with the grace of a cat.

"Well, what are you waiting for? Since when haven't you been able to scramble out of a boat?"

"Since I began wearing a dress."

"I thought that might be your excuse." He took my arm, lifted me onto the dock and held me in a close embrace.

"That scarf should be blue—as blue as your eyes, as blue as this lake. Take that foolish hat off. I want to see your hair."

We followed a narrow path that led to the marsh: our "secret place" when we were young, where we had shared our plans for the future and the first feelings of mature love.

"Take your sandals off, Maija. You haven't forgotten how to play in the mud, have you?"

We shed our shoes and plunged our feet deep into the mud flat.

"Has the mud deepened?" I asked.

In answer, Janne rolled up his pants and took another step from the shore. The mud came to his knees.

"Well, I guess I'll have to settle for dipping my feet," I said.

"Why?"

"That should be obvious."

"If you are afraid of getting your dress dirty, take it off," he suggested. "Why do you think I brought you here?"

"Why *did* you bring me here?"

"To give you a mud bath." He scooped a handful of oozing red earth to his face and inhaled the fragrance of the mud. "The dust of our ancestors is in this, and all the healing properties of our land. Here." He offered it to me. "Our land, Maija. Smell its lustiness. Rub it on your face and let it heal you."

I inhaled the scent of the rich, moist earth which seemed to contain all the sweetness of Finland—a scent compounded of thousands or millions of creatures and minerals: God's bouquet. I patted some on my face and then scooped up a handful for my arms and legs.

"Take your dress off and join me, Maija." Janne had unbuttoned his shirt and tossed it onto the pathway.

"Come on, my red Indian. You can't sit there half covered with mud and try to look demure. How many times have we bathed together in the nude?"

"We were children then."

"Let us be children again." He painted a villainous mustache on his face. "I promise," he said, making a cross in the mud over his heart, "that I shall behave myself. I shall—reluctantly—turn my back if you will only take off that dress, come over here and bathe in this glorious stuff."

He turned his back, and the temptation to push him facedown into the mud was too strong to resist. While he floundered, trying to get to his feet, I tucked my dress under my breasts and stepped deeper into the mud flat. When Janne finally stood up, he was coated with red black earth. "Ah," I said in a very serious tone, "at last we have achieved integration of the races in our fair country."

He wiped the mud from his face, so that the green of his eyes was visible again. They signaled retaliation.

It was impossible to run away in the mud; there was no escape for me. My dress was around my head when I emerged from the dunking. I knew I looked ridiculous, but at least my modesty was preserved, for I was completely encased in mud, as if in an earthen gown.

Janne produced a mud-soaked handkerchief. "I will be delighted to assist in the cleanup," he said solemnly.

I pulled the dress over my head, turned and offered my back to Janne.

At first I thought he was wiping the mud off, but then I realized he was gently spreading it across my skin. His fingers made definite movements on my back. He was writing something. I stood very still, trying to guess the message in his fingertips. The up-and-down movement of what might be an *M* was followed by an upward stroke, which was dotted, and another up-and-down symbol. The final letter was rolling and plump, with two small pokes over it: an umlaut.

"Do you know what I've written?" Janne asked in a husky whisper.

"Minä?"

"Yes, 'mine.' I would write love messages all over your body if I hadn't given you my promise of good behavior. And I've run out of *acceptable* writing surfaces."

I crawled onto the pathway, my bikini panties glued to my hips. I laid the ruined dress over my bosom and stretched out in the sunshine, encased in the earth of Finland. Janne scrambled from the mud flat and picked handfuls of grass, which he placed on my face as a shield against the sun. Then he lay down beside me.

We did not speak; we just listened to the breeze that rustled through the reeds. As a child, I had imagined the sound to be the furtive movements of trolls, but I had no fear of trolls with Janne beside me. The warnings, the insinuations—they all seemed so distant and irrelevant at that moment. Perhaps it was the time for me to have questioned Janne, to have confided my fears and sought reassurance, but I was content in our silent rapport.

After the sun had dried us, Janne stood up and said, "You'd better go for a swim to wash the mud away. I'll use the shower in the cottage, then find something for you to wear. If you wash out your dress and panties, you can spread them on the rocks, and they should be dry by the time we return from the village. Then you won't have to make embarrassing excuses when I take you back to your grandfather."

"But what could I possibly wear till then?"

"I have some appropriate clothing. Ritva didn't take many of her things when she left. I suppose she expected to find someone who could buy her more expensive clothes. Will you mind?"

I would mind, of course, but decided it was time to accept the fact that he had been married to another woman. "I'm sure they'll be better than this," I said, glancing at my mud-streaked dress.

The lake's edge, where the water was crystal clear, was hidden from the open lake by marsh grass. I stripped off my panties and entered the lake, feeling almost guilty about muddying the water. But then I reminded myself that I was only returning the earth to its source.

Within a few minutes Janne approached and set a bundle of clothing on the pathway. "You'll find something suitable here," he said and held up a bar of soap. "I'll also give you this if you can tell me who I am and then say it backward."

I laughed at this reminder of our childhood game and promptly answered, *"Saippuakauppias,* the soap merchant, and backward you are still *saippuakauppias.* In America, I taught the twins that word, and they used it to astonish their friends with their Finnish expertise and showed them that it's the same word spelled forward and backward."

"Quite an accomplishment," Janne said. "Were you able to teach them Finnish?"

"Oh, a few sentences," I answered. "Mostly they learned a few improper Finnish words when I lost my temper and, of course, they pronounced them perfectly! They loved to tease me about my accent, especially my *V*s and *W*s. They found it hilarious when I called an automobile wheel a 'veal' but said we were having 'wheel' cutlets for dinner. It became a family joke."

"I envy them your company," Janne said. "Well, hurry and dress, and we'll go into the village. A cold beer sounds pretty good, doesn't it?"

I applied the soap liberally to my body and even managed to wash the mud from my hair. Janne had also brought the pink hairbrush, which I used in braiding my hair into a long, fat plait.

Before choosing clean clothing from the bundle, I washed my shift and panties in the lake, making another silent apology for polluting it with soap. As I washed the garments and spread them on the granite rocks along the shoreline, I thought of my female ancestors who had performed the same task. It was tedious and backbreaking work, but the closeness to nature gave more purpose to the chore than the manipulation of a machine could ever afford. But I soon decided that the novelty would wear thin if I always had to do my laundry in that manner. Finally, as I smoothed my clothing on a flat rock and secured it with stones, I was thankful that I lived in the push-button age.

My skin, after the mud bath, no longer felt tender, and I selected a bright-yellow blouse and a pair of jeans from the bundle. I slipped into my sandals, walked to Janne's cottage, put the unused clothing on the porch steps and returned to the dock, where Janne was waiting for me. We headed the boat toward the village.

Janne had changed into clean denims and a white pullover, which emphasized the luster of his black hair and the green of his eyes. His skin was ruddy, and even the lines of his face seemed less deeply etched. I sighed in contentment, certain that nothing could upset me again.

CHAPTER ELEVEN

As we neared the village pier, Helge appeared from the wooden box that was his "office," jumped up and down, grinned toothlessly at us and gestured for Janne to throw him the rope. *"Hyvää päivää,* good afternoon, *Herra* Peltonen, *Neiti* Maija," he bellowed as the roar of our motor subsided, and he assisted us up the ladder.

The significance of his addressing Janne formally by his last name was not lost on me. Neither was his obsequious manner, nor his perpetual grin and repeated winks. The news from Grandfather's island had spread to the village: Janne was to be the owner of the Leinonen mill and now rated the title *Herra* Peltonen. *Neiti,* or "Miss," was still good enough for me; after all, I would be only the owner's wife.

Helge could contain himself no longer. "Ah, soon it will be Midsummer Eve. What a night that will be, eh? *Eh?"* He winked boldly at Janne.

So the invitations had already been issued by my presumptuous grandfather. I decided not to air my outrage in front of Helge.

Janne, ignoring Helge's bid for further information, placed some change in the old man's hands. "I'm sure an ale would go well after your efforts. Thank you, Helge."

The old boatman bobbed in agreement and thanked Janne profusely. As we walked to the tavern, he trotted

117

beside us and maintained a constant stream of gossip, none of which interested me since I had been gone from the village so long. It didn't seem to interest Janne, either, for he answered in monosyllables and looked off in the direction of the mill island. Its large buildings and mounds of logs were visible from the village pier.

Suddenly I found myself listening to what the old man was saying.

". . . and so I told the Gypsy that I hadn't seen *Neiti* Leinonen since she got home but that I would take her message to the island. But you know how secretive those Gypsies are."

"What?" I said in astonishment. "A Gypsy has a message for *me?*"

"That's what I've been telling you," Helge said in an injured tone. "Haven't you been listening?"

Janne was also attentive and he said sharply, "What's this about a message for Maija?"

"Ah," Helge said angrily, "that's how it is when you grow old. The young refuse to listen." He looked as if he were so offended that he would not repeat his story.

"Forgive me, Helge," Janne said, giving him a man-to-man poke in the ribs, "but you can guess where my mind is!"

Helge chuckled, seeming to forget that he had been offended. "One of the Gypsies has been looking for Maija. She said she has a message for *Neiti* Leinonen. I told her I hadn't——"

"Yes, we heard you say that," Janne said quickly, in an attempt to keep the old man from repeating himself. But Helge was not to be cut short.

"——seen her since she got back to the island. Told her I would take the message over myself, but you know——"

"Yes, we understand, Helge," I said. "They can be suspicious. Imagine not trusting a good friend like you."

"Don't know if I *am* a friend of that Gypsy," Helge muttered, offended again.

"I mean *our* friend, Helge. I know that Grandfather considers you to be one of our most trusted friends. I've often heard him say so."

What Grandfather actually said was that if you want a story from the island repeated to the north of China, tell Helge. But the lie seemed justified, and Helge was pacified.

"Right! But she refused. Said she would only talk to you."

"There's nothing to it, Maija," Janne said. "She must have heard about the wedding. You know how the Gypsies like to play on a wife's desire to look into the future."

Gypsies and Finns may seem an unlikely combination, but the people of Romany had wandered into our far-northern land and mastered our difficult language, though living somewhat apart and retaining their own customs. There was a large Gypsy encampment on the edge of our village, and they had become accepted members of our society. The government had even provided them with low-cost housing. Some of them worked at the mill, but most still followed their age-old occupations as blacksmiths, tinkers, and, of course, fortune-tellers.

The day-shift workers from the mill had arrived at the tavern and were refreshing themselves before going home. Their greetings were friendly, but few could resist making ribald allusions to our marriage, which Janne ignored. There was no need to explain why my face was red—why I looked like the typical blushing bride-to-be.

Paavo was established at a long table. He was surrounded by a group of admiring females, and the barmaid saw that his glass was always full.

Janne seated me at a small table and was ordering a pitcher of beer when a man from a nearby table came over and greeted him. He was introduced as

Mika, the supervisor of the graveyard shift. "I'm sorry to intrude," Mika said, "but could we talk for a minute, Janne? It looks as if we are going to run into production snags this evening."

"Do you mind if I join the men for a bit of shop talk, Maija? It should only take a minute. Order us a plate of sandwiches, will you?"

I ordered the food, asked if Reino was still on duty and was told he was in his office. "I think I'll go see him," I said to the waitress, who looked as if she were going to say something, then shrugged and walked off.

As I approached the door of Reino's office, I heard the sound of voices. There was no answer when I knocked, but the voices fell silent. I was about to return to my table when Reino called out, *"Kuka siellä?"*

"Maija," I responded.

The door opened immediately. Reino rushed out and caught me in an enormous hug that lifted me from the floor. His wide, handsome face beamed with delight. "How good to see you again. I heard you'd returned."

"But I'm afraid you're busy, Reino. I heard you talking to someone." I glanced at the outside door of the office. "Did I interrupt you? Perhaps you'd rather come to the island for a visit when you have time."

A shadow seemed to cross his normally good-natured face. "No, no, you haven't interrupted anything. Mother was just here to inquire when I would be home for supper."

"Well, that's all the more reason for me not to disturb you. Please, won't you come to Grandfather's and visit?"

"No, I couldn't do that, Maija. I mean—well, I suppose you've heard that I'm married now. What with the tavern and my wife and mother, I never seem to find time to visit anymore."

I sensed there was more in his refusal than the lame

excuse he offered. Grandfather's remark about Kaarina's "crush" came to my mind. Grandfather believed that Kaarina was destined to be a spinster, but there had been a time when I thought that she and Reino would marry. He had always seemed to like her and had even aroused her femininity. If it were true that he had been pushed into an arranged marriage by his domineering mother—and I didn't doubt it—it would be awkward for him to be around Kaarina. Surely Helge would have informed him of Kaarina's return.

I wondered what Reino had seen in Kaarina. Perhaps he was attracted to domineering females; certainly he had always bowed to his mother's wishes. I could understand why his mother, Mrs. Kauppi, had desired to break up the relationship with the strong-minded Kaarina and arrange for a docile daughter-in-law. She wouldn't want to lose control over her son's life.

"So you are still the tavern manager," I said, attempting to change the course of the conversation. As soon as the words were out of my mouth, I realized I'd touched on another embarrasing subject.

Reino's shoulders slumped, and a hopeless expression, which often marred his handsome face, descended. He shrugged and forced a smile. "Of course. What else would I do?"

His surrender to his mother's wishes irritated me. "You could have become an architect, as you always wanted."

He shifted his stance and avoided my eyes. "Ah, that. Well, we all had our childhood dreams, didn't we?"

Yes, I thought, we did; but what right did I have to challenge my old friend about his unfulfilled life when I had made such a botch of my own?

Reino's cheerful smile returned. "I hear that your dreams are finally to be realized." His pleasure tore at my heart, and I was unable to return his smile.

"What's the matter, Maija? *Herra* Leinonen issued

an invitation to the entire village to attend your wedding to Janne. I thought you'd be happy."

"So Grandfather has invited the entire community?"

"Maija," Reino asked, "aren't you happy?"

I wanted to tell him the details of the story, but I couldn't trust him to keep them to himself. He had no talent for deception, and I was afraid his inquisitive mother would ferret out the Leinonen scandal.

"I'm not sure."

Reino nodded his head, seeming to understand my answer. "It is always hard to be sure of what one should do. . . ." His words trailed off, and he glanced at the back door, as if evoking the image of his mother, who, evidently, had just left.

"Perhaps, Maija, I have no right to express myself, but. . . ." He stopped, and the hopeless look returned.

"Please go on. I want to hear your opinion."

"I just want to say that you shouldn't expect too much from a man. I think women do, you know. Men have, well, weaknesses. Overlook them if you can."

"Reino, please be more explicit. What are you trying to tell me?"

He sighed and ran his fingers through his shock of hair. "Oh, nothing, really. Just that we've all done things we've regretted."

"Janne has told me about his marriage, if that's what you're referring to; but I don't think it is. What else has he done to regret?"

"Ah, I'm making a botch of this. I wasn't referring to Janne."

"I think you were."

Reino shook his head in frustration and started another confused sentence but was interrupted by a loud knock on the outside door. He appeared to be relieved, but the look vanished as the door opened. *"Tanya,"* he said, "I've told you not to come here." He flashed a nervous glance at me.

"It is *Neiti* Leinonen I seek," the Gypsy replied.

She walked into the office, swinging her hips in an exaggerated motion that made her skirts whirl, and turned her back on Reino. She looked me over thoroughly and apparently decided I was no rival for her dark beauty. "They told me I would find you here. I have brought you a message."

My curiosity was piqued, but her insolence annoyed me. I remembered Janne's prediction that she wanted to make a bit of money by predicting my future.

"I don't want my fortune read," I told her.

She pulled up her outer skirt, reached into an inner pocket and withdrew a soiled note. "This is for you," she said, but instead of giving it to me, she held it behind her back with one hand and took my outstretched hand in her other one. "I have another message for you, too, and it is written in your palm." Her voice became cajoling as she examined my palm. "Ah, I could tell you much about the man you plan to take for a husband. It is all here."

I pulled my hand away, suddenly afraid of her. "I don't want to hear." My voice was firm, but my hand was shaking, revealing my fear.

A sneer spread across the girl's face, and she shrugged her shoulders. "Then, you must encounter your own destiny without my warnings." She took the note from behind her back.

"I told you I don't want your messages." Fear drove the words out more angrily than intended.

She dropped the note at my feet, walked to the doorway and stopped to look back at me. Her eyes projected insolence. "I do not need your palm to tell you about the man you think you will marry." She laughed as she saw the blood rush to my face, then slammed the door behind her.

Reino averted his face. As I picked up the note, I suddenly felt angry—angry at all the insinuations, and especially angry at myself for allowing them to keep me from forming my own opinion.

I unfolded the note.

He caused me too much pain and suffering for me to remain silent. I'll see that you suffer even greater humiliation if you refuse to meet me. I'll tell the authorities about him, and I doubt you would want that. Tanya will tell you all.

I read the words again and then handed the note to Reino. "What is this?" I said, my voice cold with fury. "What is it that everyone is trying to tell me about Janne?"

Reino read the note, then looked at me with a puzzled expression. "I swear, Maija, I don't know what it means."

"But you know that girl. Don't lie to me, Reino. What connection does she have with Janne? What are you trying to hide?"

His face seemed to crumple, and his hands waved about as if to grasp an explanation from the air. "I—I know her. Tanya has been in the village only a few months, but she has become, well, popular."

"I see."

"Maija, you don't even know if that note refers to Janne. You're assuming. It could be . . . anyone." His complexion became dead white.

I made my decision. Whatever that girl knew, I was going to find out. I extended my hand to Reino. "We'll talk again another day."

His hand was shaking, but his voice became firm as he said, "Yes, we will talk again . . . soon. As soon as I've had a chance to think."

It was my turn to avert my eyes. I couldn't help but agree with Grandfather's analysis of Reino: no *sisu.*

The tavern was a babble of conversation as more and more people gathered after their evening meal. As I worked my way through the crowd, everyone was intent on offering congratulations on my forthcoming marriage. I murmured something to each well-wisher while all the time searching for Tanya, who, I assumed, was in the tavern and was waiting for me to seek her out.

At last I caught a glimpse of her near the entrance, pushing through a group of newcomers. I thought I detected fear on her face as she looked back over her shoulder. I pushed and shoved my way through a blur of faces, but when I reached the door, Tanya had left.

The sunlight was blinding, and I shaded my eyes to squint along the pier. There was no sign of her. As I shut the door of the tavern and the din of voices was muted, I heard Tanya cry out, "Please, *Herra*, you are hurting my arm!"

"If you persist, I'll do more than hurt your arm," a familiar voice threatened.

"I shall not, *Herra*—my solemn oath, upon the virtue of the Mother of God!"

The voices seemed to come from behind a stack of barrels, and I had started in that direction when someone called my name. It was Paavo, swaying in the doorway of the tavern.

"Where are you going? Come inside. I have drunk too many bitter ales to your future happiness. I have become intoxicated from toasting my loss."

Paavo grabbed my waist, dragged me into the tavern and pressed me against his chest. He swayed drunkenly. Instinctively, I put my arms around him to keep him from falling.

"Paavo," I whispered, "we must remember who we are."

His body shook, and his voice wavered. "Please, little niece, tell me who we are."

"Feathers," I heard myself say as I fought waves of nausea. "Feathers in a strong breeze."

"That's the only thing you've ever said that's made

sense to me." Paavo attempted to whirl me about but lost his grasp, so that I was flung away from him.

A pair of strong arms prevented my fall. "Well, I see it wasn't wise to leave you alone."

"Let me out of here!" I screamed.

Janne pushed a path through the crowd. As soon as we were outside, I pushed his arms away, stumbled to the edge of the pier and vomited into the water.

"Come," he said, "you've had too much of our Finnish beer. We'll get in the boat and take you home." He lifted me down from the pier, and I slumped across a seat.

"Can you catch?" he asked.

I nodded weakly and caught the mooring rope, instinctively bracing for the impact of his boarding. My stomach was empty and sore, but my soul was sick with the memory of Janne's voice: *"If you persist, I'll do more than hurt your arm."*

CHAPTER TWELVE

Instead of starting the motor, Janne took the oars and rowed away from the pier. I felt his eyes upon me, but I gazed at a distant shoreline, not wanting to look at him. He made powerful sweeps of the oars until we were a distance from the lights of the pier. Then he shipped the oars and secured them. As the boat rocked tipsily, I noticed that large clouds had gathered in the sky and winds were beginning to lash the water. A storm threatened.

Making no effort to move closer to me, Janne said, "I was foolish to have left you. I promised that I would take good care of you, and I failed. Did you eat anything?"

I shook my head.

"But you obviously had plenty to drink with Paavo. Haven't you any sense?"

I laughed weakly, then clutched my stomach. "No, I don't have any sense."

"I'm sorry. I shouldn't lecture you when you're ill. But it frightened me when I couldn't find you. I felt like a fool, being so worried and then finding you with Paavo. It was as if it were all happening again."

So, I thought, he had known of the "comforting" Paavo had given his ex-wife.

"I wasn't with Paavo until just a few minutes before you saw us. I had been talking with Reino."

Janne bowed his head and sighed. "I'm sorry. I

jumped to a conclusion—a failing of mine. Mika and I got involved in our conversation, and when I became aware of how long I had left you, the tavern had become crowded and I couldn't find you. I even went out on the pier to look for you."

"Was that your only reason for going outside?" I asked, raising my voice against the sound of the rising wind and waves.

"What do you mean?"

"I mean Tanya."

He didn't reply immediately. Thunder crashed, and a far-off streak of lightning flashed across the silver sky. Finally, Janne said, "She did contact you. I suspected that when I saw her making her way to the door. That's what upset you, isn't it? What did she say?"

I put my hand to my breast pocket, felt the note that I'd shoved into it, but didn't draw it out.

"You don't have to answer. I can guess."

I looked at him but still said nothing.

"Well, it's true. I have been sleeping with her. I should have told you that myself, but I didn't want you to know. I can see now that it was foolish. She means nothing to me, and I never pretended otherwise. Her assumptions are based entirely on my physical needs. On the other hand, she was more than willing to have her own needs satisfied."

Oh, God, I thought, and it seemed as if the next clap of thunder was a divine response. Was it all that simple, I wondered—nothing more than a rejected woman's attempt to seek revenge, to arouse awful suspicions that would alienate Janne and me? Rain mixed with the tears that streamed down my face.

"Maija!" Janne took me in his arms and pressed my head against his shoulder. "Forgive me. It meant so little in my life, but I didn't want you to be upset. When Helge said that a Gypsy was looking for you, I suspected Tanya was going to make ugly accusations about me. She threatened to do so if I didn't continue to see her—or at least pay her. I told her I wouldn't be blackmailed. I should have told you the truth before now. We must learn to trust one another. I'm sorry about what I thought when I saw you with Paavo. Can you forgive me?"

I pressed my head into his shoulder and felt the pounding of his heart as he drew me closer to him. I could also feel Tanya's note against my breast. As my body yielded to his, I wondered if that note would always come between us.

The rain pelted down, but we were unaware of it as our bodies strained closer together. A bolt of lightning seemed to tear the sky just above our heads.

"A sign if I ever saw one," Janne said. "No, God, please—not in a boat in the middle of a lake." He pushed me away from him and took a deep breath before moving to the rear and starting the motor. "And surely not two days before Maija will be officially mine."

"I haven't agreed to marry you," I said, but the roar of the motor obliterated my words.

He adjusted the motor and said, "You're trembling. It would be just my luck if you were to come down with pneumonia." But the rain was warm. It was my emotions that made me tremble.

Janne turned full attention to maneuvering the boat through the choppy, wind-swept water, and soon we reached the channel.

"I must get home," I said as he secured the boat to his dock.

"I know, but you want your dress, don't you? It'll be soaked, but I thought you'd rather be seen in it. Stay in the boat and put that life jacket around you. It might help to keep you warm."

I sat in the boat, clutching the life jacket around myself and wondering what took him so long. Finally, he reappeared and yelled down, "I can't find your things. They must have been blown away by the wind."

"Forget it," I called back and climbed up to the dock. "I'll climb the tree to the balcony so no one will see me."

"I don't want you to break your neck," Janne said sharply.

"How many times in the past do you think I've climbed that tree?"

"Ten years in the past, if you'll remember."

"Ah, but you forget that I have been taking care of two very active boys, and getting them out of trees was part of my job."

Janne shrugged and drew me to him in a gentle embrace but made no move to kiss me. "Be careful. I don't want anything to happen to you. You can find your way down the path, can't you?"

I was surprised that he didn't offer to accompany me but supposed he was as anxious as I to get into dry clothes. "I'll be fine. The rain is stopping."

"Right. Now, get going, and be careful." He gave me a loving slap to speed me on my way. I would have preferred a kiss, but he looked very stern. I turned toward the path without protest. When I looked back, Janne was gone.

The forest was full of sounds after the storm. Dripping leaves, I told myself, but suddenly I was running. The sun was emerging from the clouds, and I was reminded of the ancient Finnish belief that an egg had been thrown up to heaven, so that the yolk became the sun and the white became the moon. The yolk-sun played tag among the clouds, creating shadows on the pathway.

As I neared the house, I saw light in the kitchen windows. I bent over and began to creep beneath the windows, but was brought up short by the sound of angry voices, Grandfather's among them.

"I won't hear another word. If I failed to make myself clear, I'll be blunt. Your relationship makes me sick, and I have no pity for your situation. You are being used, boy, can't you see that? It's bad enough when a man lets himself get entangled with a scheming woman, but. . . ." He sputtered, searching for words to express his disgust.

Heikki's voice was high and hysterical. "I don't care what you say about me, but leave Arvo out of this. You can't possibly understand the sensitivity of our relationship. You've never understood anything but your own way. Well, you'll find a time when you can't have your way."

"Just what does that mean?" Grandfather's bass voice and calm delivery contrasted sharply with the hysterical tone of his stepson's.

"You'll see." It was, in fact, a child's answer, but Heikki's voice had resumed its normal tone, and the words sounded mature and ominous.

I raised my head to peek over the bottom of the window and saw Heikki leave the kitchen. Then, as I heard the front door slam, I stepped around the corner of the house so he wouldn't see me. He seemed to pause on the porch, and then I heard his feet crunch on the walkway. When his footsteps receded, I again crept under the window, trying to make my way to the tree and the balcony, but once more I was halted. Grandfather stood looking through the window. It was obvious that his gaze did not see in front of him but was turned toward some inner vision. His face was twisted grotesquely, and he raised a trembling hand to cover it.

I waited until he turned his back to the window, then slunk past the kitchen. Testing each rain-slick branch of the tree, I climbed to the balcony and entered the bedroom, where an old-fashioned cradle had been placed between the two beds. It was hand-carved (I guessed that Mummo had used it for her children) and lined with a linen sheet. I had unbuttoned my blouse and dropped it to the floor when I heard footsteps on the stairs.

Eero was saying, "You heard him just now with Heikki. Do you really think he'd give me a better hearing?"

I couldn't make out Mummo's words, but she spoke in a soothing tone.

"Mother, listen to me. I wish you'd pay as much attention to me as you do to that brat."

"You don't have to be foul with the child just because you're upset," Kaarina said vehemently outside the bedroom door.

When I saw the handle turn, I stepped outside and hid on the balcony, not realizing the foolishness of the act. The baby was hiccuping, and Mummo patted him gently on his back. "Patience, son," she said to Eero. "Haven't I always tried to make you children see the value of patience? *Herra* is tired after his journey, and Heikki picked a poor time to talk to him. Besides, he hasn't been himself lately."

"No, he's been worse than himself," Eero said irritably.

Mummo talked on in the same placating voice, as if unaware of her son's interruption. "You must wait for the right time. Now, listen to your mother and be patient."

"Mother," Eero began, his voice heavy with condescension, "I know I can't expect you to understand that I must maintain my position in the literary world. I know you don't understand the necessity to raise the money to print my book, but I insist that you stop speaking to me as if I were five years old. I am sick of hearing your lectures on patience!"

"And *I'm* sick of both of you," Kaarina said. "Get out of here, Eero. I want to go to bed, and I don't want to hear any more about your literary problems. Can't you see? We are all in the same position. He won't give us any money. And, Mother, I want you to put that child down. You've had him mashed to your bosom all day. He'll be thoroughly spoiled. Now, get out of here, both of you!"

Mummo made a series of clucks but relinquished the child. "You see? You see? Now we're all upset and quarreling among ourselves. Patience, children——"

"Out!"

"Yes, Princess Kaarina," Eero said angrily. "Her Highness has spoken—— Ah, to hell with it. I must get out of this house and walk. I'm so upset now that I can't possibly compose." He slammed the door, and I could hear him banging angrily down the stairs.

"Daughter," Mummo began, but she was immediately cut short.

"Mother, I am tired. I don't want to talk. Please stop fussing with that baby and leave."

"I just want to say that everything will be all right."

"I think I will scream if I hear one more word. *Please!*"

Several weary sighs escaped Mummo, but she said no more and left the room, closing the door quietly behind her.

It was hardly the time to return to the bedroom, but I couldn't continue to hide half-naked on the balcony. I glanced into the bedroom and saw Kaarina seated on the edge of her bed, rocking the cradle. It was hard to imagine that she was the same screeching woman I had heard a minute before. She didn't lift her eyes from the baby as she began to remove the pins that held her tight bun in place. When her black hair was fanned about her, she lifted the heavy mane and let it settle about her shoulders. A soft smile replaced the usual harsh contour of her thin lips. She rocked the cradle with one hand as she unbuttoned her dress. Her smile broadened, and she began to hum, then sing a lullaby. She pulled the dress over her head and slipped out of her undergarments, pausing now and then to rock the cradle.

Her body had always seemed too thin and angular in the severe dresses she chose to wear, but now I could see that she had a good figure—high breasts and lean, elegant planes. She looked down at the baby, then threw her head back, sighing deeply, and ran her hands across her stomach and loins in a peculiar sensuous movement.

I drew back, knowing it was more impossible than ever to intrude on her. Even if I had been able to hide my own embarrassment, she would never forgive me for having witnessed such a private moment. Still, I couldn't remain on the balcony indefinitely.

Kaarina was clad in her nightgown, and her hands moved swiftly as she braided her hair. I wished that she would leave for a moment to go to the bathroom, but instead she lay on the bed and drew the sheet and blanket around her.

I crossed my arms across my naked chest and cursed myself for being a fool. Why hadn't I just entered through the front door, instead of placing myself in such a truly embarrassing predicament?

The evening sun had fully emerged from the storm clouds, and I wondered what I could do if Kaarina didn't fall asleep immediately. I could hardly continue to stand on the balcony, with so many people moving about on the island. My embarrassment would be compounded if someone should see me cringing, half-naked, outside my own bedroom.

Kaarina thrashed about restlessly. She wasn't going to oblige me by falling asleep. Then the baby began to whimper, and Kaarina turned to shush him.

If I attempted to climb down the tree, Kaarina would surely see me. And that would really require an explanation! I decided on another alternative and climbed onto the railing of the balcony. I had often scrambled across the rooftop from balcony to balcony when I was a child and decided there was sufficient cause to risk it again. I hoisted myself onto the ridge and began to crawl across, carefully planting each hand- and foot-hold. Then, ridiculous though it seemed, I had the feeling that someone was watching me.

Securing my position, I looked about. Pai-Pai, the cat, was crouched on the peak of the roof, apparently bemused by the sight of a distraught, half-clothed woman inching her way toward him. I was so startled by seeing the creature that I lost my hold and slipped on the roof. Though I finally managed to stop my slide, I had made a horrible noise.

"Who's up there?" Kaarina called out.

Oh, God, I thought, every action I took only made things worse.

"I said, who's there? I know someone's on the roof." She sounded hysterical, and I didn't blame her.

Pai-Pai yawned, stretched, walked across the roof-top and jumped to the balcony, emitting piteous meows.

"So it was you scratching about the roof again. Well, don't think you are going to stay in here!"

I took advantage of Kaarina's distraction, scrambled across the roof and dropped quietly onto the "Lords'" balcony. The adjacent bedroom, which Eero and Heikki shared, was unoccupied. I ran to the bathroom, locked both doors to the adjoining bedrooms, stripped off the rest of my clothes and pulled on a robe that I found hanging in the closet. As I put my jeans in the laundry hamper, I remembered the blouse I had dropped on my bedroom floor, with the note in its pocket. I would retrieve the note as soon as I was able to sneak back.

Returning to my bedroom, I opened the door quietly and listened, but no sounds came from Kaarina or the baby. Though heavy draperies were drawn across the windows, I could see the outline of Kaarina's body under the bedclothes. Even her head was covered. I tiptoed across the room and slipped into the nightgown that was tucked beneath my pillow, then crawled under the covers.

I fell into an immediate sleep of utter exhaustion, but my sleep was not sound and deep. I was jolted into momentary wakefulness by nightmarish scenes and sounds that tormented me throughout the night. It seemed as if there were a constant procession across the rooftop, down to the balcony and into the bedroom, but I was too tired to care or to try to separate dream from reality.

CHAPTER THIRTEEN

An incessant roar or wail alerted me to full consciousness, though it took a moment to separate the sounds. The roar was that of a motorboat, pulling up to our pier, and the baby was supplying the wail. He was very damp but was somewhat mollified as I rescued him from his bed.

I glanced at Kaarina and wondered how she had been able to sleep through the combined roar. Then I saw a bottle of pills on her bedside table and guessed that she had taken a sedative. That explained why she was still fast asleep and why I hadn't wakened her the night before.

The baby gurgled happily as I removed his diaper and nightgown and redressed him from the stack of garments Mummo had provided. As I bundled up his soiled clothing, I remembered the blouse I had discarded. I had been standing between the cradle and my bed when I dropped it, but it wasn't there; it was under my bed. Evidently I had kicked it there as I got into bed. But the note was gone. The blouse pocket was very shallow, and I thought it might have slipped out. I looked under the bed and on the floor, but it was nowhere to be found.

I became rigid with fear as I remembered its awful implications. What if someone found it? What would they think? As my mind became less confused, I realized that the words would be meaningless to any-

one else. They had been written to instill fear and
suspicion in me. If the note were found, there'd be no
clue to whom the allegations had been directed.

The baby began to whimper again, and I knew it
wouldn't be long before he made a full-fledged appeal
for food. It was time, I told myself, to begin acting
like a mother. No doubt Mummo had decided against
entering the bedroom to get the baby after Kaarina's
outburst the evening before.

I walked downstairs wondering who had come to
the island. I hoped that Grandfather wasn't going to
become involved in another conference. I simply had
to talk to him—to find out what he had learned about
the child, to find out why he felt he could issue
that wedding invitation to the entire village when I
hadn't agreed to the marriage. At least, I hadn't given
my verbal consent. I admitted to myself that I wanted
to marry Janne, more than anything in the world, but
I felt I should have the privilege of stating that fact
and making my own arrangements.

Voices came from the kitchen, where Grandfather,
Mummo and Janne were talking to a policeman, who
was showing them something. Their backs were turned
to me, and no one seemed to notice my approach.

"*Herra* Leinonen, *Rouva* Leinonen, can you identify
these garments?"

Mummo gasped, but Grandfather just stared at the
apparel. His back seemed tensed, as if he were awaiting a blow. He glared at the policeman and asked,
"Just what are you trying to say?"

"We found the body of a nude woman in the reeds
of *Herra* Peltonen's channel. These garments were
floating in the water."

I should have entered the room, but some instinct
caused me to back away down the hallway, into the
interior gloom of the house, where I was not readily
visible but could see and hear everything. The baby,
fortunately, was silent and docile in my arms.

"Maija was wearing those clothes when she left yesterday afternoon with. . . ." Mummo stared at Janne, her blue eyes wide and fearful.

Janne did not return her look but sat woodenly on the bench, his face expressionless. All the blood seemed to have emptied from Grandfather's face, and again I saw the terrible twisting of his mouth as he sought to gain control of his emotions. He turned slowly and looked at Janne.

"And I trusted you! I was ready to give her to you in marriage!" Grandfather lifted his arm as if to strike the younger man, but Janne did not change expression or make any attempt to ward off the threatened blow.

"*Herra* Leinonen, I am sorry," the policeman said urgently, "but you have misunderstood——"

Janne finally spoke. "I'll tell him. Those are Maija's clothes, but the woman they found is Ritva." His voice had been carefully controlled, but it broke as he added. "All that blonde hair floating about. . . . I, too, thought. . . ."

"Where is your granddaughter?" the policeman asked, breaking the silence that followed Janne's disclosure.

I forced myself to move toward the kitchen, though my mind demanded more time to think—to examine and sort out the thoughts that I could neither accept nor reject.

"She wasn't home last night when Kaarina retired and I brought the baby to bed," Mummo began to explain.

I stepped into the kitchen doorway, hoping my face showed more composure than I felt. "I've been standing in the hall."

Janne stood up and started toward me, but something in my face must have stopped him. "You heard?"

"Yes."

The officer showed me the wet garments. "Are these

yours? *Rouva* Leinonen indicated that you were wearing them when you left here in *Herra* Peltonen's company yesterday afternoon."

I nodded but said nothing.

"I'm sorry, but I must ask you how these garments came to be near the body of the dead woman."

I still could not get my mind to function correctly. *It had been Ritva, not Tanya. It was all right—it hadn't been Tanya. No,* I thought, sickened by my acceptance of anyone's death, *it wasn't right. But Ritva? That was the name of Janne's former wife.*

"Maija, speak up!" Was it fear that made Grandfather sound so angry?

"I took them off," I said stupidly, my mind still focused on thoughts that I couldn't quite hold and make into sense.

"I see. You took them off. When and why did you take them off?" The policeman sounded exasperated, and I noticed that he looked very tired. There was mud on his uniform. He, too, had been through an ordeal, and I wasn't making it easier for him. But I had to think.

"I can explain, if *Neiti* Leinonen will allow me," Janne said.

"I would rather she tell the story herself, but since she seems unable. . . ." He let his words trail off with a gesture of tired acceptance.

"She has been placed in an awkward position," Janne said and walked to my side. He took the child from my arms and handed him to Mummo. "Come, Maija, sit down, and we'll explain.

"*Neiti* Leinonen was wearing those clothes when we left here yesterday afternoon, but we stopped at my cottage and went swimming. Her clothes fell into the water, and I gave her some dry clothes before we went to the village."

There was silence as everyone absorbed this information. Mummo's eyes darted from one face to another. Grandfather bent forward and stared intently at Janne. The policeman stood stony-faced and gave no clue to his reaction, but there was irony in his voice when he finally spoke. "Miss Leinonen is somewhat smaller than you, *Herra* Peltonen. What sort of clothes were you able to supply her?"

"Women's clothes," Janne said evenly, returning the gaze of the officer. "Ritva's."

Another short silence. "I see. Then, your former wife was in the habit of visiting you? I had been given to understand that you were divorced nearly a year ago."

"And I have not seen her since she left me. She simply didn't bother to take all her things with her."

"And you kept them?" Neither the policeman's face nor voice revealed any emotion.

Janne's jaw muscles tightened. "I didn't *keep* them, I simply didn't bother to get rid of them. I'm not home much and I just—well, I just didn't care. Until now, that is." He took my limp hand into his.

"I see," the officer said noncommittally. "I am sorry to have to ask you another awkward question, *Neiti* Leinonen, but did you know whose clothes you substituted for your own?"

"Yes." I tried to make my voice strong, but the word came out in a whisper.

"I have told Maija about Ritva, if that is what you're getting at."

"Have you ever met *Rouva* Peltonen?"

"No," I said and then realized that I must explain myself further. "I have just arrived from America. I've been gone for ten years and have been home only a few days."

"Ah?" The officer raised his eyebrows and glanced at Janne. "Well, *Herra* Peltonen is to be congratulated on having won your acceptance in such a short time. I believe your wedding is to be held on Midsummer Eve—this Saturday?"

Grandfather's voice boomed out. "Urto, you know perfectly well when Midsummer Eve is. But you always were a sly little fellow. Why don't you just state what you're thinking? But I don't think you *are* thinking, at least not clearly. You are trying to imply that either *Herra* Peltonen or my granddaughter is responsible for the death of that unfortunate woman. Why? For what motive? Janne and Ritva were divorced. She wouldn't have been any barrier to their marriage. And as for your implication that their decision to marry was suspiciously quick, they have been corresponding with one another for over a year now. I personally put them in touch.

"I've encouraged this whole thing. They always were fond for one another, as you well know, Urto—if you'll forget for one moment that you are now a policeman and remember that you grew up in this village. They had a lovers' tiff that sent Maija flying off to America. Very tragic. But now they are marrying, and with my full blessing."

I hadn't recognized Urto in his uniform, but now, after Grandfather's reduction of his importance, I saw that he was one of the village boys. Indeed, Urto's face was flushed, and it took him a moment to regain his official demeanor. "*Herra* Leinonen, I have not been implying anything. I have simply been trying to find out why these clothes were found near the body."

"Well, then, ask them directly. You thrust a knife into a bear; you don't kill it by cutting off one hair at a time. Get to the point."

A flush reappeared on the policeman's face. He was angry and didn't relish being made a fool of, even by *Herra* Leinonen. "Well?" he asked us.

Janne's hand tightened on mine, but he made no effort to answer. He seemed to be waiting for me.

"I left those garments on a rock to dry while we were gone. If you'll remember, there was a sudden storm yesterday afternoon, and when we went back to look for them, they were gone. We assumed they had been blown away by the wind." My tongue spoke the decision that my conscious mind refused. In saying "we," I lied.

"You looked through the marsh?" Urto's quick response showed that he was again in command of the interrogation.

"Yes, we looked among the reeds. Of course, it was still stormy and the light was poor. We might have overlooked them."

"Might you have also overlooked a body?"

The pressure of Janne's hand increased, and I answered firmly, "There was no body there at that time or we would have seen it."

Not "we," I thought numbly. *"We" hadn't looked for the clothes. Janne went to look for my clothes— and was gone so long!*

"I might suggest that since you did overlook the clothing, you might also have overlooked the body."

"That is possible, of course," Janne responded.

And it was possible that Janne had not seen the body, I thought. *How long had she been there?* I asked the question aloud.

"It is impossible to ascertain at this time," Urto said.

"Why?" Grandfather demanded.

Urto appeared quite satisfied with his answer. "Because, *Herra* Leinonen, a medical examiner must establish the time of death, and even then it is only an estimate."

"I realize that, but surely, boy, you can tell if she'd been there for days or hours. Or *can* you tell the difference without having to consult your 'medical examiner'?"

"Of course I can tell," Urto answered heatedly. "It could only have been hours. She was seen in the village earlier——" He stopped, and the flush became even brighter. Grandfather had extracted more information than Urto had been authorized to reveal.

Grandfather concealed his delight in having tricked Urto into supplying the information and asked in a respectful manner, "How did Ritva's body happen to be found?"

The young policeman showed momentary resistance to giving any more information but then shrugged and said, "Helge saw a boat floating in the lake but couldn't see an occupant. He phoned us, and by the time we got there, the boat had found its way into the channel. *Rouva* Peltonen's body was caught in the reeds near where the boat was stuck."

"Yes," Grandfather nodded, "the current runs in the direction of that channel. We've discovered all kinds of flotsam in the grasses. That's why you found the boat, the body, *and* my granddaughter's clothing in the same area. It's a natural catch basin."

"There might be those who would object to the use of the word *flotsam* to describe a human body, *Herra* Leinonen," Urto said frostily, "but we have taken that fact into consideration. As I said, the presence of these garments is a confusing issue."

"I see nothing confusing about it," Grandfather insisted. "I just gave you the logical explanation."

"*Herra* Leinonen," Janne interceded, "I think it would be best if we let the officer proceed with his line of questioning."

Urto gave Janne a look of gratitude, and in that instant Grandfather smiled and winked at me. He was trying to provoke the policeman.

"Thank you, Janne," Urto said, forgetting his formality. "I would appreciate being allowed to proceed. *Neiti* Leinonen's clothing has caused confusion because at first we were quite certain about what had happened to *Rouva* Peltonen.

"Early last evening she was seen in the Gypsy quarter, and many people heard her quarreling with the girl named Tanya. No one seems to know what the quarrel was about, but all agree that it was violent and that both women appeared to have been drinking. Several people expressed surprise about their sudden falling out. Evidently *Rouva* Peltonen had been living with Tanya—at least she was seen at the Gypsy girl's house quite often of late, and that assumption was made. That's why I asked *Herra* Peltonen if he had seen his ex-wife. . . ." Urto glanced nervously at me and let his sentence go unfinished.

"He told you he had not," Grandfather said.

Janne gripped my hand so hard that I thought he would break a bone, but my nerves were so taut that the pain was only a mild distraction.

"So I remember, *Herra* Leinonen. Now, if I may proceed?" Urto asked sarcastically.

"Of course you may proceed. That's what I have been urging you to do," Grandfather replied blandly.

The young man took a deep breath in an obvious attempt to control his anger. "We were called out in the early morning. One of Tanya's, uh, customers"—he bobbed an apology in Mummo's direction—"reported he found her on the floor of her cabin with a knife in her body.

"When we began our investigation, we were told of the quarrel and began searching for *Rouva* Peltonen— among others. Tanya was a—well, many people passed through her house."

Grandfather raised his eyebrows. "Yes, I think we are all aware of Tanya's popularity in the village."

"Precisely." I detected a tinge of embarrassment on Urto's face. "Helge's report was received about that time, and subsequently we found *Rouva* Peltonen's body. It seemed obvious what had happened, until Dr. Tami, who accompanied us, identified these clothes as having been seen on *Neiti* Leinonen."

Grandfather ignored the last statement and said, "So

Ritva stabbed the girl, took a boat and rowed out far enough so that she wouldn't be observed. She stripped herself and no doubt threw her clothes and the knife— Or did you find her clothes and the knife?" Grandfather asked, interrupting himself.

The officer shook his head.

"So she threw her clothes and the knife overboard. I imagine she used something to weigh the clothes down. The knife, of course, would sink easily. Then she began to swim to remove any traces of blood from her body and hair. You say she had been drinking? Well, she must have become confused and swum too far from the boat, tiring herself and drowning."

"There was a blow on her head."

"She struck it on a rock, then; but I would guess that the blow came after she drowned. There are many boulders on the island's edge, particularly in the vicinity of the channel. You have been dragging the lake's bottom?"

Urto nodded, resigned to the patriarch's domination of the interrogation.

"Very good. The water is clear today, but don't forget that storm yesterday. It stirred up the bottom, so that the clothing and the knife may be mired.

"You are to be congratulated, Urto. I always wondered what you would make of yourself. A fine officer. A bit too long-winded, perhaps, but that is all part of the role, eh?" He threw him a conspiratorial wink, and even the roots of Urto's blond hair seemed to turn red.

"Thank you, *Herra* Leinonen," the young man managed to say between tightly clenched teeth. "Now, if I may, I must ask all of you where you were last night and early this morning."

Grandfather again took the lead and responded firmly that he had been in bed, asleep. Mummo stated that she had stayed up until almost ten, when Eero and Heikki returned from their evening stroll, and then had gone to bed.

Eero, Heikki and Paavo had entered the kitchen quietly during the middle of the interrogation. Eero had nothing to add to Mummo's explanation for his absence but assumed a bored expression toward the whole proceedings. Heikki paused before correcting his mother's impression that he had come back to the house in Eero's company. "I got in a little after ten, but my brother Eero was in bed at that time. We share a room together."

Paavo began to laugh when he tried to account for his whereabouts, but the laughter proved too painful and he clutched his head between his hands. "To be perfectly honest, I don't remember when I got home. In fact, I have a feeling that I was fortunate to get home at all."

"Then, you may have returned to this island late last night or in the early morning?"

"Well, it's obvious I got back here."

"You returned alone?"

"Ah, yes. A pity, but that's how it turned out."

"Did you see the boat that *Rouva* Peltonen was in?"

"Urto, I was lucky to see the boat *I* was in. I assure you, it took all my concentration to navigate my way home."

Kaarina had come downstairs to the kitchen, her eyes heavy with sleep. "I retired early, took a sleeping pill and didn't leave my bed until I was awakened by the voices here in the kitchen."

"Neiti Leinonen?"

For one mad moment I thought I would blurt out, *I came home, slunk about my grandfather's house, overhearing conversations and climbed a tree to reach my bedroom balcony. Then I huddled there half-naked, and crawled across the roof to find a way to get to my own bed without embarrassing myself or Kaarina.*

"She was with me in the cottage," Janne said. "She didn't leave until a little after midnight. I didn't think to look at the clock, but when I walked her home, this house appeared to be quiet and settled for the night."

I was appalled by his glibness, but Urto copied his statement into his notebook with no indication of belief or disbelief. He looked at me again, waiting for my response.

"There is nothing I can add," I said, trying to control the tremor in my voice.

"Did you see anyone or hear anything during the night?"

Yes, I overheard a quarrel between Grandfather and Heikki, and Heikki threatened to get revenge on his stepfather. I eavesdropped on Eero, Mummo, and Kaarina and then witnessed a very intimate moment in Kaarina's life. And yes, I encountered the cat—in case you are interested in his whereabouts last night.

I heard every sort of nightmare sound during the early morning hours, and in my tormented sleep I saw the face of the Gypsy girl. She smiled knowingly and handed me a note, but I couldn't read the words because the paper was soaked in blood and the blood spurted into my eyes and I was blinded. I could see nothing but blood until the man who sits beside me, calmly holding my hand, wiped my eyes and told me, over and over again, "Trust me."

"Nothing," I said.

CHAPTER FOURTEEN

"I saw no one. I share a room with Kaarina, and she appeared to be asleep when I went to bed."

"But you, *Neiti* Leinonen, don't remember when Maija came to bed; is that correct?"

"My title is *Doctor,*" Kaarina corrected him. "As I said, I had taken a sleeping pill."

"I see," Urto said, shutting the notebook that recorded so many lies. "Thank you. I think that is all I will require in the way of information for the time being."

Mummo placed a large platter of cold meats and bread on the table and poured cups of steaming coffee.

"You'll stay and have breakfast?" Grandfather inquired.

Urto cast a yearning look at the coffee and food and said, "Well I should get back to the village, but perhaps I could take time to tell you what we've learned about the identity of——"

He didn't get the opportunity to finish his sentence or even sip the coffee. Moving more swiftly than one might expect for a man of his years, Grandfather grabbed Urto's arm and forced him from the room, covering any protest the officer might have voiced with a barrage of words. "Terribly competent handling of what could have been a very awkward situation. You are to be complimented, and I will see that your superiors. . . ."

149

The front door shut and we couldn't hear anything further. For a moment we all seemed to be fixed in place, a cast of characters bereft of a director. Then, of one accord, we shifted positions, took our places at the table, began to sip the coffee and commented on the various inconsequential thoughts that came to mind. It was as if everyone was unwilling to resummon the horrible reality of the deaths that had been thrust into our lives.

"Mother, I really cannot eat this porridge," Paavo said, pushing away the large bowl she had set in front of him. "I don't know what gave you the idea that porridge is good for a hangover. Just coffee, please!"

"Didn't Urto look handsome in his uniform?" Mummo asked of no one in particular.

"I'm sure he'd be relieved that you didn't tell him that," Eero commented, casting a look around the table for confirmation of his superior insight. Because everyone was caught up in their own thoughts and failed to give him their attention, he cleared his throat and asked a question that made everyone look at him.

"I suppose they had what might be called a 'competitor's quarrel,' don't you think?" He looked directly at Janne.

Janne seemed to have voyaged to a far place in his mind. "They?" he asked, not seeming to comprehend Eero's meaning.

"Tanya and Ritva." Eero's tone was calculated but casual. "Surely I need not tell *you* what trade they plied?" He turned his head coyly and stared at Janne through the hooded eyes of a bird of prey.

Janne returned the look, and there was a palpable presence of hatred in the room. Carefully, he placed his coffee mug on the table; then his hands gripped the table's edge so hard that his knuckles turned white. "I remind you, Eero, that both of them are dead. Your innuendos cannot hurt them, but they might hurt you."

"Bravo!" Grandfather said from the doorway. "I

couldn't have given better advice myself. Now I will give more advice—for all of you." He sat down at the head of the table and buttered a thick piece of bread. "A very unfortunate event has occurred, but I am certain that my analysis of the circumstances is correct and that the official findings will bear it out."

No one spoke as he bit into the slab of bread. He chewed slowly and allowed his eyes to roam from face to face.

"You may recall what I said to you about Maija's child: 'He that is without sin among you, let him first cast a stone.' I suggest that you would again be wise to heed that admonition. And if what I say is too subtle, let me be more blunt. Don't attempt to blame anyone for these tragic deaths."

He selected a slice of sausage to put on his bread and added, "It won't work to try to turn Janne and Maija into murderers—or to turn them against one another. If I see any evidence that you are attempting to do that, I will be forced to change my opinion of the circumstances of the two deaths and look for a murderer—a live one." The awful words seemed to hover over us, as if etched in the air in invisible blood.

"Maija, eat something," Grandfather commanded. "I understand you had an accident and have not been well. May I remind you that your wedding is tomorrow evening? I'm sure you will want to be fit. I'm sure we *all* want to see Maija looking her best."

I took a spoonful of porridge and put it in my mouth.

Kaarina seemed far removed from the rest of us; even her stepfather's ominous words seemed not to have penetrated her isolation. She ate a slice of bread and butter and sipped from her coffee cup, which Mummo refilled. I wondered if she were still under the influence of the sleeping pill. Then, as if she were waking, she looked up. "If she had followed my advice, she would have stayed in bed," she said as if I weren't present.

"Dr. Tami thought it advisable for me to get some air," I reminded her. *"He* is my physician."

"I am curious to know what other advice he may have given you. Did he recommend vigorous exercise, too? I should have thought that unwise after your having been ill. But, then, you were never a delicate sort of female, were you?"

"That's quite enough, Kaarina," Grandfather ordered. He took a piece of sausage from the platter and fed it to Pai-Pai, who sat at his feet. "One feline in the house is sufficient. Besides, you wouldn't want anyone to think you were jealous, would you?"

Kaarina drew herself up and left the room. Heikki pushed away from the table, abandoning his pretense of eating. "Paavo, could you use some help in the store today? I simply must get away from here." Paavo, still suffering the effects of the previous evening, gestured his indifference.

Mummo said, "I'll pack you both a lunch."

"Don't bother, Mother," Paavo said. "We'll get something at the tavern."

"No doubt," Grandfather muttered as the two men left the room.

After the encounter with Janne, Eero had retired behind a book. Without excusing himself, he closed it and also left the kitchen.

"Lilya," Grandfather said, "a load of laundry was sent back aboard my boat, and I need clean underwear and a shirt to wear to the mill. Will you see to them?"

"Yes, *Herra,*" Mummo replied with a trace of a curtsy. She hesitated, then seemed to summon heroic courage. "But I don't think you should go to the mill today. You need rest. You know you haven't been well."

"I will judge my own state of health!" Grandfather responded angrily.

Her rosy cheeks flushed even brighter, and this time

she actually dipped into a curtsy, but her worried expression signaled her concern.

"Perhaps you *should* rest," I suggested after Mummo left.

"Don't pay attention to that old woman. I know how I feel."

But Grandfather was unable to control the trembling of his hands and a droop of his eyelids. He did indeed look ill, but under the tired lids his eyes were blue flame, and his voice was firm. He looked at Janne and me and asked, "What are you suppressing?"

It would have been embarrassing to have told him of my strange actions the previous evening, but he would have understood why I hadn't wanted to encounter anyone in the household and why I hadn't revealed my presence to Kaarina after witnessing her private behavior. He wouldn't have thought I was seeking to hide any sinister motive of my own if I admitted I had lied about the time when I'd returned. Why couldn't I just speak out? Because, I told myself, to do so would expose Janne's lies—and I was not sure of his innocence.

"Are you two just going to sit there? Didn't I tell you I don't have much time? Your wedding is scheduled for Saturday. If something has happened that I should know about, tell me now. I sense that some sort of wedge has been driven between you."

"I lied when I said that Maija and I were together until almost midnight," Janne confessed. "She left me about nine o'clock. I suppose Maija lied because she wanted to protect me and she——" His voice broke as he looked at me. "She thinks I killed the women."

"Do you think that, Maija?" Grandfather asked.

"I don't know what to think. That note and——"

"What note are you referring to?" Grandfather asked.

"Tanya's," I replied in a whisper. "She came to

Reino's office while we were talking and said she had a message to deliver to *Neiti* Leinonen. It was so nasty —it warned that she would go to the authorities if I didn't see her. It didn't make much sense, but it was obvious that the note referred to Janne. I don't know— coming on top of all of the allegations. . . . I didn't know what to think. I tried to follow her, but she left the tavern. Then I heard Janne warning her."

"What did Janne say to her?"

"He—he said, 'If you persist, I'll do more than hurt your arm.' Janne didn't know I overheard him, but later, when he was taking me home, he could see that I was upset. He guessed that Tanya had contacted me. I didn't tell him about the note, and he convinced me that she was only trying to be vindictive—to upset me so that I wouldn't go through with the marriage."

"And why should you think differently now?" Janne asked in a quiet voice.

"Because I finally realized that the note couldn't have been written by Tanya. She told me it came from someone else, but that really didn't sink in until I heard about Ritva's death. Now I'm sure that your ex-wife wrote the note; it couldn't have been written by Tanya. The wording—it just didn't sound like her.

"Where is this note?" Grandfather asked.

"Gone," I said. "I put it in the pocket of my blouse and then forgot about it. When I looked in the pocket this morning, the note wasn't there."

"And you think you may have dropped it and I found it, read it and became so afraid of whatever allegations it contained that I went back to the village stabbed Tanya and then drowned my ex-wife?"

"I don't know," I said miserably. "But if you aren' afraid, why did you say we were together late las night? Why didn't you deny it when I said that we bot searched among the reeds for my clothes? Why didn' you offer to walk me home?"

Janne sighed. "I can see how it must look to you

When I went to look for your dress, I did see Ritva."

"What?" Grandfather and I said in unison.

"She was alive, very much alive," Janne added. "Her boat was pulled into the reeds, and she was sitting in it She seemed startled, but then she said she had to talk to me. Maija was already so upset by what had happened that I didn't want her to have to face Ritva and any more unpleasantness. So I lied to Maija and let her walk home alone so that I could talk to Ritva and 'get rid' of her.

"As soon as Maija was out of sight, I went back to Ritva, but she was gone. And instead of searching for her, I went to bed. I suppose I should have told Urto that I saw Ritva last night, but I knew he would. . . ." He made a gesture of despair.

"Yes," Grandfather said thoughtfully, "I see what you mean. It is always well to keep sorrow to oneself. You were quite vocal a year ago after she left you."

Janne turned to me to explain. "One night in the tavern—a day or two after Ritva left me—I got drunk and one of the men asked me about her. I told him if I ever heard him or anyone else mention her name, I would kill him. And that I would kill Ritva, too, if I ever saw her face again."

"Ah, the ghosts of ill-conceived words! How they come back to haunt us. Was she drunk when you saw her?" Grandfather asked.

Janne shrugged. "I couldn't say for certain. She didn't make much sense, but I didn't talk to her long enough to tell if she'd been drinking. She was huddled up, like she was trying to hide something. Or maybe she was just afraid of me. I don't know." His face paled. "I found the knife and Ritva's clothes this morning when I was awakened by the police boat. Fortunately, I got out on the porch before the police arrived. Her clothes and the knife were inside the bundle of clothes I had given Maija yesterday. I threw the whole thing into a clump of bushes."

Grandfather said, "I think I'm beginning to see what happened. After killing Tanya, Ritva knew she must hide, and she remembered the channel. Perhaps she also remembered she'd left some clothes at Janne's and hoped to change into them, but when Janne discovered her, she had to leave. So she came back later, and this time discovered Maija's clothes. A plan came to her—a way to free herself and to make Janne look like the killer of both Tanya *and* herself. Then she'd be free to assume a new identity.

"She left her bloody clothing and the knife on Janne's doorstep, no doubt planning to make an anonymous call to the police—to tip them off—something to the effect that Janne had been seen with Tanya, whatever would bring the police to Janne's to make the gruesome discovery.

"When she went back to put on Maija's clothes, the boat had drifted away, and she attempted to swim for it. She must have struck her head on a rock when she went into the water."

But a piece was missing from his explanation, and something nagged at me, driving darts of fear into my heart. Janne reached for my hand but I pulled it away, unwilling to let him touch me.

CHAPTER FIFTEEN

"If you didn't know about the deaths when you found the knife and clothes, why were you so afraid to let the police find them?"

Janne's face paled, and it seemed like several minutes before he replied. "I don't know. It was just an instinctive feeling. I can't explain my reaction any better than that."

"Maija, why are you looking at him that way? Don't you think that's possible? I think it is. Sometimes we can't explain our reactions. Janne has always been rash, but I think it was well this time that he heeded his impulse."

Janne tried to speak to me but couldn't find the words. He pressed a hand against his eyes and then looked at it as if he had never seen it before. I, too, stared at his hand. Had it thrust a knife into the Gypsy girl? Had it also killed his wife, so that she could not tell the authorities what pain and suffering he had inflicted upon her?

"Maija, you must not look at me that way. You must not. I thought you loved me, but how can you love me if you can think such things of me?"

I asked myself the same question. Can one love and not trust? Yes, I admitted, as I looked at the two men who sat near me. I loved my grandfather, although I didn't have perfect faith in his mental condition. And my feelings for Janne transcended logic. Logic warned,

"Beware! Look at the facts." My love said, "I don't care. None of it matters." My love was the blind and selfish attitude of one possessed by passion. I felt as if I were drowning, fighting against an inexorable pull. I could almost experience the perverse pleasure of giving up the fight—allowing nature to take command, to extinguish pain, to obliterate thought.

During my ten years abroad I had learned to accept myself and take pride in my competency. I had even learned to love myself. Could I give that all up just because the child-woman in me wanted to believe in the two people who were an integral part of my life? But how could I discard my childhood memories? Grandfather's hand enveloping my own, Janne's casual domination—both men had dominated me. But does one relinquish one's very beginning? Both men had been part of my life as long as I could remember. They were my loves.

Somehow, in those brief moments, I knew I would be deciding both my physical and my emotional destiny. I rejected the thought that I was simply bowing to dominance and weakness. Love must be based on trust, they had told me. Yes, they asked for trust. But if I trusted them, it would not be because of their demand. Trust was mine, to give or to deny. I held it in my hand during that moment. I knew I had to feel it before I could offer it.

I walked to the window and looked at the lake, at its calm, mirrorlike surface—a gift of God, ruled by his divine knowledge. I envied the lake. There was no questioning in that body; it accepted and adapted to whatever condition was thrust upon it. It had no reasoning power, the curse and the glory of the human mind. I leaned my head against the windowpane and prayed for an answer, for a bolt of illumination; but, as is often God's way, none came. No special words were spoken, but as I offered him my indecision and longing for guidance, I felt a lessening of mental anguish. I thought again of that little word, *trust* and felt I was beginning to understand its meaning. It is not blindness but an instinct.

I turned and saw that Janne's eyes were blank, but Grandfather's seemed to glow with an intense flame. I guessed that he longed to purify me with words and reasons but that an instinctive warning checked the impulse.

I said, "I wish I could tell you both that I believe we have taken the right path. I can't. I suppose we will have to let the future determine that. Janne, you have asked for trust and said that love cannot exist without it. I believe that trust must be built. If I were to say to you, 'I trust you implicitly,' I would be lying, and I don't think love can exist on a lie. I am frightened about the future and don't half understand what has happened. Don't lie to me, please. I know that the events of life cannot always be glibly explained. I don't know much about the world, but I think I have learned that.

"Grandfather, I now have enough courage to say that you cannot impose your own thoughts and beliefs on me. I don't want to marry Janne simply because you feel it is a solution to a problem. I don't even know that I believe that anyone has tried to kill you. And I don't believe that you do, either. You've experienced strange happenings—very strange ones—but there's no evidence that they were murder attempts. If you were honest, you would admit that you do not love any of Lilya's children. You never have. You closed your heart to them from the first. Oh, I know they aren't a lovable bunch. Remember, I grew up with them and know their ways much better than you. But what can you expect? Their mother always spoiled them and you cared for their bodily needs but reserved your respect."

"Respect!" Grandfather choked on the word, and his face became inflamed with rage.

"Yes, respect. Every human being needs that. If they are denied it, how can they become worthwhile?"

"I made my *own* respect, child. I never looked to others for it."

"You are a strong man, but not everyone is. Most people are beset by self-doubt. You were fortunate that you learned early in life to believe in your own worth. That is a great strength, but, Grandfather, it is also your weakness. You believe too much in yourself and your philosophy. You impose your thoughts on others and wonder why they resent it. You must learn the worth of others and respect their viewpoints. Yes, even Paavo's, Eero's, Heikki's, and Kaarina's."

The old man shook his head sadly and replied, "You are wise while being a fool. Those are lovely platitudes, my dear, but don't overlook the very real fact of evil. It does exist, even if you choose to ignore it."

"That is exactly what I am trying to straighten out in my mind. I know evil exists—two women have been murdered. I can't just take Janne's hand and say, 'I trust.' I need time to think this all out."

"There may not be time, Maija," Grandfather said, his voice hoarse with emotion.

"What do you mean?" I said.

"I have placed you in a serious position. You do not wish to believe that there have been attempts on my life. All right, the evidence wouldn't stand up in a court of law. But I *know*. I *feel* it. That is why I believe Janne when he says he hid the knife and clothes before the police arrived because he had an instinctive reaction. I am not afraid of death, but by all the gods of this earth and the Supreme One, I know someone has tried to kill me. And now I have placed you in danger. The same person, or persons, will realize that now it is necessary to kill you. We have no time for all these emotions and beliefs. You *must* believe—for your own sake. Janne, don't just sit there; say something to this woman!"

"I can't ask Maija to marry me if she feels I might

have murdered two women. I want more from our relationship than a docile woman who says one thing with her tongue and feels something else in her heart."

"Oh, if I could only be sure that you love me," I said, my voice breaking with emotion.

"I think I love you—I know I want to—but if this always remains between us, I'll never feel free of your suspicion. Will you always wonder if I murdered my ex-wife and Tanya just to keep some unsavory information from the authorities? Maija, I have never been a saint, but I swear to you that I am not a murderer. Perhaps it isn't fair to ask that you give me your faith —blind faith, at that—but I must have it. We will never have anything together if you don't believe in me."

It was as if the room had developed a heartbeat of its own: the click of the clock's pendulum, the baby's contented breathing while deep in sleep, and the settling creaks of the old house. They combined into an urgent throb, a life-force that demanded I commit my emotions. I walked to Janne and took his hand. "I will be your wife. I love you. I always have. Love me in return and forgive my fearfulness. I admit to fear. Please, please take it from me."

His arms enveloped me, and he murmured in my ear, "I shall try, my darling Maija. Place your belief in me and it will give me the confidence to make you truly happy."

Grandfather cleared his throat elaborately and staged a coughing fit that necessitated blowing his nose and wiping his eyes. "Well, so so. *So, so, so.* Now we must talk of *important* things."

The baby, waking from his midmorning nap, began to fret. His small mouth puckered and twisted as he sought the comfort of a nipple. Grandfather picked him up, pretending great distaste for his soggy condition, then wrapped a blanket about him and rocked him into a gurgling, happy disposition.

"This young chap's bladder seems to function well.

If that's a sign of health, he's a splendid specimen."

He handed the infant to me but peered intently into his face. "There is a certain refinement of features in his face. I find it hard to believe."

"What?" I asked, immediately aware of my earlier puzzlement.

"Urto told me that it is believed the child is . . . *was* Tanya's. Although she never showed him to anyone, several people said they heard an infant crying in her house. She told them to mind their own business, but she seemed to hint that the father was a very prominent man.

"There are no reports of a stolen child; so we must assume that this baby was born under secret circumstances. I have a feeling that my first suspicion was correct. Why would someone send the child to me if he weren't connected with a member of this family?"

"It's possible that Tanya, or whoever the mother is, simply put the basket in Helge's boat just to get rid of it," Janne suggested.

I shivered to think of such an act but thanked God that they had not done worse.

"We should be able to learn more about the child," Grandfather said, "after the authorities have delved further into Tanya's past—though I am sure it will turn out to be complicated. It's even possible they may never be able to determine the child's true parents."

"I disagree, Grandfather. If the child was Tanya's, one of her relatives will claim it. Gypsies are different from us, but they don't desert their children—or the children of their relatives."

"Ah, but I wouldn't put it past that girl to have stolen this child."

"To what purpose? And if she did, the authorities would be aware of the kidnapping."

"Well, within a day we should know. I still believe that someone on this island is responsible, and I want you to go on pretending that you're the mother. If someone here is responsible, it will put him in a very compromising position. Guilt will show even though compassion is missing.

"Now, however, I want you to find Lilya. I told her to bring your grandmother's wedding dress from the attic. You are about her size. It is a traditional Finnish wedding costume, which she saved for her daughter— but, as you know, a daughter was never born. I believe she would be very pleased if you wore it on your wedding day."

"Grandfather, I don't know what to say."

"So do as the wise do: say nothing. Now, run along and find Mummo so the two of you can do all those womanly things—tucking, pressing—whatever it is that you do. Janne and I must talk and then get back to the mill. Run along, and take the young one with you."

I picked Johnny up, and Janne came over and wrapped his arms around both of us. "Take special care of yourself today. We'll be tied up at the mill until after supper, but if I can, I'll be by later to see you."

"You'll send word if you hear anything about . . . anything?"

"Of course," Grandfather answered. "Now, off with you. But one more thing, young woman. Don't leave the house today. You can find enough to occupy yourself without wandering about the island."

Again the specter of violence, alleged and real, rose up. Even on the day before my wedding, violent emotions surrounded me. But were they as violent as Grandfather felt them to be? The awful deaths of Tanya and Ritva didn't touch any member of our family, or so I had been told.

"All right," I agreed, tired of fighting for reason and common sense.

"The crayfish will be delivered sometime today. Lilya will appreciate your help in preparing the food that she'll insist on stuffing us with tomorrow. Kaarina will be far too busy being 'professional' to be of much assistance. I've asked Reino to send two barmaids to assist with the preparations for the wedding and the Midsummer Eve celebration."

I went directly to my bedroom, where Kaarina was pinning her long hair into a bun. She was wearing the white smock of her profession. I laid the baby in his cradle and began to rediaper him.

"I thought I would take over the clinic for Dr. Tami today," Kaarina said. "He's going to be occupied with those two tramps."

"Kaarina, how can you say such a thing! They're dead."

Her normal mask of indifference changed to one of hatred. "Dead or alive, they were tramps. And you intend to marry a man who was married to one of them and who slept with the other whenever he couldn't find a decent girl to violate."

CHAPTER SIXTEEN

"How dare you speak like that? Are you so virtuous that you have no compassion for human frailty?"

"Frailty? No, I don't suppose I have compassion for weakness. It's a misconception, just an excuse for not being able to control animalistic instincts."

"And you've never had an animal instinct?"

Her sharp eyes darkened. "Not that it is any of your business, but I have learned to channel that energy into productive work."

I knew I shouldn't say it, but she had provoked me with her self-righteous attitude. "I saw Reino."

She pulled the customary mask into place, but not before I heard a slight intake of breath. "So you saw Reino. What of it?"

"Oh, Kaarina, just for once can't we talk as women? I know you once cared for Reino. What happened?"

"You do not lack impertinence, do you? Reino is far beneath me. He is amusing, but I never seriously considered marrying him. He would have held me down, been an embarrassment in my career. I made that quite clear to him."

"Is that why he won't come to the island anymore?" I asked.

"I couldn't say, but that's possible. No one likes to be rejected and humiliated. For heaven's sake, Maija! You are going to prick that child if you aren't careful."

Johnny was squirming happily as I tried to tuck a

fresh diaper around his plump bottom. "Sorry," I muttered, though I wasn't certain that I had been careless.

"And the diaper is wrapped too tightly. That's bad for an infant's circulation. Oh, give him to me and I will show you how to do it."

She pushed me aside and bent to the task. Again I noticed a softening of her features as she finished dressing the infant.

"Kaarina," I said, "tomorrow I am to be married. We've never had the opportunity to really get to know one another, even though we were raised together. I know I've always seemed like a silly child to you, but now we are women."

She didn't raise her eyes to meet mine but sighed and said, "I'm your aunt and I am available to you for moral guidance. That is my duty. I doubt that I need instruct you on sex, but I could recommend a manual if there is a specific marital question."

"I'm not talking about moral guidance or sexual instruction. Kaarina, we must begin to be a family. Won't you be my sister?"

"I'm afraid that's physically impossible. Besides, I am a sister to too many as it is. Maija, you can't just demand love; it doesn't work that way." For a moment her voice softened and she seemed to be talking to herself or perhaps repeating words that had been spoken to her.

"Then, be my friend." I was not going to let this time of relative harmony pass without making an attempt at establishing a better relationship.

Her eyes met mine, and I saw a flicker of emotion cross them before the usual cover descended. "I am your aunt by law, and I shall always endeavor to remember that. You have much sorrow ahead of you in life since you seem bent on following a disastrous course. So I will do my moral duty and warn you not to marry Janne. Now I must leave for the village. A number of inoculations have been scheduled for today.

And please don't hold that child so much," she said, glancing at the cradle. "I've already warned Mother that he is being spoiled."

She buttoned her smock and smoothed a wrinkle from her skirt. Then she checked the contents of her medical bag, picked up her handbag and left without a further word.

Even so soon after his morning nap, Johnny seemed content in the cradle, examining his fingers and toes. As I dressed, I wondered if he was Tanya's. Although his eyes were the standard infant blue, there was a hint of another color in the iris. The fuzzy hair on his head was light blond, but his skin wasn't particularly fair. He grinned at me as I bent over him, and again I had a fleeting impression that I had seen that smile before.

I hoped that his identity would remain unknown— and was immediately shocked at my thought as I remembered that his mother might still be alive. I dismissed my selfish fantasy and had finished dressing when the stillness of the island was broken by the roar of motorboats. From the balcony, I saw Kaarina leave in one boat and Grandfather and Janne in another, as a third boat pulled up to the pier. Two young women wearing coveralls climbed up the ladder. I assumed that they were the temporary maids Reino had sent to help Mummo.

I was glad of their presence, for I had felt a pang of fear when I saw that Janne and Grandfather were leaving the island. Foolish, I told myself. Mummo was here, and from the balcony I could see Heikki and Eero, cutting birch branches. Evidently Heikki had changed his mind about going with Paavo or Paavo had declared one of his frequent holidays and closed the shop. I watched as Heikki tied the branches together. The birch boughs would decorate our doorways and boats on Midsummer Eve. Even trains and automobiles were similarly festooned for the ancient festival.

I braided my hair into a thick plait and thought it must be washed for my wedding the following evening. My wedding—it still seemed unreal. I longed to walk in the forest, but I had promised I wouldn't leave the house. What could I do to make the endless day pass— to keep all the threatening thoughts at bay?

I hoped that Mummo would let me help with the preparations. As a small girl, I had always begged her to let me help but had been refused with "No, *Neiti* Maija, Mummo will take care of everything. That is my job." How I had longed to work alongside my step-grandmother, rather than being relegated to my uncompanionable uncles and aunt. My musing was interrupted by a soft knock on the door.

"May I come in?"

"Of course, Mummo."

"Ah, he is awake," the old woman said, walking directly to the cradle. She started to pick the baby up but stopped, as if heeding Kaarina's warning about "spoiling" him. She shrugged and smiled. "Babies grow so fast, you know. You must enjoy him while he is little."

What will she think of me when she hears the truth about the infant? I wondered. There were lies on top of lies in the household, and I longed to tell her the truth, but I had promised Grandfather not to.

Mummo contented herself with rearranging the baby's coverlet and lavishing him with compliments, for which he thanked her with a series of twisted smiles.

"So," she said, reluctantly taking her attention from the infant, *"Herra* has instructed me to get the first *Rouva* Leinonen's wedding dress for you. I'm afraid it is badly wrinkled from having been stored so long, but I am sure we can make it acceptable. Do you wish to see it and try it on?"

My heart started to pound as the actuality of my wedding became manifest. Try on my wedding dress?

It *wasn't* just a dream—it was really going to happen!

I followed her out of the room, leaving the door open so that we could hear if the baby started to cry. She led the way down the corridor to the small bedroom she occupied. (She and Grandfather had never shared the same room.) The two girls I had seen from the balcony were coming up the stairway with mops and pails, and Mummo stopped to tell them to strip all the beds and to deposit the old newspapers, magazines, and other litter in a large carton in front of the linen closet.

They received their orders with half-bobbed curtsies but at the same time managed to appraise the bride-to-be. As they went to their assignments, I heard them giggle. Was their laughter caused by my unbridelike appearance—the jeans and sweatshirt—or by speculation on the reason why Janne was marrying me? The whole village was aware that Janne would gain control of the mill after our marriage. Did they laugh at a woman who couldn't get a husband without a financial enticement?

Mummo's small bedroom was tidy and radiated her soothing warmth. Snow-white pillow covers, trimmed with old-fashioned handmade lace, encased the two plump pillows on her bed. A knitted blue quilt was folded at its foot, and next to the quilt was my wedding gown, spread out on the bed. Mummo had evidently tried to smooth it by hand, but decades-old creases were etched into it, and the odor of mothballs rose from the homespun material. I wondered if my grandmother had spun and woven the cloth herself.

Part of the costume was a bright-blue ankle-length skirt, which was still unfaded after so many years. Red and yellow stripes ran the length of the skirt. A matching vest of the same vibrant blue was decorated with red and yellow piping. A simple long-sleeved blouse in an off-white, to be worn under the vest, had soft folds gathered around its high neckline.

"I was not able to find the apron," Mummo remarked with a frown, "but if you would allow me, I would like to lend you mine. It is very old and delicate. My mother made it for me when I married the children's father. I think it will complement your costume. I made the lace for the apron myself." She sighed, and I tried to picture her as a young girl preparing her modest trousseau.

Even though she hadn't been much more than forty when she married into the family, she had always seemed and looked much older. Only in occasional moments when her gentle smile, which seemed to be a set feature, slipped away did one catch a hint of what she may have looked like in her youth, before she had become a subservient functionary.

I doubted that her first husband had been loving toward her. At any rate, her children had become her whole life. I was touched that Mummo wanted me to wear a garment that had been part of her wedding costume. I put my arms around her and tried to hug her, but she pulled away and shushed me.

"There is so much to do today. Would you mind looking for the apron? I'm sure I put it in the linen closet—well wrapped in tissue, of course. I seem to remember that I placed it on one of the high shelves. I must go and supervise those girls or who knows what they will try to get away with. Why don't you try the skirt so I can see if it is the proper length? You can slip it on over your pants. The waistband is elastic and will fit without adjustment."

I stepped into the skirt. When its material was unfurled, there was a large stain in the front, and I cried out in disappointment as I looked down at the ugly blotch.

"Oh, my," Mummo gasped, "that will never do! It almost looks like grease. Now, now, don't fuss. I have something that will remove most of it, and the apron will cover that area, anyway."

She opened a cupboard and took a bottle that, when uncapped, filled the room with the potent odor of cleaning solvent. She gave me a towel to hold under the garment, then soaked a rag with the solvent and rubbed vigorously at the stain. I was surprised to see it dissolve —amazed that the spot would yield so easily after so many decades.

"There! That's most of it," Mummo said, stopping to inspect her work. "Hardly a trace left, and when you wear the apron, no one will notice the stain."

The fumes were making me light-headed, and the front of the skirt was damp with the fluid. I lifted the skirt and held it away from my body.

"Why don't you wear it a bit so the fumes will have a chance to evaporate? It might also be a good idea if you practice walking in it. It seems that you modern girls are not used to wearing long skirts. You all seem to want to wear trousers." Her tone was mildly disapproving.

"You're right," I agreed. I laughed and whirled about, enjoying the swirl of the full skirt. I hadn't worn a native costume since I was a child, and even then it had been reserved for special occasions. Now I was readying myself for a *very* special one. I held the blouse against me while Mummo checked to see that the sleeves were the proper length. Although I slipped the vest on over my sweatshirt, we could tell that it, too, would be a perfect fit.

"Try the headdress, dear," Mummo said, handing me the elaborate affair. The crown was formed by a stiff ribbon, from which a flap of soft material fell to cover my forehead. Other lengths of ribbon encircled the crown, completely covering my head and concealing my hair. The headdress was not unlike a nun's wimple, modestly framing the face and lovely in its simplicity. A delicate blue crocheted stitch edged the entire headpiece.

I looked at myself in Mummo's small mirror. Because

I couldn't see the full length of my body, I jumped up and down like a child to get a better idea of the skirt. The face I saw in the mirror looked very foreign, framed in the ancient headdress. "I *do* look like a bride, don't I?" I said in wonder.

"Of course, dear," Mummo murmured, but I could see her sober face reflected in the mirror as she stood behind me adjusting the folds of my skirt, and I wondered if she was preparing for a good cry. I had never seen her cry—she was always so controlled. Did she view me as a granddaughter and delight in my coming marriage, or were the preparations just another chore for her?

I turned from the mirror and looked at her with all the pent-up affection that I had somehow never been able to express. In a sense, she was my mother and my grandmother. I wanted to know her feeling, and I wanted her to know mine. She had always been kind to me, but there had never been the full warmth of real maternal feelings. I suspected that she was aware of my mood and uncomfortable in this knowledge, for she hurriedly gathered up the cleaning things.

"I must go and hurry those foolish girls along," she complained. "They must have finished their duties upstairs by this time—and they're probably just standing about gossiping—and with so much yet to be done in the kitchen! You won't forget to look for the apron right away, will you? I remember that I put it in the linen closet, but I might have put it in a box rather than in tissue paper. Well, that doesn't really matter. Now I must get those girls started in the kitchen."

"Of course," I said, "and then I'll come down to help."

"No, no, I won't hear of it. This is your day to rest, to prepare yourself for your wedding. After you've found the apron, bring it to the kitchen and I will see that it is pressed. You can be certain that I will do it myself. It's much too old and precious to trust to young girls—and that means you, too, *Neiti* Maija."

As she turned to leave the room, I stopped her. "Mummo, I know how busy you are, but could we chat just a bit longer? I need to talk to someone."

Her rosy face turned brighter, and she fingered a wisp of hair that had escaped from the tight bun on the back of her neck.

"Of course, dear. I quite understand, but I should have thought that with your child. . . . Well, I mean. . . ." She stopped in confusion, and her bright eyes darted about the room as if seeking some task that demanded immediate attention. "Perhaps Kaarina would be the one to instruct you?"

"I'm not referring to marital relations," I told her, circumventing the word *sex,* which I knew would send her fleeing from the room. "I'd like to ask you about my grandfather."

"Herra?"

"Tell me, do you think he has become, well, *imaginative* lately?" I couldn't be as blunt as I wished.

To my surprise, she sighed deeply and sat heavily on the bed. Her shoulders slumped, and she put her head in her hands. When she raised her face, tears glistened in her eyes.

"He's been saying those awful things again, hasn't he? Is that why you came home, Maija? I will be honest. *Herra*'s mind has been confused. Kaarina suspects he's had a—I can't remember the medical word she used, but that something has happened within his brain. He's made dreadful accusations. Maija, you can't believe the things he's imagined! And he's *forcing* you into this marriage, isn't he?"

I hesitated before replying. "No, that's not so. I love Janne, but it would have been so much nicer if. . . ." I left my sentence unfinished for fear of hurting Mummo further by repeating the allegations that had been made against her children. But I suspected that she was aware of them.

"Dear, I can understand your attraction to Janne. He is much like your grandfather. They are both vital, attractive men, but do you have any idea how difficult it is to be married to such a man? You have asked me to speak, and I will. Can you understand what it will be like to live with a man who only looks upon you as a *convenience?* Who never says a tender word? Ah, you do not see it now, but I have observed Janne, and he is much like *Herra*. Why do you think your grandfather trusts him?"

I sat beside her and attempted to take her hand in mine, but she pulled away as if she feared my touch.

"It is only natural for you to love your grandfather —it is your duty—but you *must* see that he is using you. I begged him to write you during all those years you were gone. I know it is painful for you to hear, but he appears to care as little about you as he does for my children. When I attempted to speak to him, he would silence me."

"If only you had written me," I said.

"I am not a well-educated woman, Maija. Words do not come easily, and it wasn't my place to intrude in your grandfather's life. I shouldn't be intruding in yours now, but I sense tragedy in store for you."

"Tragedy?"

She looked into space, and her mouth tightened. "I see death. I said that I am not an educated woman, but my people have always been close to the soil— peasants—and we have always had the gift of far sight. Do not marry this man. Go far away. Go back to America." Her normally soft voice hardened, and its forcefulness chilled me.

CHAPTER SEVENTEEN

I had never seen Mummo as I saw her then. It was as if another woman spoke through her. There was no trace of the subservient woman. Even her round, nondescript face seemed to take on distinctive planes and angles. When she turned to me, I was shocked at the strangeness of her gaze.

"Will you go before it is too late? I will help you, and no one will know where you have gone. Go, Maija, *now*—before you, too, lose yourself."

"Do you feel as if *you* are lost?" I asked.

"I was lost long ago. Now I live through my children. I have always thanked God for granting such a simple woman as myself such superior children. All my dreams are realized through them. They are so beautiful and talented, and someday their abilities will be recognized by everyone. Then I will be rewarded for all that I have done.

"It can be the same for you, too, Maija. You can live through your child. We women think when we are young and foolish that a man will give us purpose and satisfaction, but all they give is pain and humiliation. Spare yourself my fate."

"But I love Janne," I protested.

"Do you, child?" She shook her head and smiled sadly. "Then, I pity you all the more, because that type of love is an illusion that fades in the light of reality."

"I can't agree with you," I said, suddenly angry.

Again she looked at me with a strange, far-seeing gaze. "Don't you sense your fear? Take your child and flee. Give your love only to him and then you will know real happiness. Still, I won't pretend that children can't be trying at times." She shook her head, but her smile signified dismissal of the countless 'trying' deeds her children had perpetrated.

But they weren't children any longer, I reminded myself, and I felt a surge of pity and annoyance for a woman who loved only the fruit of her body. Somehow it was wrong—a twisted form of love. Although I didn't doubt the sincerity of her warning, every instinct told me she was wrong—wrong to live for and to love only *one* thing, whether children, a husband, or a possession.

She foresaw death, and I didn't doubt that she was warning me against premature death. But, I thought, isn't death a part of life? It lurks about as we perform our daily chores; it hides within our very organs and in the passions of those with whom we come in contact. My compassion cooled as I realized that she had chosen a living death by denying herself any form of love other than maternal.

I asked a very personal question: "Didn't Grandfather ever . . . ever offer *tender* love to you?"

Her cheeks flamed, and abnormal fire lit her eyes. "He spoke of that foolishness when we were first married, but I knew he was only trying to make a fool of a middle-aged serving woman. I am not clever, but I know when I am being laughed at. I told him it was not necessary. As his wife, I intended to fulfill my marital duties without being wooed like a barmaid."

So he had tried to love again and had been repulsed. No wonder he despised the children, on whom she lavished affection. I always assumed that his arrogance had fostered such a loveless match, but now I saw another side of truth. His arrogance and independence were armor against further pain. His love was channeled into work among those who labored with him. He treated his employees well and enhanced the entire economy of our region. These were hardly the acts of a cold, self-centered autocrat. Rather, they were the acts of a man who had to find release for his natural affection.

A web of lies, suspicion, and thwarted emotions had entangled me since my arrival. It was time to tear it apart. My marriage to Janne would not be based on vague suspicions of a lurking murderer, a would-be killer who may have stalked only the damaged cells of Grandfather's mind.

I had succumbed to mind-numbing, heart-stopping fear, half believing that Janne was responsible for the brutal death of two women. I had for a time accepted the possibility that my childhood friend—and love— would deliberately arouse my passion and murder for self-seeking motives. Even Grandfather preferred to substitute "respect" for "love," because his own love had been foiled, first by fate and then by rejection. That would not be *my* fate, I decided.

I wrapped my arms around the morose woman who sat stiffly beside me. She didn't respond but said in a sad, soft voice, "I sense that you have made your choice, Maija. It was my duty to warn you, but you must do as you are impelled. It is not possible to turn our footsteps onto a pathway that fate has not chosen."

"Don't say that, Mummo. You make it sound as if we have no free will. It's not too late for all of us to learn to love and accept one another."

"Sometimes, my dear, it *is* too late." When she turned to me, the far-off gaze was gone. "Now I *must* go," she said. "Do you hear those silly girls giggling in the hallway? And Eero—he must be amusing them. Such a witty boy."

Mummo, smiling again, had regained her composure. "Don't forget the apron," she said. "You must get it right away so it can be aired. I will take Ya-ne with me so he can have his lunch. You do not mind? I enjoy caring for him."

"You are very kind."

She evaded my look, as if regretting her outspokenness. "There is another thing—unless you feel it too presumptuous—a few pieces of my jewelry. Would you care to look at them and see if there might be something you can wear on your wedding dress?" She took a small box from the dresser. "Look them over and choose any piece you might fancy. They are of little worth, but some of them were my mother's." She handed me the box, then went into the hallway to disperse the maids and talk to Eero.

Among the few pieces of jewelry—which included a silver belt buckle and a child's bracelet—was a lovely string of pearls. I could tell by their yellow sheen that they were real. I had never seen her wear them—or any adornment, for that matter—and guessed they were a gift from Grandfather. Pearls are meant to be worn, and these had been stored—a tacit rejection? I wondered.

Then a simple pin caught my eye, and I knew at once that I wanted to wear it on my wedding dress. It was silver and slightly tarnished, but the tarnish only seemed to enhance it. It was a circular brooch, topped with a sort of medieval cross. A sword bisected the circle, and two small pyramids were at the bottom. I wanted the pin to be a link between the past and my future. I put it in my pocket, replaced the jewelry case and stepped into the hallway.

Eero was bending over the large box of debris that had been collected from the various rooms, rummaging through it and tossing scraps of paper on the floor. He looked up when he heard me and appraised my partial trousseau. "How I wish I could sing a little *Lohengrin*. How do the English words go? Ah, yes: 'Here comes the bride, all dressed in blue. . . .' No, that's not quite right. At any rate, you look like a souvenir doll on one of Paavo's shelves—very fetchingly Finnish. You'll no doubt be touched to know that Heikki is weaving a crown of birch leaves for you. I would like to say 'for the virgin,' but I'm afraid the little fellow you brought home denies you that status. Ah, well, I am sure the great god of commerce will overlook that, even though our old gods may 'tsk, tsk' a bit."

My euphoric mood was fading, but I clung to what remained and overlooked the intent of his remarks. "I am touched that Heikki would make a wreath for me. Have you been helping prepare the bonfires?"

"Paavo has taken over that chore. He declared a holiday before the holiday, closed the store and gathered a group of workers to come to the island to assist him. All female assistants, of course. He's romping about the island gathering wood—and whatever. With the start he's getting on our dual celebration, we won't have to light the bonfires with matches. We'll just ask him to breathe on them."

Determined to retain my good mood, I asked, "How is your writing going today?"

"How do you think it's going with all these women running about? Someone emptied my wastebasket, and I've had to rummage through this filthy box to rescue several valuable pages of my manuscript." He waved a few sheets of paper in the air.

He had strewn papers and litter all over the floor and obviously was not going to pick up after himself. Because the box was blocking the door of the linen closet, I asked, "Could you help me move this or possibly take it downstairs?"

"We have servants for that sort of thing," he answered loftily and went to his bedroom, leaving me to shove the box aside so that I could open the door of the closet.

It was dark inside the large closet, and I fumbled

for the light chain, but the light didn't work. Hearing footsteps in the hallway, I called out, "Would you bring me a new bulb? This one seems to have burned out, and I can't see a thing."

There was no answer, but someone seemed to have bumped against the box and pushed it against the door, because it suddenly slammed shut. At the same time, the door handle was knocked loose and crashed to the floor of the closet. Though the door was thick and solid, I heard footsteps on the stairway.

"Help!" I cried. "Let me out of here!"

I waited a moment, but no one came to my rescue. I took a deep breath and tried to master the feeling that was creeping over me. Then I banged on the door and yelled with full force, but no one came.

My childhood horror had come true, I thought. I was trapped in the linen closet, where the trolls would get me. For a moment that childish myth made the situation seem ludicrous, but mixed with the scent of violets and rose petals were the strong fumes of the cleaning solvent that had soaked into my skirt. They seemed especially noxious in the unventilated closet.

As I tried to replace the doorknob, my childhood imagination returned, and I felt I was being watched. I looked about in the dark room, then screamed in terror at two close-set eyes that glared at me from above.

CHAPTER EIGHTEEN

As I screamed, a monstrous mouth closed on my arm and shoulder. It was Pai-Pai, the cat, who had been napping on one of the high shelves, among the fragrant linens, and had been frightened by my scream. I stroked his ruffled fur and gingerly dislodged his claws from my sweatshirt.

As my eyes adjusted to the darkness, I got down on my hands and knees to search for the doorknob. Besides the cleaning solvent, I became aware of another smell, which I couldn't immediately identify. Pai-Pai yowled and clawed at the door, then jumped onto a shelf and hunched down, his eyes wide open and filled with fear. *It was fire!* The box in the hallway, just outside the closet door, must have caught fire. The closet seemed to fill with smoke.

I banged on the door and screamed, but there was no response—only the insidious crackle of flames on the other side of the door. The cat backed into the deepest corner of the shelf, cringing and twitching his tail. Choking from the smoke and fumes that rose from the bottom of the door, I stuffed the crack with sheets, hoping to retard asphyxiation.

Surely someone else would smell the smoke as it filtered downstairs! But that hope died when I remembered that in the kitchen they were baking and cooking and roasting. Who would suspect that the burning and smoke came from *up*stairs? Moreover,

bonfires were being lit all over the island, and the
windows would be open, so that one's first thought
would be to connect the smoke with the traditional
pyres of Midsummer Eve.

The sheets had begun to smolder and burn. As I
stamped them out, I placed my hand on the door and
felt that the wood was growing hot. Then I realized
that my solvent-soaked skirt could ignite at any instant
and I would be a human torch. I pulled the skirt off
and threw it on an upper shelf.

I began to cough uncontrollably and backed away
from the door. The poor cat was gagging and howling,
and his eyes were glazed with fear. Then he butted
his head against the wall, rose on his hind legs and
scratched at the ceiling, as if to tear a hole in it. The
flames in the hallway cast fearful shapes of light
beneath the door, and as I watched the cat's frantic
clawing, I saw a square marking on the ceiling. I
climbed up the shelves and, crouching on the top shelf,
felt along the ceiling.

The smoke was almost blinding, but my fingers
traced a break in the plaster. I wedged my finger into
the break and felt a trapdoor crack open. It refused to
open completely, but the opening was wide enough for
the cat to leap through. The air that poured from the
opening gave me the strength to push on the door until
its hinges yielded.

I wound the skirt around my neck before attempting to twist upward through the trapdoor. As the paint
on the interior of the closet door popped with blisters,
I pulled myself through the hole and into the attic,
where I momentarily collapsed.

Soon I looked for an exit—I knew there was a door,
for I had often crept up to admire the attic's ancient
treasure-trove. But the door was locked from the other
side, and through its cracks I could see that flames
already filled the stairway to the attic and were

spreading down the hallway. I thanked God that Mummo had taken the child downstairs.

And Eero? I remembered hearing footsteps on the stairs. Had he left his room and not noticed the smoldering debris? I was certain I had heard someone outside the closet. Had he deliberately started the fire or known that I was trapped in the closet? Now I was trapped in the attic.

Where was everyone? Why hadn't someone heard me? But the old house was solid, each floor soundproofed against the other, and I was on the third floor, high above the ground. If everyone was in the front of the house, or outside, how long would it be before the fire was noticed? I was supposed to be relaxing— dreaming the dreams of a bride-to-be. Mummo would have told everyone to leave me alone.

The small attic window was so covered with dust and grime that I hadn't noticed it at first. And even before I made the effort, I knew it wouldn't open. The cat had found a tiny break in a vent and escaped to the roof, but the window was my only hope. Wielding an old-fashioned iron and closing my eyes, I bashed the iron against the window and made a small hole in the middle of the pane. Jagged pieces of glass projected from every edge of the molding. I knocked out the fragments above the sill, looked through the opening and saw that it was a sheer three-story drop to the ground. There was no balcony or ledge or gutter or downspout, and it would be suicide to jump from that height.

Far below, the blue water of the lake seemed to taunt me with its serenity. Then I heard a motorboat and prayed that it was heading for our island and that the operator would see me waving from the window. The boat slowed, plowing the water into a creamy froth, and pulled up to our dock. When the motor was turned off, I yelled with all my power, but there was no indication that the man, whose golden hair gleamed in the sunlight, heard me. He tied the boat to the dock and stood staring at the pathway that led to the house. It was Reino.

"Reino, up here! It's Maija! There's a fire!"

He continued to stare toward the house but neither saw nor heard me. In frustration, I flung the heavy iron out the window, but it scudded noiselessly through the boughs of a tree. I searched frantically for something that would attract his attention.

Seizing an antique hunting horn, I leaned out the window and blew into it with all my might. But it produced no sound at all. Perhaps the ghost of an ancient hunter came to my aid, for on the next attempt the horn gave an ear-splitting blast.

Reino looked about, as if in confusion, and I prayed that I could reproduce the sound. Then he looked up at the window, and I waved and shouted.

"Up here! The upper floor is on fire! Get someone quickly! Do you hear me? *Fire!*"

It seemed to take an eternity for him to move, but at last he was under the window, shouting up at me.

"Can you jump? No, of course you can't. Do you know where there's a ladder?"

"In one of the sheds—I don't know which one. Go in the house and warn everyone. For God's sake, hurry!" I prayed that for once Reino would act decisively.

Smoke billowed from the attic door, and flames erupted through the closet's hatch. I stuck my head through the window and drank deep lungfuls of air. Instinct told me to save my strength, and I sagged against the wall, keeping my face to the window. There was no indication that help was coming.

I took my wedding skirt from around my neck and dropped it from the window. It was caught in an upward draft, billowed into a parachute and drifted into a tree. At least it would be preserved for a more fortunate bride. And less than an hour earlier, I thought, I had ridiculed the notion of fate.

Maija would not walk in the pathway of destiny, and she scorned the demons of pessimism, hatred, and death that lurked within the house. Her love, her faith, would conquer all. All, that is, but the trolls, who had captured her after all.

Even the precious air from the window was ineffectual against the evil army of trolls. I heard the shouts of their generals as they marshaled their troops and issued orders for my capture.

"Don't pull the nets too taut!"

I sat on the floor awaiting my capture, and the trolls became imperious. "Jump!" they commanded. "Maija, jump!"

I pulled myself up and rested my head on the window sill, ignoring the shards of glass. When I heard the trolls' sirens, I knew that death was near. No human can hear such sounds and live.

"Jump! Jump!" they demanded.

Flames had burst through the trapdoor and climbed to the roof of the attic. But beyond the attic, just outside the window, was a shaft of pure air that one could breathe—without pain or limit—while plunging to the earth below.

I forced myself into the window frame, dropped my head and hurtled into space.

CHAPTER NINETEEN

Lungs that would not fill automatically—enveloping blackness. I was a weak animal who fought for breath, and terror was the condition of my being. Then my head was pushed backward and air filled my lungs as two hands pressed against my chest in rhythmic movement. The oxygen restored my awareness, so that I realized the air was coming from an incessant pressure against my mouth. I gagged and tried to escape.

I was caught in a strong net, but I didn't care. All that mattered was that I could breathe. I wiped my hand feebly across my mouth and looked at the restraining meshes, which, I realized, had saved my life. I was also captured by a pair of strong arms and taunted by a voice that whispered in my ear.

"You are the worst-looking mess I've ever seen, and ungrateful at that. I kissed you to give you life and you fought against me. Now I kiss you for love."

The lips I had resented moments before pressed mine, but now they were tender, and the arms that held me trembled. "My God, Maija—I almost lost everything."

"Everything?"

"You, you idiot. What else did you think I meant?" Janne answered, his voice harsh. "I'm going to lift you out of these nets and see if you can stand."

I saw that I was entangled in layers of fishing nets. I also saw Reino, Grandfather, and Heikki.

"Put her down carefully, Janne. She could have a sprain or a broken bone," Grandfather said. "Heikki, get the bottle of vodka from the kitchen. Reino, see that those girls stay out of the firemen's way."

I was wobbly, but I could stand unsupported. No special point of pain indicated serious injury, but I felt as if I were bruised all over. I resisted the urge to retch and slowly inhaled the fresh air. As my head cleared, I heard the sirens and bells of the fire boats —the sounds of the "troll army." At the attic window, a smudged but cheerful face looked down.

"The flames are out, *Herra* Leinonen, but we had to cut through the roof. The linen closet is gutted, but the fire didn't travel down the back stairs or burn through any of the bedroom doors."

"Hah!" Grandfather yelled back. "You think I used flimsy lumber in my house? Is it safe to go into the kitchen?"

"There's not much smoke there, but it would be best if you stayed outside a while longer."

"When you're through destroying my house, bring all the men down and have a drink."

"*Kiitos!* That will be most welcome. Is *Neiti* Maija all right?"

I raised my arm in a feeble wave and Grandfather answered for me. "It's not easy to kill a Leinonen."

The young fireman grinned, slipped a mask over his face and withdrew from the window.

"Oh, my God, the baby! And the others?" I was clear-minded now. "Mummo, Eero——" My fear sent me into a coughing spasm.

"Calm yourself," Grandfather commanded. "Lilya went with Eero to the village for some last-minute shopping, and she took the child with her. The maids were cleaning the sauna; that's why no one heard you or detected the smoke. One of the girls finally went back to the kitchen to check on some food they were helping Lilya prepare, and she noticed smoke in the

back hall and had enough sense to raise our emergency
flag. A fire boat was dispatched almost simultaneously.
Hah! It's a miracle there wasn't a collision among all
the boats, what with men coming from the mill, the
village volunteers, and neighbors from the other
islands."

Reino returned. "Elsa is hysterical, but Lea is fine.
She even thought to get bread and meat from the
kitchen and is preparing sandwiches in the sauna." He
looked so exhausted that I felt hearty in comparison.

"Sit down, boy." Grandfather put his hands on
Reino's broad shoulders. "You reacted quickly and
intelligently. The true sign of a man is how he responds
in an emergency. You proved your manhood today."

Grandfather looked at me and explained. "When
he couldn't get through the fire in the upper hall and
the girls told him everyone else was out of the house,
he tried to get a ladder. When he couldn't find one, he
gathered up fishing nets and a grapple and was going
to use them to climb to the attic window to rescue
you. Fortunately, we arrived in time to stop him—
and probably saved *his* life as well. But by the great
God on high, what *sisu!*" He gave Reino a whack that
almost knocked him over.

Heikki arrived with Paavo, who brought the bottle
of vodka, and his weaving gait suggested he'd sampled
it. His face was black with smoke, and his eyebrows
and lashes were singed. Grandfather grabbed the
bottle. "What happened? Did you fall into one of the
bonfires you've been setting?"

Paavo drew himself up with as much dignity as his
condition would allow. "I have been helping to save
your cursed castle. Why, I don't know."

Grandfather gave the bottle to me, after taking a
small swig, and berated Paavo. "From the smell of
your breath, you probably ignited the fire in the first
place. Take your indignant face out of mine and sit
down."

Paavo looked at the bottle, which was being passed around, but no one offered it to him. He finally seated himself on the ground and sighed.

"Now," Grandfather said, after taking another drink, "what happened, Maija?"

I told them about the large box that had been placed near the closet door, the papers that Eero had thrown about in his attempt to find the pages of his manuscript —and the rags and cleaning solvent. I told of being trapped inside the closet when the doorknob fell off, and escaping through the trapdoor. I told them everything but how the fire started. I didn't *know* how. "Was it spontaneous combustion?" I asked.

"Spontaneous combustion can occur only through heat or friction," Janne said. "Is there any source of heat up there?"

"There are no heat ducts," Grandfather answered. "We light the stoves in the bedrooms only in winter."

"Who smokes in the house?"

"I'm the only one," Grandfather said. "I've never seen the others smoke. It's their only commendable trait." Paavo was too pacified by alcohol and Heikki too disconsolate to rise to the insult.

"How did you open the door if the box was wedged against it?"

"I pushed it about a foot into the hall in order to get in the closet."

"And you didn't shut the door after yourself?"

"No. I was trying to find the light cord, and the bulb was burned out—and all of a sudden the door slammed shut. It sounded as if someone had fallen against the box and shoved it against the door. The doorknob. . . . Well, I've told you about that."

"You screamed and pounded?"

"With all my might, and I was sure I heard someone in the hallway and then on the stairs. The door must have muffled my yells—or maybe I just imagined I heard someone."

"Perhaps whoever it was didn't want to hear," Janne suggested, his voice flat and expressionless.

"You're saying that someone deliberatey shoved the box against the door and ignited it after I was trapped in the closet?" The suspicion that I had been trying to suppress sent chills through my body.

Sunshine glanced through the trees and the filtered green light emphasized the color of Janne's eyes. "Yes," he said.

No one spoke. We were all locked in a cubicle of speculation. Nature's bouquet—of warm earth, the scent of flowers, and the breeze from the lake—could not mask the acrid smell of smoke or the fear that surrounded us.

Reino looked up, suddenly roused from exhaustion. "Elsa's a smoker. I don't allow her to smoke while she's tending bar, but she's always running out on the dock for a puff or two. I've overlooked this because she's such a hard worker. Would *Rouva* Leinonen allow her to smoke in the house?"

"Absolutely not. She can barely control her tongue when I light my pipe. She would never allow a serving girl to smoke in the house," Grandfather noted with righteousness.

"Then, I think I know what happened. Elsa sneaked upstairs for a smoke and either was startled by a sound in the closet or was called by *Rouva* Leinonen. In her haste, she didn't extinguish her cigarette, and she probably tripped over the box. And it is very probable she didn't hear you calling from behind that thick door. *Herra* Leinonen offered a very generous wage to those girls, and I know Elsa needs the money."

"It *could* have happened that way," Grandfather conceded. "Maija says that Eero dumped papers on the floor. A spark from a cigarette could have caused the cleaning rags to ignite and spread to the papers."

"Elsa was hysterical," Reino added. "One of the men took her back to the village. She kept asking if

Neiti Maija had been rescued. Shall I get someone to bring her back?"

"She could have been responsible for the death of many people," Grandfather said. "If it was her fault, she's being punished by her conscience far more severely than I could punish her. If it did happen that way, it was an accident, not a deliberate attempt at murder or destruction. I knew her parents well—good, hardworking people. Maija, Janne, do you agree?"

We nodded. I was relieved that the happening had an explanation other than the horrible one that, a minute before, had seemed the only possibility.

CHAPTER TWENTY

Through indifference, innocence, or alcohol, Paavo had fallen asleep, but his slumber was broken when his stepfather applied a sharp kick to his backside.

"Wake up, you sot. Get something to eat and take a sauna to sober up. There's work to be done, and, by God, you're going to help. Lilya will be up in the air when she returns, and Lea's been through enough today. Reino, send her back and tell her she'll receive a full day's wage. I'd also appreciate it if you'd take Maija with you and let her spend the night at your house. I want her away from here until it's time for the wedding."

Reino tried to look confident, but his voice faltered as he said, "Of course, *Herra* Leinonen. I'm sure Mother will——"

"You're not sure at all," Grandfather said, "but you've proved your *sisu* today, and it's *your* house, not your mother's."

A spark lit Reino's face but was soon extinguished and replaced by his usual look of confusion.

"It *is* my house, and we will be honored to have *Neiti* Maija as our guest. It's just that I must talk to you—the reason I came today." He glanced around nervously and gave Grandfather such a look of pleading that the older man was embarrassed.

"We'll talk this evening, after I've had a chance to organize things."

192

Relief, followed by a look of fear, paraded across the handsome man's features. "Thank you. I'll meet you at my house, if that's convenient. Will eight o'clock be all right?"

Grandfather nodded. "Janne, take Maija to the house and see if they'll allow you upstairs so she can get whatever she needs. Ah, that sounds like our motorboat. Lilya and Eero will be returning. Everyone get a move on. Heikki, come with me. You're good at calming hysterical females, and Lilya will surely require a softer touch than mine when she sees her house."

Heikki nodded but avoided looking at his stepfather. The words were explicit, but Heikki seemed sensitive to some hidden implication.

Pai-Pai, on a limb of a nearby tree, where my wedding skirt was caught on a lower branch, complained of his plight. Janne climbed the tree and rescued the forlorn garment but offered no assistance to the cat, who scrambled down the trunk and padded up beside me. He made a series of meows and tentative movements in the direction of the house; evidently I had proved myself worthy of providing him with food.

Janne and I followed the cat to the back entrance and made our way around the hoses that led up the rear stairway to the fire-blackened second story. The linen closet was a fire-gutted cavern, and a shaft of sunshine slanted across the hallway from the hole in the roof. The cat refused to accompany us up the stairs and wailed in displeasure when he saw we weren't going to the kitchen to feed him.

From Mummo's bedroom I took the headpiece, blouse, and vest that I had left there, then went to my bedroom to pack a few necessities. There was an odor of smoke in the bedrooms, but neither room had been blackened, attesting to their stout walls and doors.

When I caught sight of myself in the mirror, I almost fainted. My face was black with soot, and my eyes were red. Across my neck and arms was dried blood from cuts I had sustained while making my escape.

Janne laughed at my expression. "Never mind—who said all brides *have* to be beautiful?"

"That's supposed to be funny, I suppose?" Tears poured from my eyes as I traced the scratches on my neck. Then I turned my head from side to side, expecting to find ugly gashes on my face. There were none, and I was somewhat relieved to find that I wasn't totally disfigured.

"I'm sorry," Janne said, "that wasn't a good joke. I only meant that it is not for your beauty that I am marrying you. That is only a bonus I will receive."

"The main prize is the mill, you mean," I said.

Janne's skin was also black with soot, but beneath it I saw the angry rush of blood to his face. He grabbed me by an arm. "Will you never believe? *Yes*, I want the mill, but I want you, too. Should I go to Leinonen and tell him I refuse the mill? Will that make you happy?"

I shook my head as my misery and doubts increased the torrent of tears down my face.

"We both know he is obsessed by the idea that someone in this family is trying to kill him. The obsession *alone* will push him to a premature death; have you thought of that? He wants peace of mind and the opportunity to dispose of the business he worked all his life to make prosperous—that makes the lives of so many others prosperous, as well. Do you really believe that any of his stepchildren are capable of running the business? Or *care* to? Can you seriously believe they will be able to form a cooperative family corporation? They'll sell it as soon as possible, then hate one another even more when *that* money runs out.

"Maija, it's important to him that he leave the mill to a blood relation. It gives him a feeling of immortality. I don't know if that's a sin of vanity, but I understand it. There is no one left in his family other than you. A man wants to have his own family, provide for them and feel that a little of himself lives on through those he's helped create and mold. It was as if a part of myself had been killed when Ritva told me she aborted my child."

"I understand all that, but——"

"I know. You want perfect reassurance that I love you and am not marrying you for personal gain. But how can I prove it to you? Tomorrow we'll exchange an oath under the eyes of God, and then we'll sign a paper. Will that prove anything? Love and trust do not come from words or documents, they come from time and sharing. I know, or can guess, that you've even thought me capable of planning your death as soon as I take control of the mill."

I closed my eyes and turned my head, unable to look at him.

He held my chin and forced me to face him. "And yet you appear to be ready to marry me. Why? Just because your grandfather tells you to? You said this is your own decision, and I can't believe that you would be so subservient to your grandfather. You have *sisu,* and you have something else—as much love for me as I have for you. Is it because I haven't seduced you that you feel I am indifferent? Well, a signed document won't prove my love and desire for you, but perhaps a physical demonstration will."

There was no gentleness in the way he pushed me on the bed and no consideration for my bruises as he kissed me with so much pressure that I almost suffocated. He separated my legs and lay between them, his hands roaming over my body. His kisses traveled across my face and stopped in the hollow of my neck, while he unbuttoned my blouse. Then he lowered his mouth to kiss my breasts. I wrapped my legs about him instinctively and thrust my body upward against his.

My virginity was preserved only through the inter- vention of a red-faced fireman who stood aghast in the doorway and, in confusion, averted his gaze and looked down at his boots.

"The chief asked me to see if you were finished. . . . Oh, God!" He drew a deep breath and continued doggedly. "We have to inspect the rooms for possible smoldering. . . ." The young man grimaced in agony, as if attempting to withdraw his explanation.

Jahne grinned and said, "Thank you. We'll be out in a second. I commend you on your professional techniques."

"Thank *you, Herra* Peltonen," the young man said, as flustered as ever, and left the room as if it were on fire.

CHAPTER TWENTY-ONE

As I adjusted my clothing, I wished it were as easy to adjust my emotions. Janne said nothing as he watched me, but he administered a smart swat to my bottom as I scrambled off the bed.

"Thank you," I said in mock formality. "That was the only part of my body that wasn't black and blue already."

Janne picked up the wedding headdress and put it on me so that it covered the scratches on my neck. "You will be so modestly covered tomorrow by this costume that no one will see your injuries, and after the ceremony I will see that every bruise and scratch is kissed away." His tone was serious and tender, but his green eyes glinted as he added, "Unless, of course, you prove to be uncooperative. In which case you can look forward to even more black-and-blue marks. And that is a joke, so don't start up again. Now, do you have all you need?"

I looked at the cradle and the stacks of baby clothes but knew I couldn't take the child. Mummo would be happy to care for him. I also knew, or sensed, that it was only a matter of time before the child's identity would be revealed. Urto had intimated to Grandfather that the authorities would soon be coming for Johnny.

"Reino is waiting at the pier for us," Janne said, "and the firemen have to check the rooms. The child will be a diversion for Mummo—and heaven knows she'll need one to distract her from this mess." He had read my thoughts. "We'll leave by the back way, without seeing anyone. It's obvious that *Herra* Leinonen wasn't convinced that the fire was Elsa's doing. He will make his suspicions evident, and there will be further tension in this house tonight. Your presence won't help anything."

I nodded in agreement; then an ugly thought hit me. "But what of Grandfather? If someone is trying to prevent him from signing over his fortune, won't they try again tonight?"

"Trusted men from the mill will guard the house and prevent any attempt on his life."

We gathered up my bags and went down the stairs without encountering anyone, but we heard Mummo's moans and Heikki's reassurances coming from the kitchen. Grandfather was outside, seeing that the fire fighters were served with food and drink.

"Until tonight, Maija," he called to me. "Reino will see to your safety and comfort. Janne, go to the mill as soon as possible to see that all is well there; then get home and rest for tomorrow. You both look like survivors of the Winter War—but you're supposed to look like that *after* your wedding, not before!"

We walked to the wharf. Janne made no attempt to kiss me. Instead, he took my hand formally and said, "I will see you tomorrow evening at our wedding."

Lea and I climbed into Reino's boat and sat in silence, enjoying the spray on our faces as the motorboat plowed toward the village dock. Helge was there waiting for us, jumping up and down in his eagerness to hear the details of the fire.

"Elsa said the whole house was gone, but it didn't appear so through my glasses. She was so hysterical that Dr. Tami had to be called, and he gave her something that knocked her out," he told us, savoring an event that had livened the routine of his life.

His bright eyes looked from one face to another, as

if begging for details. But we were too tired to tell him more than that the fire had been brought under control with minimum damage and that no one had been injured. His wizened face registered annoyance and disappointment with such sketchy information.

Apparently the excitement over the deaths of Ritva and Tanya had faded. The police had made no arrests, and the consensus among the villagers—Helge acted as their spokesman—was that Ritva had had a falling out with Tanya, stabbed her and then either drowned accidentally or committed suicide. Finns have a philosophic acceptance of violence and passion.

Reino, always sensitive to the feelings of others, sensed my exasperation with Helge and suggested that he go into the tavern and have a drink, or several drinks, and spread the news that all were safe on the island and that the midsummer festival and the wedding were still scheduled for the following evening. The old man trotted off, delighted with the prospect of free drinks and "inside" information from *Herra* Leinonen's.

Lea refused Reino's offer of a drink and said she would see if Elsa was all right. I, too, declined and said I'd wait on the dock while he checked into the tavern to see that all was running smoothly. I looked across the water, in the direction of Grandfather's island. Although I could not see the house, I saw a dark cloud. Smoke, I wondered, or evil spirits?

Janne would be at the mill, I thought. Soon he would return home, take a sauna, and—— What does a groom do on the eve of his wedding? Wasn't it traditional to get drunk? Would he do that? I pictured him taking his bottle from the kitchen shelf, pouring a glassful and seating himself at his wooden table. What would he be thinking? Would he remember the pleasure of our bodies pressed together? Would he think of the coming evening, when our desire would not be thwarted? Or would he think of—— Good

Lord! I forced myself to stop my speculations and wished I could lie down and be released from all thought.

Reino returned and guided me to his cottage, which was tidy and cheerful, but I couldn't help thinking that it was far too small for a husband, wife, and the husband's domineering mother. What hell it must be for a girl, cooped up with a widowed mother-in-law who commanded and controlled her husband.

CHAPTER TWENTY-TWO

"Reino? What are you doing home so early?" The old woman's voice was querulous as she called from the kitchen. "Wipe your feet—we scrubbed the entrance-way today. I suppose you've been wasting your time at the old man's house this afternoon. I checked at the tavern, and they said you'd gone there. You might have been injured, and then what would have become of us? Duty begins at home, boy. *Herra* Leinonen doesn't need your help. He could build a hundred homes if he wanted to.

"Liisa, get a move on with those potatoes. My son will be hungry, and a good wife provides food for her husband despite his thoughtlessness in not observing regular hours. No, no, don't *peel* those potatoes. . . ."

"But, Mother Kauppi, Reino likes them with the skin removed."

Both women were bent over their culinary tasks. It was only after Reino had coughed several times and stamped his feet on the polished floor that they looked up and saw me.

"*Neiti* Leinonen, what a . . . surprise." Mrs. Kauppi was in a flux of conflicting emotions: outrage that Reino had brought an unannounced visitor, curiosity about my battered condition, and embarrassment that *Herra* Leinonen's granddaughter had heard her remarks. She wiped her hands on a spotless white apron and, seeming to suppress an automatic reaction to curtsy, extended a cold hand as her eyes took inventory of my scratches and bruises. "Well, shall we have some coffee?" she said in an attempt at heartiness.

"Liisa, come here," Reino said to the young woman who stood in a corner of the kitchen. "I don't believe you've met my wife. Maija, this is Liisa." The nervous girl made a curtsy, as I grabbed her hand and squeezed it.

"I'm so glad to meet you, Liisa. I knew Reino would have a lovely wife." The white lie brought a pink flush to her pale complexion and a small spark to her clouded blue eyes.

"She's frail, but she's a willing girl," Mrs. Kauppi remarked, relegating Liisa to the status of maid and quenching her momentary pleasure. Liisa murmured a reply and returned to the potatoes.

"*Herra* Leinonen has given us the honor of lodging Maija for the evening, because of the fire at his house. He feels it would be best if Maija spends the evening with us, so that she will be refreshed for her wedding. I thought we could give her your bedroom, Mother, and you and Liisa can share our bedroom. I will sleep on the couch."

"There will be no disruption of your household on my account," I told him. "You and Liisa must keep your room, as always, and Mrs. Kauppi must have the comfort of her own bed. I am the intruder, and a grateful one. *I* will take the couch." There was a chorus of protests, but I overruled their objections.

"Now, dear friend," I said to Reino, "I will forgive you for all the times you pulled my braids when I was a helpless child if you will light your sauna so I can bathe in the proper Finnish style." Reino hurried to do as I asked, and his mother followed him, issuing directives.

I sank into a chair and sighed at the pure physical comfort. Liisa peered at me and, in a voice almost too soft to be heard, asked if I would enjoy a cup of coffee. I wondered how often she was allowed to play hostess in what should have been her own house.

"What I would really like," I said, "is a good stiff drink. Do you have anything?" Despite Reino's position as tavern manager, Mrs. Kauppi was a leading member of the temperance league—a hypocrisy that didn't seem to bother her.

Another pink flush gave a healthy look to Liisa's peaked face. "I keep a bottle for Reino in our bedroom wardrobe."

"While you're getting it, I'll look for a glass in the kitchen—no, *two* glasses. Or do you drink?" I asked.

"Not often," the girl admitted but then drew herself up and said in a strong voice, "You will not stir from that chair. You have been through an awful ordeal, and tomorrow you are to be married. I will serve you—and join you." She took a deep breath and added, "And Reino will join you, too! If *she* doesn't like it. . . ." She looked perplexed, as if at a loss for what to add. She abandoned the attempt and scuttled off, much like a mouse, to the bedroom.

I relaxed in the chair and would have fallen asleep if Liisa had not immediately returned. She put the bottle of vodka in the middle of the table with a brave thump, then took three glasses from the cupboard. Her face was no longer pale. Her cheeks seemed to flame with a bold, exciting look, and I wondered if she had sampled the bottle to give herself courage. She looked at the bottle and the three glasses, then turned to me. I read her thought and nodded, and she took down a fourth glass and placed it a distance from the others.

I don't know if it was false courage or my acceptance that prompted Liisa to sit at the head of the table and pour two very full tumblers of vodka. She handed a glass to me and raised her own in salute. "What shall we toast?" she asked.

"To *me!*" I said, suddenly lighthearted and heady.

"And to *you*. And to *Reino*. And to *love*." I paused.
"And to *freedom*—freedom from all oppression, even
from those we love. Freedom from *Rouva* Kauppi,
though I know you honor her."

As I leaned forward to clink my glass against hers,
I heard myself speaking words that had long dwelled
in my heart. "We do not need courage from liquor; it
is important to remember that, Liisa. We toast and
drink because we are celebrating the beginning of a
new life—for Janne and me and, pray God, for you
and Reino, too. Our courage must come from ourselves. Did you take a drink while you were in the
bedroom?" Our sudden closeness made the question
less impertinent.

"No," she said. "I thought of it, but I decided I
didn't have to."

"So," I said, "even before we drink the artificial
courage of this liquor, we have tasted bravery—mice
that we are."

Liisa's mouth fell open. "You?" she said. "*You* feel
like a mouse?"

"All women do at times. Liisa, don't you know that?
I've often been told that people consider me beautiful,
but do you think that makes me feel beautiful? It's
not facial features and body build that give one a
sense of beauty—it is how we view ourselves. I have
not yet touched this vodka, so you know this comes
from my heart. Tell me, have you ever compared yourself unfavorably with *Rouva* Kauppi, for instance?"

"Yes," she said. "She is a very commanding woman,
and beautiful despite her years. I am only twenty-six and
not nearly as handsome. Don't reassure me—I have a
mirror. I was chosen to be Reino's wife because I am
—well, what I am. Reino has no passion for me, at
least no more than he feels for any woman, and
probably less. *She* selected me because I *am* a mouse,
I know that. I have always been this way, even among
my own family. I was the fifth of seven children. I've

always known that I am in no way special. Even if there were no mirrors, I could see it reflected in people's faces. I am a mouse."

Though I couldn't help laughing, Liisa did not appear to resent my mirth. "So, you are a mouse, and I am a feather."

Liisa moved the glass to her mouth and then shuddered at the potent fumes of the vodka. *"You?* The beautiful Maija Leinonen considers herself a feather? Well, Maija—oh, please forgive me—*Neiti* Leinonen——"

"I am *Maija.*"

"Maija, if you insist. But how much more beautiful a feather is than a mouse."

I thought about that for a moment, as a Buddhist might ponder upon the sound produced by one hand clapping. It seemed important. I said a silent prayer that I would find the correct words.

"A feather, when attached to its host, *is* important. It gives importance—beauty. Wafted in the air, prey to every gust of wind, a feather is mindless, useless. Pretty, if someone bothers to admire it, but mindless and devoid of self-direction. I think I would prefer to be a mouse," I said. "At least a mouse knows its purpose and probably accepts its worth without question. But that is not to say that *you* are a mouse. Now, let's drink and stop this ridiculous musing."

Liisa brought her glass close to mine. "I do not really understand what you have just said—all the words—but I *feel* as if I know your meaning."

"Of course," I said. "Words mean little, but if one *senses,* there has been communication. Now," I said and clinked my glass against hers, "we drink." Our eyes met over the rims of the glasses, and we giggled like schoolgirls as we sipped the vodka.

Reino and his mother chose that moment to return. Mrs. Kauppi was so stunned by what she saw that she was, for once, speechless. I later decided it was divine inspiration that made me lift my glass to her and say, "To your generous hospitality!"

Reino looked at his wife as if he had never seen her before, and indeed he had probably never seen her as she appeared at that moment. Her features were animated, and a happy glow transformed her pale-blue eyes to the delicate color of an early-spring sky. There was no hesitancy as he walked to the table, took the overfull glass from Liisa and divided its vodka equally among the other three glasses. He handed one of the glasses to his mother, who appeared to have turned to stone, and solemnly extended his glass to each of us.

To Liisa he said, "To love," and clinked his glass against hers. Turning to me, he said, "To friendship," and we, too, tapped glasses. Then he faced his mother squarely and said, "To you, dear Mother. To your acceptance of the fact that I am now a man, a man who is deeply grateful for the devotion you have always shown me, but who must declare his independence while continuing to honor you."

CHAPTER TWENTY-THREE

Reino's mother took a sip, then showed every indication that she planned to continue sipping the formerly forbidden drink. But Reino gently removed the glass from her hand and said, "I think Maija should have her sauna and Liisa and you should continue fixing dinner. I'm sure she will be starved after her bath. Besides," he added with a twinkle that gave his handsome features the sparkle they had lacked, "I don't want the *kalakukko,* which is tantalizing me with its aroma, to be spoiled by inebriated cooks."

The flush that came over his mother's face wasn't totally the result of the small amount of vodka she had sipped. The old woman defiantly took back her glass, took another sip and said, "Liisa made it— with my instructions." She was unable to totally relinquish her superior position.

"That's true," Liisa admitted, "but I added a few special herbs."

Her mother-in-law looked startled, but Reino's hard stare forced her into saying, "It *does* smell delicious. Liisa, you must share that mixture of herbs with me."

"I shall be happy to," the girl said shyly.

"And then," Mrs. Kauppi ventured, after another sip of vodka, "I will show you a particularly intricate crochet pattern I learned from my grandmother. Your small hands should be able to master it easily."

It was the proper moment for me to disappear, and

I did, making my way to the small sauna, which was only a few steps down the garden path. With momentary hesitation, because of my last experience in a sauna, I opened the door, undressed in the entry room and stepped into the blast of hot, dry air in the inner sauna, where my body and soul succumbed to the heat and all thoughts were driven out of my mind.

I stretched out on the highest bench, dipped a birch whisk into a pail of water, laid it across my face and inhaled the sweet fragrance of my native country. Then I turned my entire attention to the fascinating spectacle of sweat beads appearing all over my skin. I stayed in the sauna room, adding pitchers of water to the glowing rocks, until my blood felt as if it were boiling. When I returned to the dressing room, I wiped myself down with a towel, stretched out on the bench and fell into a tranquil doze.

When my body had cooled sufficiently, I returned to the sauna. This time I was able to stay only a few minutes, since my blood was already heated. I showered under an icy spray of water, my heat-saturated flesh immune to shock, and again lay down and fell asleep, until hunger finally roused me. But even then I lingered over dressing, feeling no need to hurry. All tensions were gone.

I thought again of Janne and wondered if he, too, were enjoying the pleasure of a sauna. Janne . . . my soul reached out to him. I felt a pleasurable pain as I remembered our moment of abandon and the fulfillment that the following evening would bring.

All the blood was washed away, and the mirror showed that the scratches were not as awful as I had thought. I would be a beautiful bride after all. "Damn Janne," I said aloud. Now that my nerves were unwound, I could see the humor of his remark. I preened in front of the mirror, my female vanity armored with confidence.

I am beautiful, I thought. Of course, it wasn't just

admiration I wanted, but love—love that would sustain us in future years when wrinkles intruded on my flesh. Still, I decided, it was reassuring to know that I would go to him as a lovely bride. My vanity satisfied, I left the sauna and went back to the house.

The table was set for four, and Mrs. Kauppi, seated in her rocking chair engrossed in a crochet pattern, looked up and nodded toward the doorway to Reino and Liisa's room. "They are having . . . a private moment. Do you think we should tell them that dinner is ready?"

"If we don't, I threaten to eat every morsel myself," I answered lightly. "I'll knock and tell them I'm out of the sauna."

They responded immediately to my knock, but their shared expression was revealing. Mrs. Kauppi and I occupied ourselves with setting out the food. Reino placed his arm around Liisa's shoulder and restrained her from helping us.

We ate the simple but delicious food with abandon and enjoyment. The crust on the *kalakukko* was baked to perfection, the fish was flaky and tender. The combination of herbs and bacon strips gave the dish a tang that cannot be described. The fish was accompanied by a salad of cucumber, beet roots, and eggs. I refilled my plate so often I should have been embarrassed, but I wasn't. The others ate as heartily. Thick slices of freshly baked rye bread rounded out our meal, but Reino took a helping of fresh lingonberries and cream for dessert.

Liisa insisted on washing the dishes, and Mrs. Kauppi, taking her cue from her son, relinquished that housewifely duty. She helped me prepare my wedding costume. Reino retired behind his newspaper but occasionally glanced around it at the companionable domestic scene that was making his house a home rather than a battleground.

While we altered and pressed the pieces of the

costume, Mrs. Kauppi kept up a steady stream of advice for my wedding night. I nodded agreeably but wondered how shocked she would be if I confided my true feelings about the coming experience. I was wise enough to look serious during her whispered admonitions on "duty."

Mrs. Kauppi camouflaged the stain on the skirt with a piece of handmade lace. Perhaps it wasn't traditional, she commented, but we agreed that it was a handsome addition. The wimplelike veil was starched and dried over the porcelain stove. Mrs. Kauppi insisted on ironing the headdress herself.

After we prepared my wedding clothes, Liisa offered to wash my hair. (Reino decided to take a walk in the garden, fearing, perhaps, that we might indulge in more intimate preparations.) I was treated to the luxury of a shampoo and scalp massage. My hair was toweled dry, then brushed till it shone with all the golden highlights bequeathed by my ancestors. My nails were manicured, and my scratches were treated with an herb mixture that Mrs. Kauppi concocted. The homemade salve soothed my skin and promised quick healing.

Both women helped me into an immaculate floor-length gown and a simple wrapper, and then we toasted each other with a modest libation of delicious *mesimarja,* which Mrs. Kauppi produced from a secret hiding place. Then a sudden rapping on the front door reminded me that Reino and Grandfather had scheduled an eight o'clock meeting.

CHAPTER TWENTY-FOUR

My state of glowing well-being must have been apparent, because Grandfather gave me a satisfied look and nodded an appreciative thank-you to both women as he shook their hands. He sagged into the chair that was offered, and his hand shook when he accepted the glass of golden *mesimarja* that was served in the household's finest crystal glass.

He swallowed the drink and smacked his lips. "Well," he said to Reino, "shall we take a walk?"

Reino looked at the women. "It was my intention to speak to you alone, but now I feel that everyone should hear what I have to say. It will be a shock, but I feel you all must know."

Grandfather nodded, whether from indifference or understanding, I couldn't say. He took a pipe from his pocket and made a silent appeal for permission to smoke. Mrs. Kauppi nodded, then flushed and looked at Liisa to see if she also concurred. The girl, new to her role as mistress of the household, looked momentarily distressed but then graciously nodded her assent. Grandfather bowed back, removed his tobacco pouch and motioned to Reino to begin.

The young man's jaw muscles worked silently for a moment; then he got up and poured himself a large portion of vodka. He offered drinks to the rest of us, but everyone declined. Reino swallowed the contents of his glass in one gulp and began to speak.

"This will be very difficult for me; I've never before attempted to be brave. It always seemed so much easier just to go along. You will all be hurt in one way or another by what I am going to say. I've told myself I hated to hurt anyone, but now I see that I was too cowardly to face the possibility of incurring someone's displeasure."

"Boy," Grandfather said impatiently, "you are apologizing. A man does not preface his remarks. Everyone in this room is mature, and if they aren't, it's time they became so. What is it you have to reveal?"

Reino closed his eyes for a moment, but when he opened them, they were clear and full of purpose.

"I have. . . ." His voice faltered, but he forced himself to continue. "Liisa, I have not been faithful to you—not only once . . . and not with just one woman."

The blood drained from his wife's face, but she lifted her chin and looked directly at him. "Go on," she said.

"Kaarina was one of them." As the words tumbled out, he looked at Grandfather as if he expected to receive a blow. The old man stopped tamping the tobacco in his pipe and stared at him in utter disbelief.

"Kaarina?" he asked incredulously, as if the idea were too absurd to be taken seriously.

"Yes," Reino said in a toneless voice. "Maija, you remember when you came to my office? I told you Mother had just left. I lied—it was Kaarina. She told me I had fathered a child."

Liisa looked as if she were carved out of stone. Mrs. Kauppi put down her crocheting and took the girl's hand.

"She was very agitated—rightfully so—and was about to tell me whom I had made pregnant when Maija interrupted. Liisa, Mother . . . God forgive me, but there have been so many I couldn't even *guess* who the woman might be. Maija, I was in torment when you walked into my office. When you knocked, she begged me to contact her as soon as possible and left by the back door.

"I met her later that afternoon, and she told me that *she* was the woman. When she'd discovered she was pregnant, she decided to be sensible. An abortion was repulsive to her, so she accepted a job in Germany. Her personal life was unknown there, and it was possible to work through her term and then put the child up for adoption. But when the child was born, she could not give it up. She became confused—uncertain if she should tell me or whether she should shoulder the burden of raising the baby alone in a foreign country and deny him knowledge of his natural father.

"Finally she decided that she must come back and tell me. She returned to Helsinki and hired a woman who was supposed to care for the child while she journeyed here to see me. Then she decided she needed additional time to gather her courage before finally wiring Mummo that she was returning.

"God, how she wept as she told me of her worry and shame. You must understand—Kaarina and I have been friends since we were children. I have always been fond of her, although I was never able to return the love she felt for me. I know what you are all thinking, and I have no respect for myself, either. I took advantage of her love. As I said before, I am a weak man."

Grandfather looked up from his pipe and said, "You *have* been a weak man. God grants pardon for all sins, so do not label yourself permanently when the Divine Creator has not. It is what you do in the future that will determine your ultimate worth."

"That is true," Liisa whispered. Mrs. Kauppi nodded but was unable to look at her son.

Reino, who gave no indication that he found solace in Grandfather's words, continued. "When she returned, she found that her child was here and that you, Maija, were pretending to be his mother! She couldn't imagine why you would carry on such a deception but finally decided that *Herra* Leinonen had learned of her child's birth, abducted it and persuaded you to participate in a cruel plan to humiliate her. She became hysterical and said that Maija had always taken what should have been hers and that you, *Herra* Leinonen, had always hated her and had at last found the ultimate cruelty." Reino looked at me questioningly. "Why did you claim the child as your own, Maija?"

The question echoed in my head. *Why?* How could I have become a participant in such a cruel act?

"It was my idea," Grandfather said. "Maija found the child in a wicker basket that had been placed aboard Helge's shuttle boat. She arrived on my doorstep with the baby in her arms. Janne was with me at the time, and we both assumed it was hers. By the time she explained the circumstances, Lilya and the boys had arrived home. I was convinced that the child was in some way connected. . . ." He stopped abruptly, searching for an explanation that would circumvent saying a member of his family was trying to murder him. "To be blunt, I assumed that one of my stepsons had fathered the infant and that the mother, in a moment of desperation, sent it to me. Now I realize that it was foolish of me, but, without Maija's knowledge or consent, I led the family to believe that the child was hers. I wanted to surprise a confession from one of the men."

"What nonsense!" Mrs. Kauppi exclaimed. "Wouldn't it have been more logical to confront them with your suspicion?"

We waited for his answer. I cannot imagine what passed through the others' minds, but again I experienced the conviction that Grandfather's mind was affected. I had become so caught up in the charade, I'd forgotten the senselessness of his lie until Mrs. Kauppi voiced it.

The old man passed a shaking hand across his

brow. "Yes, that would have been much more sensible. The only explanation I can offer is that I was upset and not thinking clearly. It seemed so clever . . . at the time." Then his voice strengthened. "But the next day I notified the authorities and requested a discreet investigation. I assumed the mother was a woman from our village and that it would be easy to locate her. In fact, I was convinced she was Pirkko, a maid who had worked for us. I found out that after Lilya discharged her, Pirkko left the village and told several people she was going to Helsinki. It all seemed to fit. But when the police began their investigation, they found that the girl had been run over by a motorcar just two days after her arrival in the capital. The interval made it impossible for her to be the mother of a child that age."

"Reino," Liisa said suddenly, "what did Kaarina want you to do?"

"To divorce you and marry her. Oh, God, I didn't know what to do. I was responsible for bringing a child into the world—for ruining so many lives. I thought of Mother and how she always thought I was so perfect—above the temptations of the world. I thought of what it would do to her. And I cannot tell *what* I might have done, because it turned out that I did not have to make a decision." The remark was addressed to all of us, but he looked at his wife as he explained.

"A few weeks ago, Liisa went to Dr. Tami to determine why she hasn't conceived. I didn't tell her, but he also requested that I come in for an examination. He said it is usual to check the husband as well, but my manhood was so shaky and my vanity so strong that it took several days before I consented. On the same day that Kaarina told me about the child, Dr. Tami came to the tavern and told me the results of the examination. I am sterile. There is no possibility that I can sire a child—or that I was ever able to."

CHAPTER TWENTY-FIVE

Liisa had sat stoically through Reino's story, but now she began to cry. Mrs. Kauppi put her arm around her.

"I shall never forgive myself for the cruel things I said to you, Liisa. I ridiculed you for your barrenness. Now I see that it is my fault."

"Mother . . ." Reino began.

"It's true, son. Don't stop me from speaking—though God knows you should have done so many times in the past. I have manipulated your life, deliberately placed a barricade between you and Liisa so she could never win your love from me. I hated her because she did not produce the grandchildren *I* wanted. I never thought of anyone but myself, and it is because of my sin that God made you sterile."

"*Rubbish!*" The word boomed forth with the full force of Grandfather's voice. "You are an intelligent woman, *Rouva* Kauppi—when you allow yourself to be—but now you are dealing in old wives' tales."

"Please," Reino said, "I have more to tell, and it is equally difficult. After Dr. Tami told me of my condition, I was going to confront Kaarina. I couldn't imagine why she told me such a monstrous lie."

"Couldn't you?" I asked.

His cheeks flamed. "That is another shame to add to my list. She was obsessed and resorted to a terrible deceit to win me. I basked in her admiration—a woman I thought superior to myself. I used her, then turned

216

aside from the pain my indifference inflicted on her. Obviously her mind became affected.

"Before I could find Kaarina, Helge ran into the tavern with the awful news of Tanya and Ritva. He seems to know every detail of a scandal or tragedy almost before the participants or authorities hear of it. He told me the Gypsies said that Tanya had been seen with an infant too fair to be her own."

"So you know," Grandfather said and looked at him intently.

"I don't know anything," Reino retorted, suddenly defensive.

"Then you must have guessed. Isn't that why you came to seek me out today?"

"I was confused—I had to talk to you."

"What are you talking about?" I demanded.

"The autopsy on Ritva revealed she had recently given birth to a child. We assume Janne is the father," Grandfather said. "I think I can now put together the sequence of events and the motivations behind them. Dr. Tami and I have just returned from seeing Tanya."

"But she's dead!" Reino said.

"That's what the police wanted everyone to believe. She was near death when they found her, but they managed to pull her through, and she regained consciousness this afternoon—with a story to tell. She's afraid and anxious that the truth be told so that she can be protected."

Reino rose from his chair. "No, *Herra!* Let it remain between us—a village secret if need be. What's the word of a Gypsy?"

The old man's voice rumbled into the silence of the room like a roll of thunder. "God forgive us mortals for the impertinence of questioning His ways. Reino, don't you think I berate myself for what has happened, too?"

"Speak!" I yelled in a voice so shrill the word sounded like a scream. "I can't stand your talk of shame and honor. Do you think I am afraid to hear the truth? *Janne* is the murderer. My soul has whispered that suspicion until I am almost mad. What worse torture can there be than that?"

"Reino, do you now understand that this should not remain private, even if such a thing were possible?" Grandfather asked.

The younger man sank back in his chair. "I understand, and may God forgive me for all that I have caused to come about."

"Maija, Kaarina alone is responsible for the death of Ritva and the attempted murder of Tanya. Janne is in no way involved, except through the accident of his seed—or so we assume. With a woman of Ritva's morals, that can never be a certainty."

"You're lying and covering up!" I shouted. "You are using Kaarina. You've always despised her. I won't sit here and listen to any more of your manipulations and pathetic——"

The blow that Mrs. Kauppi delivered hurled me back into the chair. "I'm sorry, but you are hysterical. No wonder—if you believe that the man you intend to marry is a murderer. I will pour you a drink. I will pour *everyone* a drink."

"When Kaarina discovered that Ritva was making arrangements for an abortion," Grandfather continued, "she offered her a large sum of money to divorce Janne, continue her pregnancy in secret and sell the child to her. She would claim it as her own, and Reino would be named as the father. After announcing her intention of accepting a position in Germany, Kaarina joined Ritva in Helsinki and waited out the pregnancy. Kaarina delivered the baby herself so there would be no official record of birth."

"But how did the baby come to you, *Herra?* Why did Kaarina allow Maija to claim it as her own?" Liisa asked. "Perhaps Ritva saw what an awful thing she had done and——"

"You have a generous nature, Liisa. Unfortunately, neither woman felt remorse. The baby came to be in our village when Ritva decided she hadn't received enough money. She took the first opportunity that Kaarina afforded her and brought the baby back to this village. She hired Tanya to keep the baby hidden. Kaarina was told she would have to come up with an additional payment if she wanted to see the baby again."

"Payment for having been given the miracle of conception," Liisa murmured.

"Kaarina had depleted her inheritance. This desperation drove her to return to my house to attempt to extract more money from me. Needless to say, she couldn't tell me the real reason for her need, and I refused."

"Did the boys know about her situation?" I asked, sickened by the thought.

Grandfather shook his head. "No, I am certain of that. Despite their weakness, I know that none of them would have abetted such insanity. Tanya tired of being a baby-sitter and waiting for the money. She decided on a blackmail scheme of her own. She heard that *Neiti* Leinonen had returned and arranged to send her part of the baby's layette and a note promising delivery of the child in return for payment."

"So that's how the baby clothes came to be in my toy chest."

"Yes, Kaarina evidently hid them there, not knowing that you were due to return. Tanya was very careful never to reveal her identity to Kaarina, but it was arranged through a series of notes that an exchange would take place. She would leave the baby on the dock, concealed in a basket. Kaarina would leave another basket with the requested amount of money."

"But if she had no money——"

"Perhaps she was going to bluff it out. We can't look for much logic in her actions by this time. Fate stepped in on the day the exchange was to take place. Tanya left her basket on the wharf, then hid herself to await Kaarina. Helge found the basket, assumed it was groceries, and loaded it on his boat. Tanya didn't dare to reclaim it. Helge would surely have had many questions, and there was the danger that Kaarina, due any second, would see her. Ah, but Tanya is stubborn and greedy. As soon as possible, she sent another note to Kaarina explaining the mix-up and demanding money for her silence."

"But why did Kaarina appear to accept our lie that the child was my son?" I asked.

"The main thing was that the child was back in her hands, and it must have been evident from the first that we were not aware of the identity of the baby or I would have challenged her. She knows I am blunt. She decided to go to Reino with her story, probably intending to weep buckets over her 'shame' and 'reluctant' to tell him about her pregnancy. She gave some pretext for leaving the child in my care until Reino saw fit to do 'the honorable thing.' If Ritva or the village blackmailer made another attempt to extract money from her, she would kill them."

"Would I have done the honorable thing?" Reino wondered aloud.

"It is difficult enough to deal with real issues, Reino. Why torture yourself with pointless questions? Ritva, in Helsinki, had not heard from Kaarina, and Tanya's telephone responses were evasive. Ritva returned to the village, discovered the Gypsy's deception, and they had a violent quarrel."

"The one that was overheard," I said.

"No doubt a real hair-pulling match, but it eventually dawned on both of them that their only hope of gain lay in becoming allies for a further attempt at blackmail. It was a daring but foolish scheme. Tanya was to keep Kaarina away from the island long enough to allow Ritva to kidnap the child. The Gypsy was to use any device to keep her occupied. To assure her own safety, she was to tell Kaarina that Ritva already had the baby in her possession."

"Tanya must have asked Helge if he had seen *Neiti* Leinonen, and he directed her to the tavern. Since she had never actually seen Kaarina, she confused me with her. The note wasn't about Janne! It referred to Kaarina and the secret of the baby." I repeated the message for the benefit of the others:

He caused me too much pain and suffering to remain silent. I'll see that you suffer an even greater humiliation if you refuse to meet me. I'll tell the authorities about him, and I doubt you want that. Tanya will tell you all.

"Yes, how clear it all seems now," Reino said. "And when she told you she could tell much about the man you sought to marry, she was referring to me, not Janne."

"But if all this is true," I said, "why did Tanya run away? Why didn't she try to divert me, as planned?"

Grandfather continued to explain: "You forget that Janne found her in the tavern and scared her within an inch of her life. It wasn't Janne's threat that frightened her but the revelation that she had again bungled and delivered the note to the wrong *Neiti* Leinonen."

"And I thought she feared him so much. . . ."

"It was too late for her to warn Ritva. She was already at the island. Janne discovered her before she could attempt the kidnapping. She hid in the channel, waiting for the inhabitants of the island to settle down for the night, but—as Maija can tell us—it was a night alive with activity."

It was no time for blushing about my bizarre behavior, and I told the story in a factual manner, adding how the note was missing in the morning.

"It was found by Kaarina, for she would have had no other way of knowing about Tanya. I would guess she discovered it when she was disturbed by the cat.

"It didn't take Kaarina long to locate Tanya," Grandfather went on, "even though she'd never met her. Everyone in the village knew her. The Gypsy said she wasn't particularly frightened when Kaarina arrived at her door. She had delivered the note to the wrong woman, hadn't she? Kaarina couldn't have connected her with the affair, Tanya reasoned. She probably had just traced Ritva and that had led her to Tanya. Someone must have told Kaarina that Ritva had been seen there. But Kaarina had already met Ritva on the island and had killed her.

"Tanya pulled her knife, but Kaarina wrestled it away and slashed the girl. Fortunately for the Gypsy, Kaarina was in too great a hurry to feel her pulse. She was anxious to get back to the island and wipe the knife on Ritva's clothes so it would appear that she had murdered Tanya.

"It must have been then that it dawned on her that Ritva had been killed in a very convenient location. Janne's cottage was nearby—and hadn't he made a public announcement that he would kill his ex-wife if he ever saw her again?"

"So Kaarina threw the clothes and the knife on Janne's porch to incriminate him," I said.

"It was a perfect two-way plan," Grandfather noted. "If the police found them, Janne would be booked for both murders and my plan to disinherit the family would be temporarily foiled. Time would be gained to find another way to get rid of me. And if the plan failed, Ritva would appear to be Tanya's murderer."

"But Janne found the clothing and knife first?" Liisa asked. I nodded. "Oh, Maija, you knew about that? No wonder you suspected. . . . How horrible!"

"But I saw her in bed," I cried out suddenly. "I almost forgot—she was in bed when I reentered the bedroom that night!"

"Maija, think! Did you actually see her?"

"Of course I did."

"*Saw* her?" Grandfather repeated in a patient voice.

"I. . . . The bedclothes were heaped up. Naturally, I assumed——"

"That is what you were *supposed* to assume. She left by the balcony. You aren't the only one who knows that means of entrance and exit. When she returned, she took a pill so it would appear that she had been awakened from a long, sound sleep."

"Where is she now?" Mrs. Kauppi asked.

"Disappeared—after she went to the clinic to take over for Dr. Tami and the autopsy report on Ritva was delivered to her. As I said, it revealed that Ritva had recently given birth to a child. Dr. Tami had left the results of Reino's examination in plain sight on his desk. The hospital informed us that they left a message with a woman who identified herself as Dr. Tami's colleague. They told her that Tanya had regained consciousness."

"She's dead. I'm sure of it," Liisa said. "A woman might be able to live with the fact of murder but not with the knowledge that the man she loves would find her contemptible."

"It would seem that you are correct, Liisa," Grandfather said slowly, measuring out each word as if speech were painful. "When we returned from the city, Dr. Tami found a report that a woman's body had been recovered from one of the bonfires Paavo set off this afternoon. Of course, she was burned beyond recognition, and no shred of clothing was left, but her bone structure resembles Kaarina's. We won't have positive identification until the dental records are checked."

Reino heaved forward as if someone had hit him in the stomach, then lurched to his feet and vomited in the sink.

"Does Mummo know?" I asked, trying to control my own nausea.

"No. I told the boys, and we've agreed not to tell her anything until the body can be positively identified.

They even suggested that the wedding take place as planned. Mummo has worked long and hard for the celebration, and it may be the last event she will be able to enjoy, after she learns about Kaarina. But, of course, everyone will understand if *you* wish to postpone the wedding."

"Are you convinced that it was Kaarina who was responsible for the attempts on your life and the other strange happenings?"

"I am. I knew there was malice and madness in the family, and I have found its source. The men are simply weak and foolish in their judgment; I can see that now. The other things were brought about by a cunning madness. None of them, thank God, possess that fearsome combination."

CHAPTER TWENTY-SIX

At five o'clock on the following afternoon, I boarded Reino's boat, which was decorated with birch leaves, and crowds of well-wishers waved to me from similarly bedecked boats. Everyone was headed for the island to witness my marriage and to celebrate Midsummer Eve.

Grandfather, grave and formal in a dark suit, waited for us on the pier. Mummo stood beside him. Despite the gaiety of the occasion and the warmth of the evening, she was dressed in a dark-blue dress and a woolen shawl. Her knitting bag was tucked under her arm. Evidently she didn't think that a wedding and a feast were sufficient to justify idle hands. She had been told that Kaarina was called away suddenly on an emergency consultation.

The fiddlers—a group of village men who banded together for all occasions, planned or spontaneous, and produced the sprightliest music—were dressed in their best. When they arrived in our midst, they bowed and struck up a ditty to accompany our procession to the wedding site. Grandfather took my arm in his firm grip as we walked side by side, returning smiles and nodding thanks for the compliments that are traditionally given a bride. A girl presented me with a huge bouquet of wildflowers, and Heikki placed a wreath of birch leaves and daisies over my headdress. I glanced back at Mummo, who wore her usual smile.

Presented to my groom, I accepted his outstretched

hand. Janne wore a light-blue suit and a medallion around his neck engraved with Finland's coat of arms. The words that joined us together as husband and wife were spoken, and Janne's hand was steady as he slipped the gold band on my finger. Our kiss was formal, but as our eyes met, Janne whispered, "Mine."

A cheer went up, the fiddlers began to play, and I was surrounded by well-wishers. There were kisses from the bold and handshakes from the shy. I caught a glimpse of Mummo, who was standing apart. Our eyes met for an instant, and she nodded, as if to say that the deed was done. Above the din, I heard Grandfather accepting congratulations as if it were his own wedding. Well, I thought, he had arranged it from start to finish.

It looked as if the entire Gypsy community attended our wedding. The women's bright skirts swirled, and the men's highly polished boots gleamed in the reflection of the midnight sun. Their dark-haired children darted about, and the infants wailed or slept among the folds of their mothers' shawls. When the Gypsy musicians joined the Finnish fiddlers, their gusty music quickened the pulses of all the celebrants and set everyone to dancing. Janne was swept away by the throng, and I was whirled from one partner to another.

"Where is your husband?" a husky voice called to me. "Has he deserted you so soon?" I laughed and sought to pinpoint the speaker. Everyone had a humorous or ribald remark for me; it was all part of the celebration. But there was a remembered quality in that husky voice.

As I was caught up in another partner's arms, I saw a Gypsy woman standing off from the crowd, and forced my partner to stop. She wore a bright shawl that was tied around her waist, and within its folds was a baby. Her eyes were downcast, but I continued to stare at her. Then she lifted her head and looked

Ladies & Gentlemen:
I am a deaf person selling
these cards for a living.

Give what you wish

**THANK YOU FOR
YOUR KINDNESS**

THE MANUAL ALPHABET

directly at me. Her eyes were gray and brimming with hatred.

I escaped from my partner and worked my way through the crowd, giving no thought to the consequences of my action. The Gypsy laughed and took the infant, naked and oddly stiff, from her shawl, threw her head back, and with a wild laugh flung him in the midst of a bonfire. Then she ran into the forest. The "baby"—even though it was a plastic doll—was a grotesque sight, twisting and melting in the intense heat.

I stumbled away from the bonfire, into the mindless crowd, and tried to find someone who would believe the madness I had just witnessed. Laughter and loud voices and music muffled my attempts to call out to Janne, to Grandfather, to Reino. The huge bonfires sent up thick pillars of crackling flames. Then a hard object was pressed into my side, and strong arms clasped me. I turned and saw Mummo's sweet smile. Her expression didn't alter as she pushed the object more firmly into my side. Anyone would have thought she held me in a motherly embrace, because the gun she pushed against me was concealed by her shawl and knitting bag.

CHAPTER TWENTY-SEVEN

"It should have been *Herra*. Three times I tried to kill him, but the devil protects the wicked." She whispered the words into my ear, though she could have shouted them out and no one else would have heard them. "I found that letter he wrote to you and knew he suspected the children, so it wasn't safe to continue my plan to kill him. I didn't dare destroy the letter, as I did all those you sent to him. I had to be patient and wait for you."

The whispered words became a roar, and the roar of the crowd that pressed around us became a whisper. "*You?*" I gasped.

"Oh, yes. You don't think I'd allow my children to do such awful things, do you? They weren't raised to be violent."

This can't really be happening, I thought. *It's another evil dream. I can't be standing in the midst of my wedding guests with Mummo pressing a gun to my side.*

"Slowly, my dear, slowly! I don't want anyone interfering in our family business. *Herra* would not be pleased if we let our troubles be known to outsiders. Smile!"

The pressure in my side increased. Then, concealed by the shawl, her free arm twisted my left arm backward, and her iron grip promised pain if I didn't follow her command.

228

"I arranged everything myself—the sauna and the fire, and even the cleaning fluid. But you are clever at escaping! You're as hard to kill as your grandfather. Even with my arthritis, I loosened the ladder on the dock and timed it for your grandfather's arrival."

I was shoved forward through the crowd, my face a grotesque, grinning mask. Couldn't anyone see what was happening? I screamed out silently. But if they did, I told myself, would they believe their eyes? Gentle Mummo. . . .

"It's a wonder you didn't hear me on the sauna roof. I wedged the door shut and then climbed on the roof and held the chain. But I've been used to hard work all my life. I even drove the crane, under those coveralls and hat. It wasn't much different from the tractor I drove on our farm. And I sent the note to Uno."

Everyone made way for us. My head bobbed up and down in response to the greetings. Mummo took care of the words.

"Ah, *Herra* Risko! How good of you to come, and you with your gout. . . . No benefit in being old except the satisfaction in seeing our children happy. . . . Everything is fine, Toini, just a bit too much excitement for the bride. Surely you remember *your* wedding day?"

Minutes before, the crowd had been my enemy. Now I silently beseeched each person to stay put, to bar our progress to my death.

"Of course, nothing worked out as I planned," Mummo hissed in my ear. "I can see now that it was God's will. But it did appear that *Herra*'s mind was affected. I used enough sleeping medication to kill him, but he is so fussy about his coffee. Wouldn't take more than a sip—but enough to make everyone think he'd had a stroke. Then nobody believed him about the other attempts."

Suddenly the band struck a fanfare and one of the players called to the crowd, "Ladies and gentlemen, please gather round. It is time to remember our heritage. We will sing of our heroes in the ancient words of Finland's epic poem, *The Kalevala*. And who is more suited to repeat the words of wise old Väinämöinen than our own *Herra* Leinonen?"

Grandfather moved toward the makeshift stand, carrying a *kantele*, the ancient stringed instrument of Finland. A cheer went up as he stood straight and tall and looked out at the crowd. Mummo was forced to stop, but her grip on my arm didn't relax, nor the pressure of the gun against my body.

"Friends, family," he began in his resonant bass voice, "you would do better to choose the howl of the forest wolf for your entertainment, but I will try to remember the words that have been handed down to us from our ancestors." All eyes were turned in his direction.

Mummo whispered in my ear, "The wicked man. It is he who has forced me to kill you. What could be more wicked than to force the death of your flesh and blood? He makes me kill you so that my children will not be disinherited."

"But they are already," I said as the first notes of the *kantele* floated into the bright night.

"No, dear. He has not signed the document that will give the mill to Janne. He is a prudent man, who never trusts anyone. I heard him say he would not sign it until after the party. But it's too late for you, of course, though you will remember I tried to warn you." She spoke in the special scolding tone I remembered from childhood.

Grandfather's powerful voice sang out: *"'There has not been here before nor will there probably be indeed in the future the manliness of this bridegroom, the beauty of this bride, the size of this crowd, the pleasure of these young people. . . .'"*

A cheer went up as he finished the couplet and I saw Janne raised above the crowd on the shoulders of two mill workers. I wanted to cry out to him, but I knew Mummo would kill me on the spot. As if hearing my thought, she urged me forward. "Maija must lie down for a bit; she's feeling faint. Please, let us pass."

We gained several feet, but many celebrants still barred our way.

"Quickly, Maija. If necessary, I will kill you in front of everyone. I intend to see my children come into their rightful inheritance."

"Lilya! Where is Lilya, our little Mummo?" Grandfather called from the stand.

"He's calling you, *Rouva* Leinonen. Your husband is looking for you," someone said.

"Come up here, Lilya. This song is for you. First spoken centuries ago, still fitting today."

Faces were grinning into ours, and I twisted about to see Mummo's. A bright-red flush brightened her rosy cheeks, and her head turned from side to side. No one could have suspected that the flush was caused by frustration rather than modesty.

"Tell him I must help Maija, someone. My old voice will not carry that far."

"Never mind," Grandfather called back in response to the crowd's shouted refusal. "Stay where you are. My bear's roar will reach you!"

He plucked the notes on the *kantele* and sang, "*Whom shall I praise here? I will praise the mistress first. . . . She has brewed the barley beer, the delicious malt drinks; sweet is her malt. . . . She baked big loaves, patted into shape the big cakes of barley made for the drinking party of the good crowd, to the joy of the good country people. . . .*"

"Enough!" Mummo shouted. "*Herra*, you embarrass me with your praise. Let the music begin again so that all our guests can enjoy themselves."

With an elaborate bow, he ended the ancient song, and the musicians began a lively dance. Everyone reached for a partner, and we were locked together amid whirling dancers. Mummo shoved me forward with a violent push.

"*Aiti!*" exclaimed an exuberant voice, and Mummo was lifted into the air by Paavo. "Come, little Mother. We'll whirl a bit to this lively tune, and then you will share a glass with me. You must toast my eternal poverty!"

I heard her scream, but I didn't look back. I rammed my way through the dancers, pushing aside everyone who innocently blocked my progress. On the edge of the crowd, I looked back and tried to locate Janne or Grandfather. I knew Mummo would have rid herself by now of her drunken son and be searching for me.

My mind was a blur of Mummo's malevolent words and the faces of the celebrants. I had to find someone to confide in. Someone to help me before I again encountered Kaarina or Mummo.

The elderly, those who were not able to dance, sat at long tables, feasting on heaping platters of food. Boiled crayfish were piled into large mounds, and the people were sucking out the succulent flesh. I looked from one face to another to find someone who would help me—who would believe me when I told them Kaarina was dressed like a Gypsy and skulking around the island and that Mummo was trying to kill me.

Suddenly there was a wild cackle, and a sharp object was pressed against my back. "You are playing games, eh?" a voice whispered.

It was Helge. The old man's nose was as red as the crayfish claw he poked at me. His eyes were inflamed and his bandy legs shifted as if he were trying to stabilize his body on a turbulent sea.

"Is the bride trying to hide from her groom? Ah, poor Janne. Let us hope he hasn't had as much to drink as Helge, or he will never find you!"

"Helge," I said, "you must help me. Find *Herra*

Leinonen and tell him I am in trouble. Mummo is trying to kill me!"

He made a tremendous effort to focus his eyes. His toothless mouth opened, and he gaped at me stupidly. Aware of his alcoholic state and his normal deafness, I shouted in his ear. "Please *understand*. I am in *trouble*. Mummo is going to kill me!"

"Ah!" he said and shook his head in sudden understanding. "*Neiti* Maija, you must not worry. You are *married* now! Let the gossips count the months. Yours won't be the first 'premature' baby in our village. Mummo will forgive you now that you are wed." He tore the claw off the crayfish, and his mouth caved in as he gummed the morsel.

I ran into the woods. My heart pounded so painfully that I stopped for rest as soon as I reached the shelter of the trees. As I looked for the path that led to Janne's cottage, my heart returned to a relatively steady rhythm.

I hadn't forgotten that Kaarina had disappeared into the same forested area. I slipped my shoes off and ignored the painful bite of pine needles and twigs. As children, my uncles and I had played Red Indian in the woods, though I had always disclosed my location by snapping a twig. But this was not a game, I reminded myself, and detection could be fatal. Each sound I made seemed like thunder, and I stopped to listen for telltale movements around me.

The sun sent shafts of light through the leaves, dappling the ground with golden pools. There was no protective darkness on this night of the longest day. Dead leaves falling to the ground or rustled by the breeze sent waves of fear through me. I was sure I was being stalked. It didn't seem possible that I could find Janne's pathway without being assaulted. Then, when I found t, I didn't trust the crunch of the path's granite pebbles and kept to the protection of the underbrush. I ran through the clearing to his cottage and crouched beside the woodpile, listening for the slightest sound that would indicate I'd been followed.

It seemed an eternity until I was able to resume reasonable control of my body. I peeked through the cabin window, but it was dark inside and I could see only my reflection in the glass. Then I heard a sound that I had heard before—the cry of a small animal, perhaps an abandoned kitten . . . or the baby! Oh, God, I thought, had Kaarina somehow managed to kidnap the child? Or was this clever but deranged woman trying to lure me into the house?

It was difficult to imagine the prim Kaarina imitating the cry of an infant, but it was possible. She was clever, and I knew that the insane are often especially cunning. Despite the warmth of the sun on my back, I shivered as I listened to the whimper. If the child was inside, he might be so worn out by crying and hunger and distress that it was the loudest sound he was able to make.

I picked up a piece of firewood and tiptoed up the steps, listening for any sound from within. I slipped inside the door and flattened myself against the wall, ready to strike back with my club, but there was no sign of life in the large room. Maybe Kaarina was hiding in the bathroom or in the connecting bedroom.

The child could be secreted in one of the cupboards or drawers, but I couldn't make a thorough search of them without revealing my presence. First I had to look in the other rooms. I had to confront Kaarina— if she was in the house—before she could seize the advantage. Necessity, not bravery, led me on.

The bathroom was empty, and I cautiously entered the adjoining bedroom, which also was empty. Nor was anyone hiding in the closets. I stood in the bedroom, the club dangling from my hand, and decided it was safe to search every cupboard and drawer for the baby.

There was no other adult in the cabin—of that I was certain.

I went to the doorway of the bedroom and looked into the main room, deciding where I would begin, when I detected—or sensed—a stealthy movement. I looked about the room and into the shadowy corners but saw no one. Then the creature leaped from above and landed in the middle of the kitchen table, in a ray of sunlight. Pai-Pai sat regally on the table, washing cobwebs from his whiskers.

I decided I would kill him. He had caused me no end of terror and now had unwittingly played his last prank. My nerves were too shattered to see any humor or make allowances. As I advanced on Pai-Pai, he regarded me with his usual bored expression, and when I raised the club, he began to lick his handsome ruff.

Disheartened, and all but undone, I let the stick fall from my hand, and I sank to the floor. Pai-Pai looked down at me, then leaped into my lap. I sat huddled on the floor, stroking his fur, while tears cascaded down my face. As I clutched his warm body to my bosom, he suddenly wiggled free, streaked across the room and jumped onto a high cupboard. An instant later, Kaarina grabbed my arm from behind and jerked me to my feet.

Her fingers dug into my flesh as she shoved me out the doorway and down the porch steps, to the place where she had murdered Ritva. Next to it, a bonfire had been laid. Kaarina held me in an iron grasp as she struck a match with one hand and threw it on the wood, which reeked of kerosene. Tall flames immediately shot up. The island was ablaze with similar bonfires. Who would notice another one? As she pushed me toward the roaring fire, I saw the glint of her knife.

"Witch!" she shrieked. "Only a witch would steal another woman's child! He was mine, and you took him from me!" Her hair, free from the prim knot, danced weirdly about her head in the heat from the fire.

"Kaarina," I cajoled, "I did not steal your child. The baby is Ritva's. Someday you will have your *own* children." Despite my extremity, I regretted the lie.

"Witch!" she repeated and slashed at me with the knife.

I saw that she was beyond reason and wondered if the knife was the same one with which she had killed Tanya. No, I remembered, she had placed it on Janne's porch, with Ritva's clothes, to incriminate him, to make everyone think he had murdered Tanya.

"The proper death for a witch is by fire, and in these flames you shall die. Enter the eternal fires of hell— your proper home." She screeched and slashed at me again, forcing me toward the roaring flames.

"Burn, witch—stealer of babies!" she screamed as she advanced toward me. Then, suddenly, she halted and began to laugh in the insane manner I had seen and heard earlier.

"I should have done the same with the other two witches. But they are dead now, and the eternal fire of hell torments them. The child was brought into the world by my love for Reino. I took him from that other witch and held him in my arms—claimed him for Reino and me.

"Why do you hesitate? *Step into the fire.* Don't you recognize your destiny, the flames of your master's world? Go, witch, and join the others of your kind."

The knife stabbed at my heart, and I fell backward into the inferno.

Fingers, deep in my mouth, extracted the mud until my instincts took over. I turned my head aside and spat out the remainder. Janne wiped the mud from my eyes and face as he cradled me in his arms. He had snatched me from the bonfire and flung me into the mud flat to extinguish my smoldering garments.

Kaarina was restrained by Paavo and Eero, but a stream of obscenities flowed from her. Her face was twisted insanely, and there was little resemblance to the rational human being we had known as Kaarina. I buried my face in Janne's shoulder.

"You are all right?" the question was more a statement than a question.

"Yes," I managed to say.

Kaarina was still muttering, but her words were incoherent. Then her body went slack, her brothers released their hold, and Kaarina sank to the ground. They stood over her for a moment, but she was subdued and intent only on her muttered litany of hate. Concern showed in the men's faces as they left Kaarina and walked over to me. I nodded at them and forced a reassuring smile.

A strange procession headed toward us, led by Mummo. Her smile was as gentle as always, but Heikki walked close behind with a firm hand on her shoulder. His face registered anguish as he guided his mother, who was obviously insane.

Grandfather followed behind Mummo and Heikki, his shoulders hunched and back bent over, Mummo's knitting bag dangling from his gnarled hand.

The crackle of the bonfire was the only sound. Even Kaarina had fallen silent. We were all locked into our individual condition—exhaustion, anguish, insanity. No one looked at the other. Mummo's round eyes seemed to stare into some far place that none of us could see.

She finally broke the silence. "The children come first." Mummo nodded at her sons and daughter, as if satisfied, but no longer able to see them in their true dimensions. Or had she ever? The words had barely been uttered before she slipped into a state which was later diagnosed as catatonic.

Because our attention had been on the pathetic old woman, no one noticed that Kaarina had recovered the knife until we heard her gasp. It was a soft, almost happy sound, as she plunged the knife into her heart with the skill of a surgeon. She was dead before any of us could move.

Mummo looked down on her dead daughter with the sweet smile that was to remain the permanent expression of her face. She nodded happily, as if she had just seen Kaarina tucked into bed.

CHAPTER TWENTY-EIGHT

Now a noise is heard in the lane,
a rumbling at the farm; it is
getting quite unpleasant, is
becoming harder to celebrate the
wedding at North Farm, the feast
at gloomy North Farm.

Janne's arms held me tightly as we listened to Grandfather: "My wife is to have the best possible care, and Finland has the finest psychiatric clinics. I realize it is too late, but she will be denied nothing."

He looked into the faces of his stepsons. "It will take considerable *sisu* for us to accept the fact that your mother is insane and will likely remain so for the remainder of her life. As I have explained, I am responsible for much that has happened, but I am not solely responsible and will not accept the full blame. If I did———" His voice faltered. "If I did, I would become like Lilya, and what purpose would that serve? No, some of this misfortune, this tragedy, has been the result of my confused thoughts and suspicious nature, but your spoiled, self-indulgent ways—which were fostered by that poor woman—contributed to these sad events. So who is to blame? Each must accept his share; but if anyone claims all the responsibility, he is defying God's infinite wisdom in the design of life. I suggest that no one do that. Come, boys, your mother is waiting with Dr. Tami. We must take her to the hospital and then see to your sister's funeral arrangements."

Janne and I stood on the dock and watched the boats depart. Word had spread, and everyone knew the celebration was over. All had withdrawn discreetly. In

239

the village, glasses would be raised to the future of the newlyweds and in farewell to the departed. Such is the sensible and sensitive heart of a Finn.

Later, as I lay in Janne's arms, we talked about the child. He said that we would never really be certain if he was Janne's son. If we were to raise him, the day would come when the circumstances of his birth would have to be explained to him.

We discussed allowing the child to be adopted by a family in a far-off place, but I think we both knew, even then, that we would make him our own and give him so much love and security that he would be able to accept life on any terms.

We made love again, and as I was falling asleep, I heard a sound like laughter. It was unearthly and more than a little ribald. I decided it was Pai-Pai, yowling indignantly outside the bedroom door, but Janne rolled over, gathered me into his arms and murmured, "The old gods approve."